DANIEL PARSONS

Daniel Parsons lives in South Wales, UK, where he writes fast-paced stories full of mystery and danger.

He wrote the first version of his debut novella *The Winter Freak Show* whilst studying English Literature at Cardiff University. The encouraging reception it got from fellow students and other readers spurred him to write *Blott*, a full-length teen fantasy novel, which also proved to be popular.

His comedy zombie story, *Necroville,* has received extensive acclaim on the story-sharing website Wattpad. There it garnered over 34,000 reads and was named one of the site's Top Zombie Stories as part of a campaign to promote Hollywood's *Pride and Prejudice and Zombies* movie. This spawned the idea for *Last Crawl*.

Daniel Parsons also writes non-fiction for creative professionals. His first title in *The Creative Business Series* is *The #ArtOfTwitter,* which was released in October 2016 to rave reviews and eventually became a US Top 100 Business bestseller.

Join Daniel's 100,000+ followers on Twitter (@DKParsonsWriter). He would love to hear from you, and responds to tweets personally.

www.danielparsonsbooks.com

LAST CRAWL

DANIEL PARSONS

The Necroville Series
Book One: Last Crawl

© Daniel Parsons 2017
www.danielparsonsbooks.com

The right of the Author to be identified as author of this Work has been asserted by him in accordance with sections 77 and 78 of the Copyright, Designs and Patents Act 1988.

All rights reserved. No part of this publication may be reproduced, stored in a retrieval system, copied in any form or by any means, electronic, mechanical, photocopying, recording or otherwise transmitted without written permission from the publisher.

You must not circulate this book in any format.

Published May 2017

ISBN: 978-1546424185

Category: Horror / Black Humour

For my fans on Wattpad.
Without your insatiable hunger for more, I might never have written this book.

ACKNOWLEDGEMENTS

Last Crawl, the first novel in *The Necroville Series*, shouldn't exist. It's true. *Necroville*, the short zombie story that inspired it, was intended to be a stand-alone. It was only after I posted it on the story-sharing website, Wattpad, that my plans changed.

Soon after uploading *Necroville*, it gained thousands of reads and a spot on the marketing campaign of a major Hollywood movie. It exceeded all of my expectations, none of which would have been possible if not for the early fans who gave it a chance. Their enthusiasm and hunger for more was the driving force behind my decision to write *Last Crawl*. So for that, I'm grateful.

On the topic of the book itself, I'd like to thank my family. They continue to be a supportive bunch, nodding at the right moments when I get carried away explaining book ideas and publishing schedules.

Then there's the crew of experts working around me that make me look good. My editor Heather Osborne has done a fantastic job of streamlining my words and filtering out all of my grammatical inconsistencies, not to mention blowing my mind by pointing out I've been spelling *meerkat* wrong my whole life.

My friend and proof reader, Joe Moore, also deserves thanks for his keen eye and his genuine enthusiasm for my work. Alongside him is my illustrator and cover designer, Zoe Foster, who has managed to draw my characters exactly as I imagined them for the cover of this book.

Seriously, it's like she can see into my brain!

Finally, my last shout-out must go to my most avid readers. You're a small tribe but your numbers grow with every book I release. Sometimes being a writer can seem like an impossible slog but you guys make all of the hard work worth it.

Daniel Parsons

CONTENTS

Part One: Fresh Meat	1
Part Two: Screaming	10
Part Three: Not Syrup	17
Part Four: Bath Salts	24
Part Five: Behind Closed Doors	29
Part Six: As One Door Closes	40
Part Seven: In the Dark	47
Part Eight: No Way Out	59
Part Nine: Armageddon	69
Part Ten: Theodor Grayson	75
Part Eleven: Secrets and Larssony	82
Part Twelve: Let's Get Mortal	91
Part Thirteen: A Little Tied Up	98
Part Fourteen: For Science	107
Part Fifteen: Sobriety Can Kill You	118
Part Sixteen: The Ministry of Myths	128
Part Seventeen: This Godforsaken Kingdom	139
Part Eighteen: Blackout	147
Part Nineteen: Lost	152
Part Twenty: Regret	163
Part Twenty-One: The Conspiracy	168
Part Twenty-Two: Away with the Fairies	174
Part Twenty-Three: Hold Tight	182
Part Twenty-Four: Reporting for Duty	186
Part Twenty-Five: Hazardous Area	197
Part Twenty-Six: Sacrifice	203
Part Twenty-Seven: Fast Food	210

Part Twenty-Eight: In Cold Blood	218
Part Twenty-Nine: Amelia's Confession	222
Part Thirty: Pressure	231
Part Thirty-One: Rescue Mission	234
Part Thirty-Two: The Gates of Hell	240
Part Thirty-Three: It Lives in the Dark	247
Part Thirty-Four: The Bar	253
Part Thirty-Five: Lost at Sea	259
Part Thirty-Six: Stranded	266
Part Thirty-Seven: Blaze of Glory	275
Epilogue	281
Get Your Free Starter Library!	285
Also by Daniel Parsons	287

PART ONE
FRESH MEAT

Beads of sweat dried cold on the jogger's forehead as he slowed to a trot. His chest smarted, but he couldn't stop. Not now. The figure hunting him was still in sight and showed no signs of fatigue.

Glancing at his digital wristwatch, the jogger let out a frustrated whimper. He had been followed for twenty minutes now. And he had been jogging for half an hour before that, so keeping ahead was a struggle. With the sun setting, he didn't want to turn and confront the guy. The paths around the student village were known to be crawling with junkies after nightfall.

Why do I always get the psychos? he thought.

Looking over his shoulder, he shuddered. The gap between them was closing, so he powered onwards, hoping to reach open streets before the daylight vanished.

* * *

A guttural, retching sound emerged from my throat, and I realised I was being strangled. It was the anxiety again, crawling up my windpipe like a trapdoor spider. This panic attack was worse than usual.

Sitting in the dark, my muscles tight, I perched on the end of my bed. The cool sheets were a soothing contrast to my flushed, sweaty skin. I wheezed, my lungs feeling shallow, as I struggled to get a grip on my nerves.

Voices jabbered on the other side of the door. Glass smashed somewhere in the building. The intruders had breached every room in the house, except one.

So, this is it?

As though in answer, a dead weight slammed against the door. This wasn't how I expected it to play out. I'd been so careful, preparing physically and mentally. Extensive preparation had gone into every aspect of my survival, and yet no amount of training could prepare me for the field.

I coughed to clear my throat. My chest was burning, so I sucked at an asthma pump resting on a nearby table. Then I discarded it, unsatisfied.

Empty, I thought.

I had spares, but they were buried somewhere in the wardrobe. I suspected they were duds, too. My doctor had told me I'd outgrown the asthma a while back. All I had now was anxiety and a shedload of old inhalers to satisfy me.

"Hey, is someone in there?" asked a disembodied voice. It was male, deep, with a nasal quality I couldn't help but associate with wealth.

I held my breath. *Maybe if I stay still, they'll forget about me.*

Sliding my hand to the desk opposite my bed, I felt my fingers curl around a cold object about the length of my forearm. It was heavy, weighted at one end. Taking it with me, I edged towards the danger, unfastened the bolt, and wrenched open the door.

"Hey, mate. You okay?"

A tall, blond boy in a white shirt with cufflinks leaned against the door jamb. He looked older than me, but I attributed it to his extra height and broad shoulders. Beads of sweat on his forehead suggested there was a pressing reason for him to knock my door.

Around him, several fresh-faced students inhabited the thin corridor connecting the bedrooms to the communal kitchen. At my feet, a tubby, ginger boy lay unconscious, still clutching a bottle of whatever spirit had paralysed him.

That explains the thud against the door.

Eyeing him with distaste, I allowed my gaze to flick up to my tall visitor.

"You okay?" he repeated.

"Fine," I responded, holding up the beer bottle I'd grabbed on my way to the door. "Just looking for a bottle opener."

If anything was going to get me through the night, it was alcohol.

"Cool. You're Milo, right? Milo Callaghan?"

"Yeah. How do you know…?"

"Oh, Wyatt told me about you."

Great. Wyatt's been making my first impression for me.

That was reason enough to close the door and forget the party altogether. Staying in and watching online videos was more my scene anyway. Some new conspiracy vlogger had just uploaded a video exposing the corruption in a major oil corporation. *The Truth Lives Among Us?* – I'd spotted the title before shutting down my laptop. It sounded really good.

"All good things, I hope?"

"Of course. I'm Monty Rosenberg, by the way. I live upstairs. Can I use your loo? Everyone else's are taken."

I glanced behind me at the vertical coffin next to my bedroom door. The university claimed it was an *en-suite* bathroom, but they used the term loosely. Everything was so close together – the shower fired tepid water directly onto the toilet. On arrival, my dad had grimaced at the infection of dark stains left in the corner of the ceiling by my room's previous tenant. I'd cleaned it after he had left. It still looked terrible, but at least the mould now smelled like bleach.

Monty wrung his hands. His eyes flicked from me to the toilet. I could tell something was wrong.

"Go for it," I said.

"Brilliant."

"No prob–"

He barged past me before I could even finish the sentence. Slamming the cubicle door behind him, I heard him calmly lift the toilet seat, then projectile vomit into the pan.

Wonderful, I thought, deciding to leave him to it. It appeared my first glimpse of Freshers' Week was going to be messy.

* * *

Suppressing the urge to throw up, the jogger supported his hands on his bare knees. He had hoped the ragged man following him would back off when he entered the student village. That didn't happen.

The man's hampered breaths were within earshot now. Turning back, the jogger shook, overcome with adrenaline. His initial concern became hard fear. As the figure rounded a corner, and his mangled body appeared only a few paces behind, terror stabbed the jogger's gut afresh.

"What do you want?"

His words were greeted by a snarl. Black vomit glazed the man's waxy coat. He looked homeless, with matted hair dangling wet in front of his eyes.

I've got to find help, he resolved. *This is getting out of hand!*

* * *

Unsure whether I should hang around to make sure he was okay, I loitered for a moment, registering someone scrambling to escape at the end of the hallway. A tail of white hair vanished through the apartment door. I recognised it as one of my new flatmates – a pale, scrawny girl, whose name I was told was Ellie.

My dad had accidentally cornered her in the kitchen while I was unpacking. He caught her name, but said she got out of there before he could ask anything else.

"Looks like you've got yourself a ghost," he had said knowingly, before leaving. "They're like Sasquatch. You hear 'em raiding the kitchen a lot, but spotting 'em in the flesh is a challenge. I had one in my first year, too. Never got his name. Odd boy, but harmless enough."

I bopped noncommittally to a distant beat leaking from the kitchen as I waited outside my bedroom door. My game of 'try to act natural' was interrupted, though, when a girl backed out of a nearby room. She was shorter than me, with dark jeans, raven hair and a black turtleneck – not your average clothes for a party. And that was without mentioning the rope and grappling hook looped over her shoulder, and the camcorder strapped to her belt. Come to think of it, the bulky pair of high-tech goggles tilted up from her forehead were also an odd fashion choice.

"Hi," I said, holding out a hand.

In hindsight, shaking hands with a girl at a party seemed overly formal, but the alternative – a hug – probably would have ended with a swift knee to the groin… or a restraining order. Her dark eyes glared as she locked the bedroom door behind her.

Definitely a swift knee to the groin.

"Name?" she asked.

"Um… Milo Callaghan."

"Noted. Now, get out of my way."

"Oh." I noticed I was blocking her exit, and stepped to one side. "Sorry."

She breezed past me, flipping down her goggles as she headed for the door.

"And your name?" I attempted, slightly taken aback by her attitude.

She paused, then sighed. "Amelia Larsson."

Amelia Larsson. There was something oddly familiar about that name.

"You staying for pre-drinks?"

She scoffed. "Hardly. I'm having a little party of my own."

"Oh, cool." I feigned interest. If I had to live with this girl for the whole year, the least I could do was be civil. "What's the theme? Spies or burglars?"

"The theme is mind your own damn business."

I paused, waiting for her to laugh. She didn't.

"Okay… Have fun!" My face brightened in a last-ditch attempt at enthusiasm, but she had already left, and probably didn't see it.

Weaving between partiers, I eventually decided to head for the kitchen, where it sounded like a chipmunk was rapping about 'big booties.' The room was small and plain, with granite worktops and basic appliances. Chairs were pushed up against the walls to make room for a table decorated with two opposing clusters of cups. A laptop hitched up to speakers balanced on top of the microwave.

A bearded boy, with the build of an American football player, hurled a ping pong ball from the far wall. It landed perfectly in his opponent's cup as I entered. The spectators erupted, and a smaller guy downed the drink inside it with fake reluctance. Then the winner took a cup from his own side of the table and chugged what appeared to be a dirty cocktail of beer and colourful spirits, as a show of sportsmanship.

"Robb-ie! Robb-ie! Robb-ie!" chanted those nearby.

Shaking the last dregs into his mouth, he upturned the cup and wore it like a crown. He fist-pumped wildly, shouting, "Let's get mortal!"

My stomach churned just imagining the liquid curdling inside him. Heading towards the hob, where two girls leaned against a worktop, I eyed the pair uncertainly. The shorter of the two was babbling about a boy she had met after her parents dropped her off, while the other one – a tall, attractive girl, who looked like the survivor of a freak accident at a glitter factory – listened with an air of superiority.

"Um… excuse me," I said to the taller one. "Could I just…?"

"I have a boyfriend."

"Okay…" I said, a little confused. "Sorry, I was actually just trying to get to the drawer behind you. Is there a bottle opener in there?"

I held up my sealed bottle as evidence. A moment of panic flashed in her eyes as she realised her mistake. Her friend masked a smirk and handed me the bottle opener.

"Hi, I'm Candice," she added. "And this is Chloe. You're… Milo, aren't you?"

"Yeah…"

I made a mental note to punch Wyatt in the arm when I found him. Too many people probably already knew a ton of secrets I was hoping wouldn't follow me to university.

Opening the bottle, I took a swig. The sharp taste of alcohol felt acidic on my tongue. I was never much of a drinker, but I guessed I'd have to become one to fit in with this crowd.

Chloe made an awkward cough, recovering from her *faux pas.* "How was your drive in? Did your parents bring you?"

"Yeah, my dad dropped me off earlier. I couldn't wait for him to leave," I lied, remembering my bottom lip wobbling as his old car turned the corner at the end of the road and vanished.

"I know exactly what you mean. My parents hung around for ages! It took us two hours to get in because of that oil tanker that overturned on the road outside. My mum was a mess – from the emotion, not the oil. She got right on my nerves."

"I like your parents, Chlo," Candice grinned. "They left snacks! And I think you seemed pretty devastated when they…" A hard glare from her friend shut her down before she could finish her sentence.

Chloe got out her phone, apparently deciding the conversation had ended. Frowning, she slapped the side of the device. "O.M.G. The signal here's terrible! No Wi-Fi or phone signal. I can't even get 4G!"

"Tell me about it," I said. "It's because the campus is so new. I read somewhere they're still building the final quarter. The construction company the uni hired are over a year behind schedule."

"Yeah," agreed Candice. "My cousin stayed here last year when they opened it. He said the uni promised to do something about the black spot for months, but they never fixed the problem. They just wanted the students moved out of the city. Anything to stop the noise complaints. Still, I think building actual walls and a moat around the student village was a bit much."

I laughed. "Absolutely. Plonking us three miles from town should have been enough. The moat's just showing off!"

"Mmm," Chloe mumbled, disinterested. "Argh! It's, like, *literally* killing me. I'll try outside." Deserting us, she pushed past me.

Candice looked apologetic. "I'd better go and make sure she doesn't run into any trouble while she's Lion-Kinging."

"Lion-Kinging?"

"Yeah, like how the monkey held Simba up on Pride Rock."

"Oh, I see." I chose not to mention that Rafiki was actually a baboon.

With that, Candice loped after Chloe, leaving me to sip my drink alone.

Well, this is worse than I imagined, I thought, lifting the bitter fluid to my lips. *Things can only get better, I guess.*

"Drink up!"

An intrusive hand knocked the bottom of my bottle upwards. Shocked, I swallowed the wrong way and spluttered, spilling beer all over my crisp shirt.

"Hey there, Kitten."

I scowled, still coughing.

Wyatt.

Apparently, I was wrong. Things *could* get worse.

PART TWO
SCREAMING

The scruffy boy stood in front of me, laughing so hard a vein bulged in his flushed forehead. Wyatt was the type of kid you could describe as having a cocaine laugh and an ecstasy personality – not without reason. He was harmless enough but didn't make the best life choices.

Electing not to go with a plain shirt, he had instead decided a ripped t-shirt and a ridiculous card dealer's visor would make a better first impression. Sucking a cocktail of bright orange juice and heavy liquor through a straw, he beamed as I composed myself.

"Don't call me Kitten," I growled.

I dabbed my shirt with a kitchen towel, regretting the tattoo of a tiger's face stained onto my right shoulder.

"But, why? It's your name."

"Not anymore it isn't. I'm Milo Callaghan, right?"

"But, I've already told everybody about…"

A bolt of embarrassed heat ran though me. I had gotten the tattoo when I was sixteen, without my parents' permission. It was the first thing I'd ever done without them knowing, and it was meant to be cool. And it might have been, if the artist didn't draw like a five-year-old. What was supposed to resemble a ferocious beast actually became a ginger kitten, and birthed a nickname I never managed to shake.

"You told everybody?"

Wyatt slapped my chest and cackled heartily, his face leaning too far into my personal bubble.

"Of course I didn't, mate. I'm just messing with you."

Scooping his arm around me, he gestured to the room with his flamboyant drink. "Meet any new friends yet?"

"Um, just some girls called Candice and Chloe."

"Ah, Chloe. *La chica*. What you think of her?"

"Um... She seems... nice."

"I agree. Stuck-up bimbo. Hot, though. Her friend's nicer. Now, let me give you a tour." He pointed at the bearded beer pong champion with his ridiculous cocktail. "That's Robbie Flowers. He's got three years of experience as a student."

"You mean, he's failed the first year twice already?"

"Shh, don't interrupt! Flowers. Hell of a drinker. Now, there's..."

He reeled off a round of quick-fire names I instantly forgot. Somehow, Wyatt had already spoken to everyone at the party – including my flatmates – and he didn't even live with me. He had waltzed in from another apartment block at the other end of the campus.

Monty strolled back into the room, chewing a mint, and sipping a neon-blue drink. His hair was dishevelled but, other than that, nobody would even have suspected he had just thrown up. Looking lost for a moment, he sidled his way into a group, and struck up a conversation with a girl in sloppy dungarees, commando boots, and blonde dreadlocks.

"Oh, that's Monty. Posh boy. Don't ask him about it, though. He'll flat out deny it, even with the Eton drawl. And the girl he's talking to, with the dreads – that's Sophia. Good girl, her. Likes a laugh."

I rolled my eyes, knowing what Wyatt meant by a 'laugh.' Judging by the size of his pupils, he'd already enjoyed a laugh or two himself.

"Speaking of which," he continued, rummaging in his pocket, "I have the best idea! There's this new stuff. According to my dealer, it makes you *smell* colours."

"I think I'm good," I said, shutting him down. Wyatt had a warped definition of what makes a good idea. Most of his were illegal. How he landed a Chemistry degree offer eluded me.

"You sure, bro? You're really missing out."

I raised a hand. "No thanks."

"Fine. Maybe Sophia'll join me. I think you'd like her. We should go over."

Panic flared in my mind. "But…"

Before I could protest, Wyatt grabbed my elbow and guided me into the circle.

* * *

"Get off! Leave me alone!"

Exhausted, the jogger batted away the hands swiping at his back. The man was practically rabid, speaking in grunts as he chased him along the pavement.

At a loss, he surveyed a row of apartment blocks ahead. At the end of the street, a large boy was hunched in a doorstep with his back to him.

Thank God! he thought.

Even sitting down, he could tell the boy was huge – big enough to overpower his attacker with ease.

"Hey!" Bounding onto a turfed area, he wheezed. "I need help…! This guy's been chasing me… for ages. Can you give me a ha–"

Fresh terror bolted through his core as the mountainous student rose and turned his way. Letting his eyes flick up to the boy's face, then his attacker, the jogger backed into a fence.

"No," he said.

He was trapped. Unable to fight back, he screamed as they both descended on him. Within seconds, he was dead.

* * *

"So, I was at Glastonbury, yeah?" Sophia was saying, mid-conversation, as we arrived. "And Figgy Blake was, like, really shredding on the guitar. It was sweltering. We'd all had a few beverages – but who hasn't when they're witnessing history? Figgy had just finished talking about the poor orphans in Malawi. And that's when I said to my mate, Shannon, I was gonna throw up. The whole day had just overwhelmed me. The sun was too bright. It was, like, *really* hot.

"So, anyway, Shan and Laura banded together and got these wonderful guys to lend us their dingy. They lifted me out of the crowd, like freakin' Jesus, and put me in the dingy, where it was cooler. Crowd surfed me all the way to the front. Figgy's security guards guided me to the recovery room after that. I swore I wouldn't drink again, but, of course, I was back at it the next morning. No rest for the wicked, eh? It was all just so, like, spiritual, y'know?"

Monty fiddled with the label on his beer bottle. "I'm pretty sure Figgy's dead," he mumbled.

"What? No. He's very much alive, my friend."

"Actually. I'm positive he's dead."

"Don't listen to everything you read in the newspapers, bro."

"I don't. Figgy's been dead for ten years. Why would he show up at Glastonbury?"

"Well, maybe, it was Phil Greene. I can't remember. I was a too busy having a spiritual experience crowd surfing in a dingy."

"Phil Greene's also dead. I went to school with his son."

"Where the hell did *you* go to school?"

"Not important."

"You some sort of billionaire kid or something?"

"What? Not at all. My family might be comfortable, but – wait. I don't see what this has to do with anything. We're discussing general knowledge, not–"

"Are you calling me stupid? You know what? It's people like you who really get me riled, wearing your elitism like a God-given right. You know nothing about living in poverty, blinkered by your white privilege!"

"You do know you're white, too, don't you?"

"There you go again, with–"

"Ahem!" Wyatt stage-coughed into his fist. "Oh, I didn't see you two there. Having fun, guys?"

The pair glared at each other but dropped their argument.

"Oh, hi, Wyatt. We were just discussing the time I crowd-surfed at Glastonbury," said Sophia. "It was so hot I nearly fainted."

"No chance of that tonight," Wyatt snorted. "It's brass monkeys out there."

"I hear a storm's predicted for later," I added.

"I heard that, too," said Sophia. "I'm not heading into town tonight. Not with it being so far away!"

"We could order a taxi," suggested Wyatt.

"We could, but we'd still have to walk all the way to the carpark outside the main gate. They're not allowed to cross the moat, are they?" Monty explained. "It was a fair walk in, after I parked my four-by-four out there. I'm just glad they let us come in to drop off our stuff."

I could already see that not allowing cars would become a real pain, especially with the onset of winter. I'd read online the no-cars rule meant lots of students stole trolleys from the student supermarket to carry groceries home. The carts were strewn across pavements all over the campus. A steward had to collect them every day.

"Think I'll just check out the uni bars in here," said Sophia.

"Jolly good idea," Monty agreed. "The uni didn't give us our very own bar strip for nothing. I suppose they had to, with thousands of us living here."

"Absolutely," said Wyatt, with the grin of a mother who was happy her family wasn't arguing at Christmas dinner.

"Just another way for them to control us, I think," said Sophia. "Damned corporate dictators."

"Er, yeah..." Wyatt backpedalled. Uncertain, he quickly added, "Fight the man, right? Oh, by the way, this is Milo."

He nudged me forward into their spotlight.

"We've met," said Monty. "Good chap." He shot me a conspiratorial glance, so I made a note not to mention the spewing incident.

"Pleased to meet you," Sophia added.

She held up her mug of liqueur, and I clinked it with my bottle. We both took a swig. I'd been sipping my beer throughout the conversation and was already beginning to feel the buzz of alcohol kicking in.

"Where are we off to first?" Wyatt asked.

"I'm not sure," said Sophia. "I've heard Armageddon's good."

"Sounds amazing," I said, feeling the buzz reach my feet.

Swigging the remaining contents of the bottle, I placed it on a nearby workspace, glad I'd run out. Wyatt immediately fished a replacement drink out of the fridge next to him, opened it with his teeth, and handed it to me.

Joy, I thought, raising it to my lips.

"Armageddon? Maybe not yet," Monty suggested. "It's barely dark. A little early for a nightclub, don't you think?

We'll be dead before twelve if we start there. How about somewhere with a bit more…. ambience?"

Sophia rolled her eyes. "Sorry, I don't think we have anywhere with a black-tie dress code."

"Not like that," Monty snapped. "I swear, I'm not even *that* posh."

"Fine. Where do you think we should go?"

"Um…" he paused. "I saw a quaint, little pub on the way in. It's clearly new, but it looks just like an old tavern."

"That sounds pretty chill," said Wyatt. "I like it. We can start off with a few quiet ones there, then move on to somewhere a bit more intense. This is gonna be lit!"

"Of course," Monty chirped. "I bet it has craft beers. And it's right next to the uni dressage building. You never know," he laughed, "if the night gets out of hand, we could all end up going on a drunken jaunt on the ponies, like back at school!"

"Sorry?" I asked, choking on my beer.

Sophia stifled a laugh. "Not. Posh. At. All."

"But… I mean…" Monty faltered.

His explanation was cut short when a horrified scream reduced the party's conversations to silence.

PART THREE
NOT SYRUP

Escaping the dread of the party, I headed towards the screaming, hoping it meant I wouldn't have to talk to anyone for a while. Like a shoal of fish, most of the room vacated in a rush of limbs and glittering bottles. The flat was on the ground floor of a multi-storey block so it didn't take long for us all to pour onto the lawn bordering the building.

Outside, the scene was chaotic. Sprawled on the grass, Chloe was sobbing. Her spoiled princess facade had dropped away like a mask. It looked as though someone had splattered her arms and face with maple syrup. The viscous fluid matted her hair and dripped off her fingers. Beside her, Candice squatted, consoling her with a bottle of water. Chloe batted it away, slurring gibberish.

I followed her gaze to a collection of large recycling containers hemmed in by trees on the opposite side of the road. Despite the party starting before sundown, it was now twilight – too dark to figure out exactly what she could see. *A fox, maybe? But, why would a fox cover her in syrup?*

"Woah. What the devil happened here?"

Monty was the first to react. While everybody else gasped and chattered like schoolgirls, he kneeled beside

Chloe and Candice. Taking off his blazer, he draped it over the traumatised girl's shoulders.

"Smooth," Wyatt whispered. "This guy's good. Wish I'd thought of that."

Monty glanced up at him and rolled his eyes. I shook my head, silently apologising on his behalf. Ignoring Wyatt, Monty addressed Chloe's friend. "Candice? That's your name, right?"

Shaken, Candice nodded.

"Okay, what happened?"

"I'm not completely sure," she uttered. "She ran out here to get reception. I couldn't find her right away. It wasn't until she screamed that I saw her."

Placing a hand on her arm, Monty leaned in closer to Chloe, inspecting her body in the same way a mechanic hovers over a car engine.

"I have a boyfriend," she said, this time between sobs.

Wyatt snorted, but Monty kept his composure. "Well, does he know where the blood's coming from? If not, you need to let me take a look at you."

Blood? I squinted and leaned closer. That's when it hit me. The gloopy fluid wasn't syrup at all. It was rich, arterial blood, and it seemed to be flowing from somewhere on Chloe's body. Judging by how much of a mess it had made, I guessed it must have squirted with considerable force.

Quivering, she allowed Monty to take her hands and slowly turn them over. A drooling hole had been torn into the flesh on her forearm. The horribly inflamed skin around it was a ruddy shade of grey. A chill ran down the back of my neck. Even though it was obvious the party was over, at least for her, I couldn't help but sup my beer, hypnotised by the drama.

"He came out of nowhere," she cloaked, finding real words for the first time. "He was, like, insane."

"Who was insane? Who did this, Chloe?"

Chloe's words emerged as an indecipherable whisper. Some of the students around me had already decided the performance was over. That her mysterious attacker was probably drunk, and already gone.

Someone would have to waste their first night of Freshers' getting the injured girl to the university's recovery room, and waiting for her to sleep off the alcohol. It appeared almost everyone was determined not to become that person. As they sidled back indoors, a small group of concerned spectators stayed to see what would happen next.

"I saw the creep just before he took off," said Candice. There were tears of panic in her eyes. "He was wild. A big guy. I think he was on something."

"We need to report this to the police," said Monty. "Any defining features? What did he look like?"

"I don't know. He was big... bulky."

"So, muscular?"

"No..."

"Fat?"

"I'm not one to fat-shame, but..."

"He just attacked your best friend!"

"Okay, he was... a little out of shape."

I shot Wyatt a warning glance, knowing he was already concocting an inappropriate joke. He just smirked back at me, relishing my concern.

"Is that a bite mark?" Monty asked, frowning.

"Yeah," Chloe whined. She was shivering, but light perspiration glazed her forehead.

"Alright. It looks like you're going to need a tetanus. Anybody not had a drink yet?"

He looked around. Forgetting myself, I raised my hand – the one containing my second half-empty beer bottle. Wyatt slapped it down.

"Come on, Kitten. We'd better get out of here before you get us roped into something neither of us want to do."

He tugged at my elbow, but I didn't budge. I couldn't leave Monty by himself. He needed help, and I needed to find a way to escape the bar crawl. Finally, I'd found the perfect excuse. A few more bottles would be the death of me.

"I'll hel–"

"Don't say it," Wyatt warned under his breath, squeezing my arm.

I ignored him. "I'll help!"

"Dweeb."

Stooping, I looped my hands under Chloe and lifted her to her feet. Between me and Monty, she practically took to the air. There were cats heavier than her. As we set her down, she wobbled, her ankles shaking atop her stilettos. Orbiting us, Wyatt, Candice, and Sophia loitered.

"Oi oi! Lookss like ssomeone can't take the pacce!" Robbie Flowers' silhouette appeared in the doorway. Stumbling forward, he joined us in the forecourt. "Oh… ooh!" The stupid grin, which contorted his alcohol-bejewelled beard, dropped as he noticed the sour faces. "Everything okay – hiccup! – out here?"

"I don't feel well," Chloe moaned.

Robbie swayed, eyeing her dubiously. "What'ss eating you?"

I ignored him, hoping he'd go away.

"Your eyes do look a little glassy," I noted. "Do you need to sit back down?"

"She'll be fine." Candice swooped in and shifted her weight under her friend like a crutch. "This is how she always gets. She's a lightweight. The drink probably just hit her because she hasn't eaten all day."

"How about I get a chocolate bar from my room?" I suggested, remembering the mountain of junk food my mother had posted through the open crack of the car window as my dad and I pulled away for our long car ride to the university.

"No," Chloe moaned. She sounded woozy. "No snacks. Eatin's cheatin', right?"

"A girl after my own heart!" Robbie beamed.

"That makes no sense," I insisted. "You need something. Come inside. We'll find something to bandage up your arm, and something you can eat to boost your blood sugar."

"Good plan, chap," said Monty. "Then, hospital, I think. That thing looks infected."

"Alright, guyss! Good luck with that."

"You're not going to help?" Monty said, his voice icy with accusation.

"We've run out of beer in there!" Robbie protested, almost falling as he jutted a thumb over his shoulder. "I should have expected to need more than one crate. The ladss are having to resssort to..." An unexpected hiccup threw him off balance. "...wine. Someone has to do something."

"This girl needs help, and all you want is beer!" Sophia flared. "Honestly, I think you need a gap year to Malawi to give yourself some perspective on life, and..."

I blanked out whatever she said next, focusing instead of Chloe, who had grown alarmingly silent. Helping Candice lift Chloe off her feet, I ogled the wound, wincing as her blood-soaked arm draped around the collar of my fresh shirt. The cold evening air chilled the wet patch as it moulded to the shape of my skin. With distaste, I eyed the ragged pit of flesh on her forearm.

"Looks like that guy's got a nasty bite on him," I mumbled, my stomach churning as the gore brushed against my cheek. *Definitely not making it to town now.* "The teeth went right in!"

"If I find him, I'll give the cretin what for!" said Monty.

"Me too. I'll ssshow him, Capt'n!" slurred Robbie, throwing up a sloppy salute. He winced, having punched himself in the face. "Anywayss, like I said... beer. I'll jusst get my bottle opener, so I can drink on the way back. Always thinkin', me."

With that, Robbie shuffled back inside. I guessed he'd be at least half an hour trotting to the twenty-four-hour student convenience store. By the time he got back, we'd be half-way to the hospital.

"You know, it's kinda beautiful," cooed Wyatt.

"I have a boyfriend."

"Not your face! The cut. It's sort of... deep, man, you know? Like a metaphor for life or something. Blood leaving the body, and all that. Makes you wonder if our souls are red."

He tilted his head towards me. His pupils were like manholes. A fat, white joint was propped between his lips, already lit. I didn't bother asking him how he'd managed to light it without anyone noticing, or what was in it. "Don't you think, bro?"

"You bet," I said, realising long ago that humouring him was the fastest way to shut down the conversation.

"Beautiful, but savage."

"He must have taken something," I offered, talking about Chloe's attacker.

"Damn right," Wyatt agreed. "My guess is bath salts. They make people crazy! Like cannibals. Wouldn't touch the stuff, myself."

If Wyatt wouldn't try it, I reasoned, *it had to be bad.* "Okay, now, let's get her moved."

"Wanna climb something?" Wyatt asked, without reason. I ignored him, not bothering to wonder how his mind had jumped from cannibalism to rock climbing.

"Come on, mate," Candice moaned at him. "She's

getting blood all over my dress, and we've got a long night to come yet! Get out the way!"

"I'll prepare a space," Monty suggested, reaching for the door. "Looks like she needs a lie down, before we go anywhere. Oh!" He froze.

"What is it?" I asked.

Raising her head, Chloe's eyes shot open, and she screamed in my ear. Candice and I held her tight as she bucked like a mule.

Blocking our route to the tower block, a hulking figure in a flowery apron, fake antlers, and a pair of artificial fairy wings growled. He had to be at least six-foot-six, though, his rotund frame and hairy shoulders bulging either side of his apron made him look bigger. I gasped, experiencing the same rabbit-in-the-headlights fear I'd witnessed on Monty's face.

Despite his mountainous size, the guy looked young, like a Fresher. Judging by the way he was dressed, I guessed he was part of some sort of society initiation, maybe for the rugby team. Their hazing stories were legendary, and apparently hilarious.

Right now, though, his getup was anything but funny. There was something unsettling about the combination of his ridiculous costume, and the dripping mess of black blood smothering the entire lower portion of his face.

"Um… Chloe?" Monty uttered. "Is this the guy?"

For our sakes, I really hoped it wasn't.

PART FOUR
BATH SALTS

Forming a barricade between us and the troll of a man, Monty puffed out his chest.

"See here, chap. I'm sure you've been given something strange tonight, and this is very out of character for you… but that doesn't excuse you. Our friend's injured, and we need to get this whole mess cleared up. You'll have to come with us."

The man-mountain didn't respond. Instead, he stood statuesque, bloodshot eyes flicking from one person to another, as if calculating his next move. His fingernails were dirty, covered in earth. It was unclear how much he understood.

"'Big' and 'out of shape'?" I snapped at Candice under my breath so he wouldn't hear me. "You didn't think to mention the antlers, apron, and fairy wings?"

"It all went so fast," she protested.

"Too fast to notice antlers!"

"I was confused."

"Antlers, for Christ sake!"

"I–"

The man-fairy-deer hissed deeply like a huge python confronted with its jaws wrapped around the ribcage of a dead horse. Dark, bile-like fluid poured from cracks between his teeth.

"Now, don't be hasty, old sport."

Monty's confident façade faltered. He was tall, but it was evident his own mass wouldn't stand a chance against the giant.

Without warning, the attacker threw up his hands, roared, and barrelled into Monty. Fortunately, he anticipated it. Ducking under the avalanche of flesh, he toppled the titan with a knee to the thigh. As the large boy spread-eagled, Monty bounced on his toes and balled his fists.

The beast seemed unfazed as he sprawled close to where Candice and I propped up Chloe. Not even taking the care to protect his face, he head-butted one of the concrete paving slabs edging the grass, and scrambled to right himself before even coming to a complete stop. A skid mark of blood soiled the rock where he hit it. One half of his face was completely grated. Without pausing, he lunged at us on all fours.

I panicked, and dived out of the way, forcing Chloe to take the brunt of his meaty hand. The impact knocked her legs from under her, dragging down both her and Candice. Seizing his first opportunity, the man-beast locked onto the first available target – Candice's leg. She wailed and lashed out with her free leg, but the blows had no effect, glancing off his torn face.

"Hey! Not cool, man! Can't we just all calm down?" suggested Wyatt, sucking his joint as he hovered nearby. Beside him, Sophia was floundering, so he handed her a spare and lit it as she sheltered the tip with her hands.

Monty made a more meaningful contribution, swooping in and punching the giant's side. When it had no effect, he clamped onto his shoulders and yanked hard, flipping him over. In an instant, the giant changed targets, lashing out in his direction.

"Argh!" A pudgy hand tripped him, and the giant dropped his full weight on him, pinning his legs to the spot.

My heart jumped like a jackrabbit with a caffeine addiction. As he looked to me for help, I panicked.

Where's my asthma pump?

I fumbled in my pocket, and came up empty, remembering it had run out in my room.

"Help me!"

I wanted to help – really, I did. But, something held me back. Confrontation was something I had always avoided, at all costs. Every nerve ending in my body was telling me to leave. This wasn't my fight.

As I struggled to step off my cliff-face of fear, Monty wrestled with the man's melon of a head. It flailed, batting him frantically with its plush antlers. Monty struggled to keep the boy's gurning jaws away from his skin. I could tell his strength was waning. It wouldn't be long before he caved and those gnashing teeth hit him.

"Help!" he yelled. "Now, Milo! Somebody!"

The giant swivelled unexpectedly out of his grip, and lunged at his face. Powerless to stop him, Monty's arms collapsed as the wall of blubber crushed them. Opening his mouth into a grizzled yawn, the man sunk closer to Monty's face.

Finally, I burst into action. Or, at least, I would have, if Wyatt didn't do it first. Sprinting forward, he swung his leg back and powered it into the side of the giant's head.

"Argh!" he screamed, hopping on one foot and massaging the other with his hands. "His head's like a rock. I knew boat shoes were a bad idea!"

The distraction was small, but enough to throw the beast off Monty's scent for a second. Given enough wiggle room, Monty slid from under him and scrambled to his feet. His chest heaved, and there was so much gore he looked like he'd slipped in an abattoir.

"Did he get you?" I asked.

"No..." He rested his hands on his knees to catch his breath. "No thanks to you."

The heat of shame rushed to my face.

"Guys, don't forget the problem hasn't gone away!"

Wyatt was talking now. He gestured at the man-beast on the ground. In all of the action, it appeared he had mangled his right arm. A lump in his forearm revealed a bone shard threatening to stab through the surface. Surprisingly, he didn't scream. Instead, he threw himself at us in great lurching movements, like an elephant seal, unable to support his weight with one arm.

"Help!" I shouted at the apartment.

Lights were on in every window of the tower block, but my cries were drowned out by loud speaker systems and drinking game banter. Freshers' was well underway. And with us living at the end of a cul-de-sac, with only trees and a high wall as neighbours, there was nobody else around to notice our struggle.

I decided I had to go inside. Taking a drunk, injured girl to hospital was one thing, but doing so with a drugged-up fairy-tale giant on our tails was another matter entirely. We needed more bodies.

"I'll be right back," I said.

"What!" Monty replied. "Where are you going? Coward!"

The pang of humiliation stung me, but I left the group circling the giant. He writhed on the lawn, covered in his own blood. I got as far as the door jamb when Robbie ploughed into me. His beard was missing a clump of hair and there was a look of terror in his eyes.

"You really don't want to go in there," he said, yanking me to my feet. Sobriety had hit him hard, clearly as a result of coursing adrenaline. I could tell right away he wasn't joking.

"What the hell's wrong n–?" My question was cut short as he clamped a hand over my lips.

Robbie pointed at the cold stairwell leading upstairs to the student accommodation. Under the din of loud music, I heard screaming. My skin became gooseflesh as I waited with my mouth clamped shut. The screams settled one by one, the voices snuffed out like candles.

When blood splattered the breezeblock wall at the top of the stairwell's first turn, I knew the situation had taken a turn for the worse. Shadows stretched against the stairwell's limey brickwork, distorting the outlines of people so they no longer resembled humans.

It can't be, I thought.

My fears were confirmed when a ragged girl in a miniskirt and blouse tumble down the steps. Landing in a pile of her own mangled limbs, she craned her neck and caught sight of us. The whites of her eyes were amber, with rims of bloodshot red in the waterlines. Opening her mouth, she emitted a throat-scraping hiss.

"There are two of them?" I blurted.

Robbie shook his head. "More," he said breathlessly. "A lot more."

PART FIVE
BEHIND CLOSED DOORS

"What sort of maniac gives out bath salts to a whole party of kids?" I screamed.

"One who doesn't stick around to find out what happens next," said Robbie, nudging me away from the door. "We *really* need to go, bro."

"Shouldn't we phone the police?"

"Not an option. This whole place is a black hole for reception. There's no WiFi and no phone signal, remember? But, there's beer." He pulled a can of some alcoholic drink out of his back pocket and grinned, waving it in front of my eyes. "Found it in the kitchen, just before all hell broke loose."

"Not the time!" I shouted. "We need to find the security guards. They'll know what to do."

A blunt *thump* brought to my attention the broken shape of a scrawny boy, who was suddenly lying on the floor at the bottom of the stairs. Peering at us with a gormless look on his face, his mouth widened in fury.

"Where the hell did he come from?" Robbie asked.

Stepping over the body, careful not to get too close, I looked up between the handrails running all along the edge of the stairwell. I wondered if anyone could survive a fall from that height.

"I think he… jumped," I said.

"Crazy," Robbie cooed, popping open the can in his hand. "He looks like he could use a drink. I know I could. Shall we go now?"

I opened my mouth to respond but didn't have time. A horde of throaty growls answered for me. Piling around the corner, more freshers clambered down the stairs to us. Each of them wore a bib of black slime dribbling from their mouths.

"Yeah, let's go."

Hopping over the mutilated boy, I ran into the open forecourt, dragging Robbie with me, as he tried to run without spilling his drink. Outside, I saw Monty. He was out of breath and his blond hair had fallen in front of his eyes.

"You're back," he noted. "I wasn't really expecting you."

Not in the mood to exchange venom, I cut straight to the point. "We've got to go. Quick! Where are the others?"

I scanned the lawn but they weren't there. The giant was on his knees now, legs shaking as he tried to rise to his feet. Just as he managed to gain balance, Monty spear-tackled him from the side and sent him sprawling.

"Chloe's not exactly looking like a picture of health, old sport," he explained. "She's got a fever, and her lips are turning blue. The others took off with her in a groundsman's wheelbarrow they found over by the bins. I offered to stay here to keep an eye on our large friend until they sent a security guard."

"What's this – a mother's meeting?" demanded Robbie. He toppled the remains of the can into his mouth and crushed it against his forehead. "Stop yakking, and get a move on. We need to go!"

"I can't. I'm staying to–"

"No time to explain," I said. "Come on."

He must have understood the urgency in my words, because he instantly changed his mind. Passing the man-mountain, he stuck in one final boot, knocking him off kilter as we jogged into the dark.

It wasn't long until we caught up to the others. Chloe lolled in the wheelbarrow, her dress soaked in dirty rainwater which had accumulated at the bottom of the pan. Wyatt manned the handles, puffing smoke from his joint like a locomotive as he trundled along the road.

"Maybe someone can help us in there," Candice said, just as I joined them in the halo of a streetlight.

She was referring to a neighbouring tower block. Next to its main door, a boy lay on his back, one of his trouser legs rolled up to the knee. A pink-haired girl in black and white make-up sat on top of him. Initially, I turned away, thinking we might have walked in on an intimate fumble on the grass. It was only when I saw the necklace of slick blood hanging from the girl's chin that the truth dawned on me.

"Maybe not there," I suggested, taking over the controls of the wheelbarrow and guiding the gang away before everyone else jumped to the same conclusion as me.

He's probably just unconscious, I told myself, not quite believing it.

"Milo!" said Candice. She sounded relieved. "So, you decided to join us?"

"Uh, it wasn't really my choice," I confessed.

"Oh?"

"We got chased," Monty cut in. "I think someone's managed to give out those bath salts Wyatt mentioned to what looks like every kid in the village."

"I hope not," I said. "There are ten thousand of us in here."

"Indeed," he agreed. "Anyway, we need to keep moving. Do you chaps know where you're going? I don't remember seeing the security office on the way in."

"Nope. We'll just have to keep moving until we find it."

"What's going on, guys?" Chloe croaked from the wheelbarrow.

Her eyelids and head were wilted. Waxy sweat had spread over her skin like lichen. By all accounts, she looked dead, so it was a relief to hear her speak for the first time in minutes.

"It's okay, Chlo. We're getting you help. Just try to stay awake." Candice brushed a strand of stray hair out of Chloe's eyes, as though it were the only thing wrong with her appearance. Offering her a winning smile, she added, "We'll be there in no time. If I'm right, there's a uni office just around the corner. They scanned my ID there on the way in. There have to be guards stationed in there, right?"

A deathly silence descended on the seven of us as we advanced along the road. I found myself receding into my own head, as was often the case when it came to group gatherings. Only the shaky creak of the wheelbarrow's tire kept me tethered to reality.

"What about that?" I asked, finally spotting a small building with a plastic sign hoisted between two poles.

"'Welcome. Meet a smiling face!'" Sophia read aloud. "Looks about right."

"This is the place," Candice confirmed. "It doesn't look like anyone's in right now, though."

She pressed her face against a window, cupping her hands over her eyebrows to block out the reflection of the streetlights.

"There's a light flickering inside. I think it's a CCTV screen," she said, after a moment. "There has to be a guard around here somewhere – argh!"

Candice recoiled milliseconds before the widow exploded, raining glass all around her. Instantly, we were on red alert.

Where the window had been, there was now a gaping, square hole. A bald man in a navy jacket and a baseball cap hung from the gap. His chin was completely gone, and his cheeks were ripped away from his teeth. A vivid triangle of gore soaking his neck and uniform gave the impression of a giant clown's mouth. Ivory teeth shone through the red, like a nightmarish smile.

"Get back!" Monty ordered, rushing forward to save Candice. Before the man had a chance to clamber through the open window, Monty drove a fist into his nose, knocking him back into the bowels of the building. He vanished, dragging a table with him on the way to the floor.

"That guy looked a tad old to be a student," Monty said, rubbing his knuckles.

"That's because he wasn't one," Sophia replied. "Didn't you see the walkie-talkie? He's a guard."

"An irresponsible guard," I said. "Obviously, he was expecting a slow night. Why else would he get high?"

Sophia scoffed. "A slow night? On the first night of Freshers'!"

"Point taken. Either way, we should get moving."

"Good plan, bro!"

Wyatt tapped me on the shoulder and pointed at the road we had just travelled. Most of the street was shrouded in darkness, but what I could see ignited a furnace of anxiety in my stomach.

"What the hell is going on?" I whispered.

Like rats abandoning their nest to a ferret, students poured out of the *cul-de-sac's* buildings. They glanced over their shoulders in wild panic as they barred doors behind them. Some sported monstrous wounds on their arms and legs, others, cuts and bruises. None seemed to be enjoying their first night away from their parents.

Down the road, the girl with the pink hair sprang from an alcove, having apparently abandoned her first victim. With electric speed, she took down a spindly teenager as he passed by. The encounter was over quickly, but a slow-motion camera would have revealed something similar to a scuffle between a lioness and a young zebra.

Moments later, a door was bashed open. A horde of viscous freshers spilled into the road, slathered in bile and blood. There were dozens of them, all crazed and driven by some unexplainable fury. Whole shoals moved as one, slowly but with purpose. One such group was headed in our direction.

As we debated what to do about it, a crocodilian grunt rumbled from the broken window. The security guard had regained his bearings.

"Time to go!" I yelled.

We took off as fast as we could. When Wyatt saw Robbie had a hold of Chloe's wheelbarrow, and was about to run it into a wall, he swept in and took over.

"Never drink and drive, bro!" he shouted. "Let me take the wheel… er, barrow."

I couldn't help but wonder if she was any safer under his muddled watch. Chloe apparently didn't notice the changeover, nor did she care. By this point, she was in a semi-comatose state, draped over the side of the barrow, her body bouncing unrestrained with every pothole.

Wyatt only made it a few hundred feet before the tire came off the wheel and the barrow skidded to a halt. At high speed, his legs came into contact with the metal bucket and he catapulted over it, like a puppy ploughing into a beach ball.

"Argh!" he winced, rubbing his behind. He scowled at the ground as though it had personally attacked him. "Piece of junk!"

"Guys!" Monty said, circling to heave Wyatt to his feet. Being the fastest of us all, he had adopted the role of scout. "We're blocked in." He eyed the destroyed wheelbarrow with surprise. "She okay?"

I shrugged, and stooped to inspect Chloe. Her eyes were closed. Thankfully, she hadn't fallen out when it came to a grinding stop. Tapping her cheek lightly, I mumbled some quick-fire questions and shook her.

"I have a boyfriend," she complained woozily, wrinkling her nose.

"She's fine," I said to Monty. "But, she'll need to be carried the rest of the way."

"I'm not sure we'll get *ourselves* the rest of the way, chaps."

At the end of the road, the shadow of what looked like an angry mob had materialised. Their arms and heads writhed, their jaws gurning – a tell-tale sign of their drug use. Many of them were missing huge gouges of meat from their sides. Their clothes were slick with gore.

That must be quite a drug, I thought.

We were trapped on both sides. The jaw of angry masses was closing in faster than we could come up with a plan.

"In here!" I heard someone shout, and turned to find Candice up against the door of a low-rise building. "It's unlocked."

Hoisting Chloe into the air, Monty flung her limp body over his shoulder. Candice ushered us all inside and locked the entrance behind her, just as a slick hand slammed against its small window pane. Pulling a chord, he released a blind, shutting out the terrors of the outside world.

Inside, deep shadows swallowed part of the room. A checkerboard, vinyl floor led to another high window which streamed streetlight into the building. Clawed hands pressed up against that, too. I raced across the tiles, skidding on the plastic, and pulled down a second blind. A wall of industrial washing machines and tumble dryers stood dormant in a horseshoe shape around us.

"What's this?"

"The communal laundrette, by the looks of it," Monty answered Sophia. "I imagine this is where the hired help wash and dry clothes."

"Hired help?" Sophia snapped, helping Candice move Chloe to a small back room, where she lay her on a pile of linen. She closed the door behind her, leaving Candice to deal with her friend. "Do you think *normal* people live like that? I mean, *slaves*? Seriously?"

Monty did a double-take. "Of course not! I said nothing about slaves! I was talking about assistants. You know – *paid* workers. Not that a hippy like you would know anything about paid work. Don't be so preposterous, woman!"

"Woman! So, you're sexist as well! I should have expected it from someone of your calibre. I've seen your kind before. My father–"

"Aha!" Monty's face wore a cruel grin. "So, we've finally found the heart of the matter. Don't think I didn't see through your disguise. I know a private education when I see one! Feeling guilty for Daddy, are we? What did he do? Is he in the sugar trade? Does he pay people to club seals?"

"Shut your face! You don't have a clue what you're talking about. You're just a Neanderthal."

"At least I'm the real me. You don't see me pretending to be someone I'm not. I mean, really. Dreadlocks? For a social justice warrior, you're very keen on cultural appropriation!"

"Uh, guys," I said.

"What!" They both turned in unison.

The weight of everyone's eyes rested uncomfortably on me. A sudden, irrational fear of public speaking clamped its hands around my throat. I wished I had my asthma pump.

"You're forgetting the problem," I said finally. "We're trapped in here, there are dozens of drugged maniacs at either door, and we have an injured girl with us, who I think has an infection. *We* might be able to wait for the police, but I don't think she can."

"So?" Monty stated. "What's your point? I don't see a way out of this. If it weren't for this place being a cesspit for junkies–"

"Hey!" Wyatt cut in. "We prefer the term, 'Maverick Chemists,' and I've been doing some think–"

"Shut it, Wyatt."

"Hold on." He held up a hand to Monty. "Hear me out here."

"No! I don't think your opinion really matters."

"Do you have any ideas?"

"Well, no. But, I'm sure–"

"Then hear me out."

"Wyatt," I sighed. "We don't have time to play games."

"We've got nothing but time, baby."

I shot a glance at Monty. "He has a point."

"Fine." Monty shrugged, then, leaning against a giant tumble dryer, slid to the floor. "Let the idiot speak."

"Right, what is it?"

"Ahem," Wyatt started. "Before I start, keep an open mind."

"Go on."

"What if these angry people aren't on drugs?"

I sighed. "Keep going."

"Look, I've seen a lot of guys on a lot of things in my time, and none have reacted like this. Even drugs that make people violent don't affect everyone that way."

"What are you suggesting?" I asked, humouring him. "A government experiment? Chemical warfare?"

"Maybe," Wyatt uttered. "Or maybe they're zombies. *Real* zombies."

A hush blanketed the room. Monty chuckled, then cackled, and finally full-on belly laughed. "See," he said, holding his ribs. "That's why you don't let a junkie come up with ideas."

"Think about it," said Wyatt, undeterred. "They're unreasonably angry, have a taste for flesh, feel no pain, no matter how badly they get injured, and everyone they bite turns into one of them."

Monty groaned. "Nonsense. We haven't seen a single shred of evidence to suggest their bites are contagious. I mean, Chloe got bitten over an hour ago, and the worst thing that happened to her was she got the lurgy. I mean, does she look like a man-eater to you?"

"Well…" said Wyatt.

"Don't answer that!"

A loud bang stopped the conversation dead. I fired Monty a worried glance, and he immediately stood up.

"What was that?" he asked.

"Something fell over?"

I could have sworn the noise came from inside the building. Monty looked at the door at the rear of the room. The wooden panel radiated pressure. I could sense it. My skin tingled, responding to the wood in the same way it would a live bomb.

"Candice?" I called.

There was no reply.

"Candice?" Sophia tried.

No luck there, either.

She was sitting on an old washing machine, which had possibly been removed for repairs. Sliding off the surface, she dropped to her feet and headed for the door.

"Better check on them," she reasoned.

"Mmm," Monty agreed.

Trailing behind, I wrung my hands as we edged closer. Muffled movement told me something was going on behind the wood.

Candice. All I needed was one word from her to put me at ease.

"Hello?" Sophia knocked twice. When there was no response, she pushed on the door. Before it even arced open all the way, she screamed.

PART SIX
AS ONE DOOR CLOSES

Oh, wait. That scream came from me.

"You're looking better! Oh…"

Wyatt's face dropped as he noticed Chloe was anything but better. The thin girl crouched on all-fours, her dress folded up around her hips as she perched like a wolf over a familiar body.

Candice was under her, her whole body slack, blood pumping from open lacerations in her neck and abdomen. Her eyes stared blankly at the ceiling. A shelf was torn from the wall. Washing powder layered the scene like fresh snow, congealed with blood and other fluids. It looked as though someone had thrown up everywhere after eating half their bodyweight in asphalt.

"Good Lord!" Monty recoiled.

Hackles raised, Chloe jolted as she saw us in the door jamb. Her top lip curled back, and she abandoned her kill. Balancing with uncoordinated legs, she lifted herself to her full height and ambled towards us. At the start of the night, her dress had been fashioned with a diagonal slit, revealing part of her toned stomach. Now, it provided a window for her bloated belly, which hung through the hole, overstuffed with human entrails.

"Real zombies!" said Wyatt. "Told you!"

"Poor Candice," I murmured, because no one had said it yet.

Chloe lunged, a maniacal death-hiss contorting her face.

"Argh! She's on me!" Wyatt pushed her away, and she spun, her grotesque belly swinging like a pendulum. There was a liquidity about the flesh, suggesting she had burst the organ wide open when gorging on her best friend.

"What do we do?" asked Sophia.

In a panic, I grabbed an industrial-size pack of washing power. The box practically jumped into the air.

Empty!

I shook the box, but launched it at her anyway. The hollow cardboard bounced feebly off her head.

"Argh!" I screamed, when she grabbed hold of my shoulder.

Stumbling back, I put distance between us. The others formed a circle. Drowsy confusion overcame Chloe as she found herself playing 'piggy in the middle' with our voices, unsure which way to turn. Her yellowed eyes snapped from one person to the next, but she was gripped with indecision.

"Now what?"

"We need weapons!" Sophia said, on the verge of hysterics.

Wyatt sprung at her, fists raised. "I've got a weapon right here – woah!"

Sliding on a spot of blood, he slipped past Chloe and tumbled into a heap next to one of the washing machines. In an instant, she was on him.

"Ah!" he screeched. "Help!"

Monty ploughed forward and smashed her off him. Teetering awkwardly, Chloe toppled backwards, her rear end falling into an open tumble dryer. Wyatt screamed, pinned to the spot, unable to edge around her and get out of reach.

"Quick! Someone do something!" he yelped.

In a moment of panic, I did the only thing I could think of doing. I hit 'spin.'

Incapable of wriggling free, Chloe started to rotate, and her manic tongue was carried away from Wyatt's head. Wyatt slumped, relaxing as the danger turned upside down. It was only when she came back around that he realised his mistake and screamed again.

I rolled my eyes and pulled him to safety.

Hands shaking, he fished inside his pocket and pulled out some sort of pill.

"That was close."

"Do you really think that's a good idea?" I asked.

He shrugged. "The whole world's gone berserk. Outside, there are real zombies. *Real* zombies, man! The least I can do is go out on a high."

I placed a hand over his and gave him a hard look, maintaining eye contact until he cracked.

"Fine," he said, and popped them back into his pocket. "But don't come crying to me when you die sober."

"Uh, guys?" said Sophia, when all of the drama had died down. "Where's Robbie?"

My eyes shot wide open. "I knew we were missing someone!"

Monty looked troubled. "Robert?" he called into the dark. There was no response. "Well, he's definitely not here." He scanned the high laundrette windows, where dozens of hands smudged red ooze across the glass. "And it doesn't look like he'd last long out there, either."

"He must have fallen," I said, remembering what he looked like bouncing along with the wheelbarrow, completely unable to stay on course. "Who knows how early he started pre-drinks. He was in no fit state for a zombie apocalypse."

A thunderous wrapping on the laundrette door made us all jump.

"It's him," I said. "It must be. He's made it!"

I bounded to the exit and lifted the blind. A pale face with jaundice eyes and a missing tooth greeted me. I frowned. Then a fist unexpectedly pounded on the door again, and a blurred figure sped past.

"Is someone in there?"

The caller sounded like a man. Peering past the ragged head, I saw the blur pass a second time. It was an older man, in his fifties, with mercury-coloured hair and a navy uniform.

Another security guard.

"Anyone?" he shouted again, speeding past a third time.

"Guys, it's a security guard."

"Jolly good," said Monty. "Let him in. Maybe he has weapons."

"Um…" I opened the door a fraction and felt the pressure of bodies piled up behind it. Dirty fingers threatened to pull it away from me, and a chorus of hisses leaked through the open gap. "Little help?"

"Here." Monty Spartan-kicked the door, sending a handful of the living dead careering in all directions.

"Over here, old chap!" He waved his arms.

The old security guard's face brightened as he noticed the open door. Dodging two zombies, he pranced between them, his uniform soaked in sweat.

"They're slow," he called, with a hoarse voice. "As long as you keep on your toes… and don't get trapped anywhere…phew… they're pretty easy to avoid."

Pirouetting around a mutilated teenage girl in a bloodstained onesie, he got closer. The strain showed on his face. This wasn't a man used to physical exercise. He was a little tubby, and limped for a second or two after every leap. His face was grey. I guessed he wouldn't be able to keep up his zombie ballet routine for much longer.

"I think it's some kind of drug they're all on," he continued. "Flakka, I believe it's called. It was on the news the other day. Did you hear about that kid in America? Ate someone's face."

He was only a few feet away from the opening when Wyatt shot forward and wrenched it shut. Through the window, we saw the man's eyes widen as his body hit the door. Bouncing off, he stumbled and narrowly avoided a fumbling attack.

I glared at Wyatt, incredulous. "What did you do that for?"

"Look, man." He gestured through the small window. The security guard tripped at that exact moment, landing awkwardly on his elbow. He didn't even have a chance to roll onto his back. Two monsters collapsed onto him, pinning him down and plunging their teeth into his shoulders. Volcanic rage blasted through me.

"You murdered him!"

"No, man. Look!"

Furious, I glared hard at the man, his arms shaking frenetically as his nerves went into overdrive. A muffled scream squeezed its way out from under the accumulating zombie dogpile.

I spotted it.

His right calf was torn open. Rich blood had streamed down it into his boot. Now the limp made sense. He had been bitten.

"Wyatt…" I said. "But…"

"I know." He nodded simply. "He was a time bomb."

"Guys, there's our opening!" Monty interrupted. "While they're distracted."

Sophia glanced at the feeding frenzy. There had to be over a dozen reanimated bodies out there, and seven or eight of them had moved away from the door to strip the security guard's carcass.

"What? Out there? Now?" she gawped. "But, we're unarmed! And we're safe in here."

"Not for much longer!" Monty explained. "The windows won't hold forever. We have – what? – five minutes until they're finished with him. Now's the best chance we've got to get out of this alive. Let's head for the village's main gate and hope they haven't spread that far yet. We can pick up stuff to defend ourselves with on the way."

I caught myself subconsciously backing away from the door. The trapdoor spider of anxiety was lodged in my throat again. There was no telling what horror lay just outside, never mind further down the street.

I can't do it, I told myself. *I won't.*

"You okay, chap?" Monty levelled his eyes on me. "You've gone a bit white."

"I can't go," I said. "You guys go. I have asthma. I'll only slow you down."

"You got asthma? You've seemed okay so far."

"It's very subtle asthma! And I hide it well. No, I've made up my mind. I'll just stay here and wait until the police or the military show up. They shouldn't be long now."

Wyatt rolled his eyes. "You wanna be locked in here all alone… with Chloe?" He gestured to the writhing girl with her butt stuck in the tumble dryer. "You know she has a boyfriend, don't you?"

"I'd rather my chances with her than with the hundreds out there!"

"Nonsense!" Monty cut in. "You'll be dead before anyone gets here. This place is a black spot, remember? Who's to say we aren't alone out here? If enough people have already been caught, it's all over. We'll never make it out alive." He opened the door again. "If we're going to make it to the main gate, we need all the bodies we can get."

"Mentioning bodies isn't helping your argum– oof!"

A powerful shove sent me stumbling into the open air.

"Hey!"

"You're wasting time," said Sophia.

The three others vacated the room and shut the door behind them, blocking me from getting back inside.

"But, my asthma!"

"To hell with your asthma! Get moving."

Defeated, I turned to the carnage ahead of me. Our nearest zombies were now thoroughly distracted by the security guard buffet. Others stumbling in the grassy verges, however, had already spotted us, and were shambling in our direction.

I gulped.

"This is a bad idea," I protested.

Despite my reservations, we banded together and sped, unarmed, into the unknown.

PART SEVEN
IN THE DARK

The further we headed away from the rear tower blocks, the quieter the streets became. By the time we made it to the pedestrianised road that boasted a strip of student-only bars, there were no bodies in sight.

"Where's everyone else?" demanded a silverback gorilla of a bouncer, glancing at an imaginary watch, as we approached what looked like an Irish bar.

He grinned, showing the usual confidence of large men in their late thirties, as we rushed up a set of steps to reach him. He had a receding hairline, black uniform, and an earpiece. Next to him, another brick wall of a man stood in silence. "All your mates decide to go straight into town or something, did they?"

"No. They're all dead!" Sophia exploded as we stepped into the light.

The bouncer glanced at his friend, and they both chuckled.

"Wrapped up like burritos in bed, then?" he continued. "Lightweights, the lot of 'em! You millennials have no idea how to drink… Woah! What are you lot dressed as? Nuclear blast survivors? It's not Halloween yet, you know."

Pushing to the front, Monty lunged to pass him. A thick arm barred his path.

"Hold up, mate. I'll need your ID. That goes for the lot of you. And it's a fiver each for entry."

"Oh, we don't want to drink," Monty replied.

"Ha! And I'm a showgirl on Wednesday nights. You must think I was born yesterday."

"It's true," said Monty. "We just need to speak to a manager."

The bouncer rubbed his chin and smirked. "That right? And why's that?"

"We need to get this bar evacuated. Everyone here's in danger!"

Another chuckle. "Good luck trying to stir up trouble in there. It's like a morgue. The place can hold three hundred, but we've only got about a hundred and twenty in tonight."

"I'm not trying to cause trouble. Two streets away, the roads are filled with dead bodies – and they're walking!"

"Like zombies?" The bouncer's voice was barbed with mock enthusiasm.

"*Exactly* like zombies! At first, we thought it was the drugs, but now we know it's not!"

"You kids are on drugs?"

"No! Not us. I mean them. But that's not important. It's not drugs. They're real zombies!"

"Hey, Mike," the bouncer said, pressing his radio mouthpiece to his lips. "See these kids on the security camera? They're telling us to get everyone out. Apparently, there's been a zombie outbreak. We're all gonna die."

He released his finger on his radio and held the speaker up for us to hear a crackle of white noise and obnoxious laughter.

Monty bristled. "This might seem unbelievable at the moment, old sport, but you have to listen. If you don't get this place emptied before they all come rushing down here, they'll take over. Not even a meat head like you could fight them off!"

Feeling the tension build, I coughed apologetically and reached into my pocket. I flashed my ID at the bouncer and slipped a folded note between his hairy knuckles. They were balled into a fist. Monty held his gaze like a rutting stag but I didn't fancy his chances.

"Good acting, mate!" I said, slapping him on the back. "You almost had *me* going there." I shot the bouncer a winning smile. "He's joking, of course!" Leaning closer, I stage-whispered, "Drama student."

The bouncer laughed again, and whispered back, "Say no more."

Persuading everyone to hand over their IDs for inspection, I ushered our little group through the door and closed it behind us. Monty's face was stoic. When I shrugged, he said, "I don't even do drama. Don't insult me!"

"Drama, politics. You say tomato…" I said.

"Coward."

"Whatever. Now, let's get down to business and find the manager."

"I say blow the lot of them!" Monty ranted. "This place is a farce. They clearly didn't want our help, so why should we go out of our way? It'll be faster for us to keep moving."

I bit my tongue, realising his need to let off steam. Inside, semi-crowded tables full of spent pint glasses covered a busy carpet. A jukebox harmonised badly with the fairground tunes of a bandit. Both devices watched over a purple-clothed pool table. Approaching an oak bar, I scanned the space for someone who looked like they were in charge.

A twenty-something woman with a black shirt and a tight ponytail wrote notes on a clipboard, while a plump boy in a *Star Wars* t-shirt pulled pints.

"Excuse me," I croaked over the din of rowdy voices, pushing in front of a handful of punters lining the bar. The woman's eyebrows knitted in annoyance and she pointed at a sign on the bar with the butt of her pen.

Please form an orderly queue, I read. "But, I'm not ordering–"

She was already gone, her ponytail swinging as she cantered down a staircase to a cellar.

"I've got this, lads and ladies!" said Wyatt, doing up his fly and strolling back from the Gents. I hadn't seen him leave. He ran his tongue along the surface of his teeth and snorted. "You go find a table and rest your legs. There's no point all of us waiting."

"I'll meet you there," Monty agreed, heading off to the bathroom himself.

I slid into a wooden booth, and fiddled with a dog-eared beer matt while Sophia thumbed her phone screen, her face illuminated in an odd contrast to the sombre pub lighting.

"There's no use," I reasoned. "It's not going to work."

"I'm not trying to text anyone. I'm playing a game." She poked out her tongue for concentration. "Relaxation Valley. It helps to settle my nerves."

Four full pint glasses slid under my nose, froth spilling onto the table.

"Bad news, peeps," said Wyatt, removing one and glugging half its contents. "Ah… that was good! The manager's busy. The guy at the bar said they're short-staffed, and she's doing a stock audit. She might be another half an hour. But, look – I got drinks!"

"You what!"

"What's this?" Monty arrived, frowning at the pints.

"Manager's busy," repeated Wyatt, distracted by the vortex of bubbles in his beer. "She won't talk to us for half an hour so I got a round in."

"Absolutely not. We're running out of time," Monty said, taking his pint and supping it. The creamy foam moustache above his top lip arched into a smile. "Oh, that's good."

"I know, right!"

Sophia also downed a portion of her drink and drew her forearm across her lips.

"Nectar of the gods," she agreed.

I grimaced. "Have you all gone mad?"

"No, but I tell you what is mad – the price of these drinks. It's so cheap here!"

"How cheap?" asked Sophia.

"Go and get some shots. You'll be surprised! I've got a good mind to stay here all night."

"Be right back." She disappeared, slipping off to get more drinks, leaving Monty and Wyatt to chat about the music.

Noticing a twinge in my bladder, I gave up reasoning with them. *What's thirty minutes?* I was exhausted anyway.

On my way to the bathroom, I passed gaggles of students laughing and singing. Packs of playing cards had been distributed. Together, they were playing drinking games, flipping cards, and cheering like a pantomime crowd. A boy snorted into his beer, struggling to drink it without using his hands.

"I swear he was on something," a girl said, deep into a story as I squeezed past her chair. "I've never seen someone so angry. Incredible, wasn't it, Chris?" A short boy in a hoodie nodded, and she continued, "We're lucky he was on the other side of bank, with the canal between us, or who knows what he might have done!"

I spotted a white stickman sign on the front of a door and pushed my way into the Gents. Two men looked startled as I entered. One left immediately, while the other moved to a row of sinks to wash his hands. Doing my business at the urinal, I strolled over to the sinks and leaned on their granite worktop, staring into a large wall-mounted mirror.

No wonder they looked like that when I came in.

I was a mess. My thick brown hair was slick and angular, styled by dried gore. On top of that, my shirt was torn and bloody. Despite my weedy frame, it certainly looked like I didn't have much left in the way of patience.

Splashing water on my cheeks to wash away some of the grime, I hand-dried myself with a paper towel. Then I re-entered the lounge. The table with the storytelling girl was in full banter mode. Passing them, I held back when someone said something that caught my attention.

"Steve walked up and gave him money, the wally. Honestly, I don't know what's wrong with the homeless guys around here today. This bloke was a psycho as well. Completely out of his tree on something, obviously! Chasing the seagulls, he was." The boy blurted a laugh. "Anyway, Steve handed him a fiver, and then the guy grabbed him! We all had to jump in just to get him off! He bit Steve right on the…" He stifled a laugh. "Well, you show 'em where he bit you, Steve. Oh, he's fallen asleep." The guy next to him, who I assumed was Steve, was unconscious, slumped in the corner of the booth.

"Long day, I suppose," continued the storyteller. "The drink's hit him hard. Anyway, the nutcase bit him on the thigh – the thigh! He was ravenous, too. As soon as we got Steve from under him, we all bolted. No point staying to reason with a guy like that."

Hurrying back to the table, I slid next to Sophia on the outside of the booth.

"Guys, we really need to speed this thing up. Where's the manager?"

Several glittering drinks of various sizes and colours waited for me on the table. A lot more empty glasses bordered them. It appeared the others had been busy in the few minutes I'd been away.

"Down the cellar still, I think, man. She won't be long. Come and have a drink. You've got some catching up to do. Next round's on you." Wyatt raised a glass in my direction.

Brushing it away, I said, "Look, we're running out of time. If we don't get this sorted in the next five minutes, we really need to go. I just overheard a group talking over there about–"

A maniacal howl echoed through the bar, bringing conversation to a standstill. Glancing over at the storyteller's booth, along with a hundred and twenty other heads, I winced. The unconscious boy, Steve, was upright and awake in his seat. His eyes bulged, and black vomit spewed from his lips as he screamed again.

"Aw, mate!" his friend complained, moving his pint. "You've got it all over me! I told you that guy probably had a disease or something. Now we've both got to nip back to the flat, and – argh!"

As the zombie sunk his teeth into his friend's tricep, I stood bolt upright. Grabbing two free cues propped against the pool table, I tossed one to Monty. Unprepared, he yelped as it hit him in the head. I faced the carnage with the other in my hand, anticipating an attack. I had no idea what I planned to do next, but I felt safer with a weapon.

"Forget the manager. We need to leave," I said without taking my eyes off the scene at the other side of the lounge.

"Yep," Wyatt squeaked in agreement. Lower, he added, "Ahem... Drink up, guys."

I headed for the exit as pandemonium broke out. Seeing the attack unfold, friends piled in to save the victim. The girl who told the original story was screaming. Behind her, the bartender arrived, having abandoned his post to intervene. Poking her head through the cellar door, the manager scowled.

Great, I thought. *Now she appears.*

Monty, Wyatt, Sophia, and I bushed past a sea of curious faces, fighting against the flow of the crowd. Reaching the heavy main doors, I flung them open and darted into the cold night air.

Bad decision.

The bouncer we'd encountered on the way in was on the ground, his head pulverised against a paving slab. His hand fidgeted with his radio, but I'm not sure he would be able to use it even if he got it to his mouth.

Three living corpses crowded him like fruit flies on a rotting peach. His silent accomplice was gone. The broad steps we had ascended were flooded with zombies – too many to avoid. Their breaths were ragged with frenzied hunger as they scrambled up the obstacle on all fours.

"Nope!" I yelped, pushing the others back inside.

"Now what?" Sophia shouted.

"Shots?" Wyatt suggested. Monty froze him with an icy glare and he raised his eyebrows in defence. "What? If we're gonna die anyway, we might as well enjoy ourselves."

"Get out of my way!" Monty wedged his pool cue under the front door's handle and propped it against a table leg. "That should hold them back for a while."

"Okay," I replied. "That sorts that problem, but what about that guy?"

The reanimated corpse in the booth was now pinned by four large men, one being the barman. Stuck, he writhed and howled like a trapped piglet. Black bile dribbled from the corners of his mouth, and his cheeks shook with ugly frustration.

"God, he's stronger than he looks!" shouted one of the punters holding down his arms. "Someone call the police! Er… and an ambulance!"

"Are there any other ways out?" I demanded, adrenaline crackling through my system again.

"Wait a minute," said Monty. "We need to tell 'em."

He gave us no opportunity to argue, striding past us to the brawl. The moment he stepped away from the door, the pool cue splintered. He rushed back to catch it. Too late. A giant spider's worth of arms punched through the gap.

"Get behind him!" Sophia ordered, pushing against the wood to help force it closed. Wyatt joined her. So did a few bystanders, though it was obvious they had no idea what was on the other side.

"What's going on?"

The voice startled me. Spinning, I faced a dozen staring faces. Jackets were being retrieved, and umbrellas collected, as people resolved to leave the quaint bar to avoid trouble. Only about two hours ago, I would have been with them. They wanted to get out – a perfectly reasonable response. But, if they only knew the truth, they'd want nothing more than to keep that door closed.

"I said, what's going on?" The voice was more forceful now. It was the woman with the fitted shirt and the ponytail. "I'm the manager here. What are you doing? Let go of that door! People are trying to get out."

"I can't really explain right now, but – believe me – we can't do that. Do you have another exit?" I asked.

"What? No."

"There has to be! Wherever it is, start escorting people to it. We're all in danger. This'll sound crazy but you have to believe me. Those people behind that door are zombies!"

"Don't be so ridiculous. You, with the blond hair. Let go!"

Monty ignored her, his arms shaking with the strain of holding back the weight behind the door.

"There are more. The door's getting heavier!" he shouted. "We aren't getting out this way!"

"That's it!" the manager growled. "I'm getting the bouncers." She grabbed a radio from behind the bar and pressed the mouthpiece to her lips. "Security to the main doors."

The response was silence. Before she had a chance to question it, I pounced.

"They won't answer you. They're dead."

"They're what!" For the first time, she looked worried.

"I'm telling the truth. Believe what you want, but we all have to get out. Think. There has to be another exit. Where is it?"

"There isn't. Security to the bar," she tried again.

Monty's muscles finally gave way and the door swung open. Bodies packed closest to the door immediately face-planted the carpet while others tumbled over them, disregarding any sense of comradery. Picking up a chair each, Monty and Sophia swung them into the crowd. The monsters didn't even flinch.

Chaos erupted, as the undead exploded into the lounge like a swarm of wasps. Students were cornered in inglenooks, screaming as zombies dived face-first into their bodies.

That was when I lost all composure. Abandoning the others, I blew headlong past the manager and fled behind the bar. My chest heaved as I ducked out of sight. The idea of placing something between me and the madness seemed to help, if only for a second.

"Hey!" the manager shouted, but her attention was torn in too many directions, and I was quickly forgotten.

"Great idea, bro!" Wyatt joined me behind the bar. Meeting me near the dark opening to the cellar, he toggled a smorgasbord of light switches. "Come on!" he grumbled, detonating a lightshow of wall lights and dance floor lasers.

"What the hell are you doing?" I said.

"Shh! One of 'em has to be for down there."

A tall girl in soiled clothes, which clung to her like a diving suit, leaned over the bar to reach me, and I panicked. Stretching back, I grabbed the first thing I touched, and swung it. Lemon slices rained over the room as the bowl hit her in the chin.

"Argh, none of 'em work! Monty, Sophia, get over here! We'll have to go in the dark," Wyatt shouted.

The pair arrived in an instant.

"Follow me!" he said, and slipped into the black cellar.

"Where's the light?" Monty shouted after him.

"Couldn't find it!"

"Oh."

I glanced at Monty and shook my head. "Well, I'm not going down there."

"Oh, you are," he said, and shunted me into the gloom.

I practically fell down the steps. Sophia and Monty followed me down to a concrete floor. Bringing a mop from beside the bar, Monty wedged it behind the door, cutting off the light from the surface.

"Wyatt! You better have a plan," he grumbled.

I couldn't see how far ahead Wyatt was, but his voice sounded distant when he responded. "Sort of! Just follow my voice. Anything has to be better than up there, right?"

I had to disagree. Since I was little, I'd always been afraid of the dark. It was home to too many monsters.

"Ugh. Watch the walls, guys. They're damp. I think it's lime. That stuff'll stain," Sophia said.

"Heaven forbid it ruins my shirt," Monty deadpanned. "Lime clashes with blood."

Feeling our way along a murky passage, we passed metallic instruments I guessed were high-pressure gas cylinders attached to beer barrels. Eventually, we arrived at a door that opened with a push. The sound of blunt tapping told me Wyatt was feeling his way around the border of a room.

"Boxes. Boxes. Wall. Boxes. More boxes... Uh oh."

I didn't like the sound of that.

"What's wrong?" I asked.

Wyatt laughed, but I could sense his nerves. Genuine humour never sounded quite so dry.

"This is a pub, right?" he explained. "It faces directly into the street."

"Where are you going with this?" Monty demanded.

"Well," Wyatt continued, "do you ever wonder when pubs get deliveries? I mean, they're open all day and late into the night, and you never see a van dropping off supplies, or employees carrying crates or barrels through the lounge, do you? They must have a back door – some way to get deliveries in without disturbing the punters."

"Right?" Hope flared in my chest.

Wyatt coughed. "At least, that's what I thought. Only thing is... this place doesn't. It's a dead end."

"Oh." The single syllable lodged in my throat. "So, we're trapped in here?"

"Yup," he confirmed.

A sharp *crack* echoed through what I now considered the dungeon. Seconds later, distant growls confirmed my fears. Something had snapped the mop wedged against the door.

Death had entered the dark.

PART EIGHT
NO WAY OUT

Wyatt swore. His scurrying intensified as the noises of the undead got louder.

"Come on, guys," I found myself saying. "Keep looking!"

A shiver ran its chilled fingers over my skin, but I ignored it, groping the polythene covers of cardboard boxes in the hope of bumbling into something which might be of use to us.

In the background, the ominous pants and bumbles of bodies escalated. A metallic *clang* told me they were halfway down the narrow passageway now and had just bumped into one of the large canisters, which aerated the pumps behind the bar.

"Here, try this," Sophia's voice suggested.

A white light flashed, illuminating a small patch of the dank cellar. Protecting my eyes from the glare, I blinked at the source. Sophia stood in one corner beside a huge bottle bank. From her vantage point, she ran the torch on her phone along a metal rack filled with industrial-sized vodka bottles and crates of cider.

The light sparked a frenzy in the zombies further up the tunnel. They hissed feverishly the moment it bathed the slick walls. We had no visual of them yet but I was sure they weren't far away.

"Thanks," I croaked. "Anyone else got a phone?"

I'd left mine in my room. Without internet reception and a phone signal, I'd reasoned it was little more than a glorified games machine. No point risking losing it on a bar crawl.

"Nope," said Wyatt, head buried in his scrambled attempt at an escape.

"No point, until now," agreed Monty. He had scaled one of the racks and was several feet off the ground, sliding his hand along dusty shelves.

"It doesn't look like there's any way out," said Sophia. Being closest to the door, her eyes darted up the corridor to the direction of our pursuers. In a frantic whisper, she added, "They're coming."

My game plan shifted gears, and I began searching for a weapon. If there was no way out, then the only other option was to fight our way back. It wasn't ideal, but it was the only plan I had. Eyeing packs of giant vodka bottles, I half-regretted not sinking a few drinks with the others before this whole scenario broke out. Some Dutch courage would have been welcomed.

I perforated the plastic holding the vodka bottles together, and wiggled one free. It was the length of my forearm, and probably weighed more than a skull could withstand.

Could I take one down with this?

The question was double-barbed. I had the strength required to swing it, but what about morals? Was it murder to kill someone who was already dead? Were they even dead at all? Who was to say this wasn't some sort of disease – perfectly treatable, given the right conditions? I pushed those thoughts to the back of my mind. Ideas like that were only going to get me killed.

"Argh!" Sophia slammed the door and wrenched up the handle. "We've got company."

A fist or head slammed against the metal door, echoing like a bomb blast in the cavernous basement. Manic jabbering followed. There were at least two voices. Two we could handle – maybe. I just hoped they hadn't brought friends.

"Alright!" Wyatt appeared at my side, with a rusted metal rod in one hand and a broken bottle in the other. "I'm ready, man. You ready for this?"

I just gulped, my eyes darting around the room. It was very apparent the moment the bottle in my hand shattered, I'd be left unarmed in the dark.

Monty dropped to the ground and strained, lifting a small tin barrel to shoulder height. "Good Lord! These things are heavy even when they're empty," he moaned. "Okay. Open the door."

Sophia did as he said, and got out of the way. The next moment was like something out of a first-person shooter, bathed in dim phone light. The monsters screeched in unison, mouths hanging open, cracked teeth dripping with blood and fragments of snagged flesh. At least ten pairs of eyes glinted in the dark.

The faces at the front of the rabble didn't last more than an instant, as the barrel obliterated their skulls. Grabbing a bottle off the rack, Monty instantly followed it up by driving its thin neck into a survivor's eye.

A forest of hands came down on top of him, and he slipped back in a feint. Before I could think about what was happening, I bounded around him, alongside Wyatt, to take down any stragglers.

Swinging like a madman, Wyatt jabbed at heads. Bodies clambered over one another. He took down two before he was forced to fall back. I was less accomplished, swinging the heavy vodka bottle in feeble arcs. None of my initial strikes made contact. The third glanced off the broad chest of a dead student and bounced, sending me stumbling off course.

"Woahoh!" I yelped, tripping over my own feet.

Driving into Sophia, I knocked her legs from under her in a tornado of clumsiness. Together, we spun. She must have let go of her phone as we fell because the cellar became a kaleidoscope of spinning lights which ended with the crunch of broken glass. Then our world went black.

"Argh!" I screamed as a wet hand closed around my ankle. Kicking out with both legs, I scooted away on my back, sliding my body onto a cold, metal surface. The biting chill of the material radiated through my clothes.

My friends' voices were shrill now, hamstrung by fear. They mainly just swore and screamed as they thrashed in the dark, unable to see the next set of approaching arms and teeth. At one point, I heard an almighty crash and assumed the whole set of metal shelves had come down on top of someone.

There was no time to investigate, though. The only thing on my mind was the predator stalking me in the dark. Its fingers brushed against my legs again like antennae, but I managed to evade, rolling out of reach. There was no opportunity to get up off the metal floor, so I stayed low, wondering how long I could play this game of cat and mouse before getting cornered.

Finally, it happened.

Shimmying back, my shoulders hit the limey wall of the cellar and I realised I had nowhere else to go. A gelatinous body dropped onto my legs as hot breath and wisps of tangled beard registered against my throat.

Screaming, I lashed out, punching the monster, and fumbling for anything I could use to defend myself. My fingers closed around a rubber-handled shaft of some sort.

A crowbar?

I pulled it hard. It didn't budge.

Raising both feet into the air, I kicked out and felt them slam into the zombie. He pushed forward into me, but was unable to move any further. Using his body as leverage, I pulled the rubber grip again. Suddenly, there was a clunk. It was like I'd just given the world an enema, as its bowels began to move.

The metal platform below me rumbled into life, chugging and shaking with aged movements. The pungent aroma of petrol flooded my nostrils.

What the...?

Without warning, the weight propped up against my legs fell away, and I heard a gut-wrenching pop. Hot liquid splattered my face and I wondered what had happened to the zombie. I lowered my legs and felt open air. They overhung the metal. The gritty concrete, there just a moment ago, had gone.

I frowned in the dark. Then my eyes widened as it dawned on me what had happened. The zombie must have slipped, landed awkwardly on the edge of the platform, and fallen. Since no noise came from that direction anymore, I guessed the blow must have been fatal.

I glanced up, as a seam of bright yellow leaked through a fracture in the ceiling, and I recognised the familiar glow of streetlight. The straight fissure grew wider as I got closer.

I'm rising!

"Guys!" I shouted.

"Me and Wyatt are over here!" Sophia replied. A noise, which sounded like a bag of meat hitting a wall, punctuated her speech. "What's up?"

"Where are you?" Monty's voice broke through a torrent of moans and hisses.

"Head to the back of the cellar," I told them, relieved they were all still alive. "Wyatt was right all along. There's a way out – but it's not a door. It's a hydraulic lift. Quick! Jump on. I can't stop it."

Scrambling and bumping sounds told me they were on their way. Reaching over the edge of the platform, I fished for a hand. One grabbed me, and I pulled it.

My eyes shot open when I realised my mistake. A slimy tongue slid along my wrist and I felt the edge of incisors press into my skin. The hydraulic door opening above me offered just enough light to reveal the outline of a bedraggled head and bulging, yellowed eyes.

I screamed, unable to pull away. Luckily, something hard hit the monster's temple like a freight train. A tremor jolted through its body, and I worked my wrist free, massaging it with my opposite hand.

Monty hoisted himself onto the platform beside me and dragged up Sophia and Wyatt. There was barely enough room for the four of us, but we clung together for balance. Slowly, a pair of rusted hatch doors rose above our heads, flooding our senses with disorientating light.

We arrived safe, but breathless, inside a concrete compound, surrounded by high walls. The rasping sound of dead voices faded as the platform reached ground level and sealed the hatch. Chilly air kissed the sweat which had accumulated on the back of my neck, but I didn't shiver. In that moment, I was just happy to be alive.

"Well, that was unpleasant," Wyatt wheezed, lying next to me.

"Milo, you owe me a phone," Sophia moaned.

Grabbing hold of a handrail bordering the opening, she clambered to her feet and got off the rusted platform. A few feet away was another identical hatch.

"Let's agree not to go into any more cellars," I said, ignoring her for a moment.

"Yeah, bro. That sounds like a good idea." Wyatt rolled onto his stomach. "Got us out, though, didn't it?"

Sophia harrumphed. "But where exactly did it get us?"

Taking in my surroundings, I sighed. The main thing which caught my attention was the serenity of the place. It was some sort of walled delivery bay, by the looks of it. Not much to look at but it felt like a panic room, given our situation.

Behind us, a brick wall displayed the back of the tavern. Opposite that, stood the high exterior wall surrounding the whole student village. A bridge probably crossed the moat on the other side to allow for delivery trucks to do drop-offs. As far as I could see, a hydraulic lift was the only way in or out, other than looming, double-breasted gates. But they were boarded with plywood panels that blocked off handholds, stopping anyone from climbing them.

"Locked," said Monty, shaking a padlock holding them together. He eyed them dubiously. "I don't think I could climb them, but maybe I could boost one of you chaps."

"Try me," said Sophia. "I'm the lightest."

"Actually, I think Milo might be easier to manage."

Sophia gasped. "How dare you!"

"Um..." Monty's eyes widened. "I mean, Milo's... taller... and you're wearing a lot of clothes, so they might... restrict your movement?"

"Oh, so you'd rather I wore less clothes?"

"No! That's the last thing I... I mean..."

I winced, watching Monty stammer as he tried to backpedal.

Sophia shifted her weight onto one leg, hands on hips. "You men are all the same! When are you gonna start looking at us as people and not just objects? Honestly, it makes me furious!"

"Okay, I'll lift you," Monty attempted. "I'm sure it wouldn't be a problem to–"

"No! You go ahead and lift Milo. Wouldn't want you pulling your back out carrying this whale to the wild!"

"Oh, come on now. You're not a whale. If anything, you could be a little underweight."

Uh ho.

"There you go again! Body shaming me because I don't meet your ideal standards. You know what? The patriarchy's been doing this since forever and it's really starting to get up my nose!"

"But, you said–"

"Guys!" I shouted. By the time they both turned to me, I was already positioned up against the gates, sleeves rolled up to my elbows, and one foot pressed against the wood for purchase. "Are we doing this or not?"

Seeing his opportunity to escape, Monty rushed to my side and linked his fingers under my shoe. I gazed at the lip of the gate far above me.

Let's hope I can't reach, I thought. I didn't know what was worse; being locked inside until help arrived, or the embarrassment of admitting I wasn't strong enough to do a single pullup.

"One, two, three, nnnhaaa!"

Monty threw me like a Scot throws a log at the Highland Games. Startled by the explosive power, I reached up and slapped my hand on the smooth wood. My fingers burned, as they slid up the grain, stopping inches from the top. Dropping back, I grimaced as I hit the ground.

"Almost!" I said. "You're stronger than you look."

"Thanks. I've been rowing since I was twelve."

"Of course!" Sophia sniffed. "Oxbridge reject."

I decided to intervene before she went on another crusade against the upper classes. "Try again?"

Monty hurled me a second time. This time, I was ready, and braced myself for the catapult. Sailing high into the air, I extended as far as I could, and slammed my fingers over the cold metal frame of the gate.

Instantly, it felt like my hands were set on fire. Screaming, I let go and dropped to my feet.

"Argh!" Holding my wrist with my opposite hand, I gritted my teeth. Tiny oil wells of blood sprang from my fingers. "They've put spikes on top!"

"Looks like that idea's off the cards then," Sophia huffed.

I shot her a livid glare, regretting my decision to step in just to keep the peace. Scanning the enclosure, we all looked for another option.

"There's always this," said Wyatt. He stood next to the second metal platform. "According to this sign, this other one leads to Armageddon."

"The nightclub?" Monty shivered, folding up the collar of his shirt against the cold. "I think I've had enough excitement for one night."

"Me too," I mumbled, massaging my raw hand.

"Look, I don't like the idea either, but what else can we do?" Wyatt explained. "The door to Armageddon is around the corner from the pub. It might not be overrun yet. If we get in early, we can get away before they reach it. If we stay here, who knows how long we'll have to wait to be rescued!"

"He has a point," Monty admitted.

"At least, this time, we know how to get back here if it all goes wrong."

All eyes rested on me, as though they felt the decision had to be unanimous for anyone to make a move. I rubbed my arms, the chill finally making its presence known through my thin shirt. The moment I opened my mouth to respond, the sky rumbled and spots of rain dotted the concrete loading bay.

"I can't believe I'm doing this," I said, caving to peer pressure.

"Yesss!" Wyatt fist-pumped with too much enthusiasm.

Mounting the metal platform, I squatted so the jolt of it bursting into life wouldn't throw me off balance. Wyatt and Sophia joined me while Monty flipped up a plastic lid on a plinth between the two hatches. Two buttons came into view.

Punching the left one, he waited for a moment. It took some time to kick in. When it finally shuddered into life, he hopped on beside us, and we huddled together, descending once more into the bowels of the Earth.

PART NINE
ARMAGEDDON

The elevator shuddered to a stop in complete darkness. Dropping off the platform, everybody headed for the exit.

"Wish I had my phone," grumbled Sophia.

"You'll survive one night without it," Monty reassured her. "Just feel your way with your hands and feet and–"

Bong! A metal surface clanged like a steel drum.

"And head?" I deadpanned.

"Ow," he drawled. "Yeah... And that."

Reaching a set of steps at the edge of the grotty cellar, I opened a heavy door and peaked through to a large room with a domed ceiling. We were behind the bar. The staff didn't notice as we slipped through the door and hurried onto a dance floor on the other side.

The club was packed with gyrating bodies and the stench of perfume. Pyrotechnics and strobe lighting lit up the dome like a smelting pot as we weaved between drunks.

On a raised platform, rocking above a sea of hands, a tall man in a blazer and a new romantic hairstyle spun on heeled boots, throwing his arms in the air. Girls laughed and circled him, despite the fact he was dripping in sweat and spilling a drink everywhere.

Drawing my eyes away from the ridiculousness of the manic dancer, I powered onwards, knowing the doors had to be close by. My chest rattled from the bass of the speaker system. If it weren't for the sticky tiles, I might have vibrated along without moving my legs at all.

Pushing open a swing door, I ushered the others up a second set of steps and into a passageway, hoping to find a quiet alcove. No such luck. I quickly discovered the DJ's beat was pumped into all corners of the building through a spider web of powerful speakers.

"Shall we look for the manager?" I shouted at Sophia.

"No chance!" she replied. "You know what happened last time."

"This place is a maze!" Monty added.

We passed a bathroom area and Wyatt waved, apparently spotting someone he knew. Indicating for us to wait for a moment, he zeroed in on a skeletal boy with slick hair and piercings. Together, they ducked into the toilet. A moment later, he emerged alone and loped towards us with his visor on backwards. There was a peculiar look on his face.

"Friend of yours?" I asked.

"An old friend, Kitten," he purred. "We go way back. Loves a laugh, does Indie."

His reference to my old nickname in the presence of the others instantly gave away that something had changed. Luckily, none of them heard. I pinned him with a hard stare. He met my gaze with two black moons for eyes, and I nodded knowingly. Disappointment rose inside me, but I forced myself to be pragmatic. This wasn't the first time Wyatt had prioritised a high over survival. Scolding him for forcing us to carry his dead weight right now would only waste time.

"Let's get going." I grabbed his shoulder and shoved him ahead of the others to make sure he didn't fall behind.

"Escape's over there, by the way." He pointed at a set of double doors.

"Fine." I readjusted him.

"You're welcome."

Bumping, edging, and apologising his way through the crowd, Monty led us in the most British bid for freedom a nightclub had ever seen. Pressing his hand against a glass door, he assured a bouncer that none of us were carrying out any drinks, and then made a path for us to venture into the cold air. It was still raining outside, but an overhanging roof offered us shelter.

Pushing through yet more bodies, I eventually hit a wrought iron fence and stopped dead. There were no steps heading down to ground level. Thunder cracked in a charcoal sky. I realised my mistake.

"Wyatt. This is a smoking area," I said.

"Is it?"

"We were looking for an exit."

"A...what?"

"An exit. You know – a way out."

"Oh, were you?"

"An escape. That thing you told us was over here."

Fishing inside his pocket, Wyatt adjusted his hat and pulled something out into the open air. Opening his palm, he grinned at a tightly rolled joint.

"Escape," he said, as if it were a perfectly reasonable explanation.

At last, I registered the leap his brain had made and gritted my teeth.

"That's not the kind of escape I had in mind! Honestly, if I wasn't already trying to save your life, I'd *kill* you right now!"

"Uh, Milo?" Monty hung over the balcony, distracted by something on the ground outside the club. "If you're going to do it, make it fast. You might not get a chance in a minute."

Following his eye line, I gasped. Yet again, the zombies were a step ahead. Havoc broke out on the street corner nearest Armageddon's main door. Like baboons, the undead showed their broken teeth, their faces painted blue and red by bruises and blood.

First to encounter them was a gang of hipsters in beanie hats and beards. A vortex of vape smoke clouded their view of the oncoming attack. Within seconds, they were dispatched, too slow to react. If there were any screams as the tide of monsters washed over them, I didn't hear one.

Security guards near the front doors spotted them just as they stepped over the hipsters. Like rhinos in tall grass, they charged through the crowd and into the action. Responding to a vague message on his radio, the bouncer stationed on the smoking area balcony abandoned his post to join the others.

Outside, a middle-aged man with a reflective jacket and a military haircut was the first to react, pulling a ravenous girl off one of the victims and pinning her to the ground with her arms behind her back.

He screamed as a second monster lowered itself onto his shoulders and scalped him with its teeth. Glittering blood poured down his forehead like liquid hair, and he fell back under a stampede of corpses.

The other bouncers were no luckier. Seeing their colleague brought down by the horde, they retreated to the main doors. One of them shouted something about drugs, and I guessed they had come to the same conclusion we did earlier in the night.

"Let's get downstairs before they block off the exits!" Monty suggested, prodding me in the direction of the glass doors.

A piercing ringing sound cut through the DJ's tunes, and I realised someone had set off the fire alarm. Oblivious students immediately glanced at each other on the balcony, torn out of drunken conversations. As one, they migrated towards the glass doors into the building.

"Come on," I said. "If we follow the crowd, we're going to get crushed when people start panicking. We need to find another way out."

"Why don't we stay here?" Wyatt smiled. "It's nice up here in the cool. Can anyone else see that?"

His mouth dropped open, as though he had just stumbled into a room with a breathing Tyrannosaurus Rex. We followed his gaze but saw nothing. Sliding past us, he edged up to a hanging wall light and delicately stroked its bulb.

"Guys, you're not going to believe this. I've found a fairy!" He pushed a finger to his lips. "And it's sleeping."

We ignored him. So, as everyone else had left the balcony, he explained his discovery to a nearby patio heater.

"Did you see any side doors?" I asked the others.

"None that I can be certain lead outside," Sophia said. "According to the uni's prospectus, this place has eight bars! It's a labyrinth."

"Right-o," said Monty. "What about the elevator in the cellar? Plan B's looking jolly good right now. At least we'll be safe in the loading bay."

Sophia shook her head. "We're too far away now to make it there safely. And imagine if the lift doesn't work straight away. We'll be trapped!"

As much as I hated the prospect of fighting our way through the meat grinder, I couldn't help but agree with her. All we needed was for something to go wrong with that elevator in the cellar and we'd be reliving my nightmare scenario from the pub. The claustrophobic memory made my throat close up just thinking about it.

Hauling Wyatt into the group, I said, "Alright. Decision made. Let's go."

We left the balcony, piling into Armageddon's sticky air. Reaching the top of the stairs, I crashed headlong into someone's chest, bounced off it, and crumpled to the carpet.

"Hey!" I growled. "Watch where you're…"

The face that stared back at me resembled a deer bolting from a forest fire. It was the tall, muscular dancer with the debonair hairstyle and blazer. Still glazed in sweat, he scrambled around me and barrelled his way through the others.

"Don't go down there!" he barked as he departed. "They've closssed off all the exitsss. It'sss happening again."

A shard of frozen fear crystallised in the pit of my stomach. *Did I just hear that right?* As the dancer careered around a decorative plant pot, and through the glass doors to the smoking area, one word stayed with me.

"Again?"

PART TEN
THEODOR GRAYSON

Circling around, I gestured for the others to follow and we raced back to the balcony. At the foot of the stairs, screaming cut through the music. Somehow, I knew nobody would make it off the main dance floor alive.

"What's wrong?" Monty spat. "We need to go. Now!"

"That guy," I replied. "Didn't you hear him? Every exit is blocked."

"He doesn't know that."

I locked eyes with Monty. "I saw it in him. He knows. And more than that, he knows what's going on. We need to talk to him."

Monty lowered his gaze. "Fine. Two minutes. But if you're not ready to leave by then, I'm leaving, with or without you."

Tentatively, I entered the balcony and found Blazer Guy curled up in foetal position next to the patio heater. His mouth chattered from the cold, and his eyes roamed, unable to focus on anything for very long. He was obviously extremely drunk. Still, that didn't mean he was clueless. He knew something. I was sure of it.

Stooping, I held out a hand. He sank further into the corner of the balcony and shook his head.

Monty immediately got to work, bending a thin bar from the balcony's ornate handrail. Working it until the join was white, he snapped it off and used the rail to bar the glass doors.

"Hey!" I attempted. "What's your name?"

"N-n-no," mumbled Blazer Guy. "You don't want to know. And don't tell me your n… name, either. I don't want to know any more namesss."

I frowned. "Why? What's going on?"

He didn't answer. Instead, he just buried his head in his arms and wailed.

"Again," he moaned. "I knew it would happen. I warned them. I tried so hard." A loud, far-off *bang* sent him into a frenzy, and I had to place my hands on his shoulders to calm him down.

"It was just a sign," I soothed. "Someone knocked over a sign. That's all. Now tell us what you know."

He hesitated. "But, I promised…"

"What? What did you promise?"

"I promised I wouldn't talk about it anymore."

"About what? What wouldn't you talk about?"

"They told me it didn't happen." he gulped. "It was all in my head."

"Alright, your two minutes are up," Monty grunted over my shoulder.

"Just a second," I said.

The doors rattled. A body had slammed against them, its contorted face pressing against the glass. It was a short girl in jeans and a t-shirt which might have once been a pastel colour. Her clothes were filthy, and her entire forearm had been degloved in some sort of terrible event. For her sake, I hoped it had happened after death.

"Too late," Monty said. "Looks like we're stuck here."

More bodies ambled up the stairs and joined the maimed girl. Only a handful managed to navigate the staircase, but there was no guarantee we could find an escape route, even if we managed to fight past them.

"Tell me what's all in your head," I tried again, ignoring a frantic panic suddenly rising inside me, telling me we were trapped and it was all my fault.

Blazer Guy jabbered but offered nothing of use.

"Why are you so angry?" Wyatt asked the zombie through the glass. His face was only inches away, like a child at a zoo enclosure. The creature on the other side scraped her teeth along the glass in a vain attempt to get at him.

"Tell me," I whispered to Blazer Guy.

"Forget it," Monty grumped. "The man's clearly mad as a box of frogs."

"Hey!" Sophia scolded him. "Don't stigmatise insanity."

She stooped next to me, zeroing in on Blazer Guy. "Come on, sweetie. You're so brave. You've been through the wars, haven't you?"

Her words seemed to have an immediate effect on him. Chin wobbling, he squeaked a quiet, "Yeah."

"I know, sweetie. Look, my name's Sophia, and I'm a psychology student. You know what that means for you?" He shook his head, so she continued. "It means, if you tell me your name, I can help you. Is that okay with you?"

I decided not to mention Sophia hadn't actually attended a single psychology lecture yet. She seemed to be making more progress than me, so I stood back and let her do her thing.

"It's Theodor Grayson."

"Theodor. That's a lovely name. Do you mind if I call you Theo?"

He gulped, his mouth sounding dry, and gestured that he didn't mind.

"Great. And what do you do, Theo?" Sophia continued.

Theo eyed me with trepidation, so I lowered my gaze.

"I teach Acting Theory here at the university," he said.

"Oh… that's fantastic, Theo. You're a very accomplished man. I'm just going to have a chat with my friend here. If you'll excuse us, we'll be back in a second, okay?"

Turning her back on him, Sophia dragged me over to Monty, and we went into a huddle.

"I know this guy," she said.

"Of course you do," Monty quipped.

Sophia's icy glare cut him off before he could say anything else. "My cousin, Beatrice, told me all about him. She was here studying drama last year. According to her, he was the most bizarre lecturer she ever had. He teaches drama theory but never hangs around with the other academics. Instead, he gets obliterated every night with the students.

"He never shows any evidence of an acting background, either. When one student asked him if he's ever been on a stage, he apparently replied, 'Not since the incident.' Then he stared into space for the next twenty minutes. He was still there when everybody packed up and left. Apparently, it was really awkward."

"So, he's crazy?" I asked, already regretting my decision to follow him.

"Oh, without a doubt."

"Great. In that case, what do we do about him and, more importantly, us?"

Rain drove into the side of the building and we all winced at the cold. I was almost jealous of the girl on the other side of the pane. She was dead but at least she looked warm.

Surveying the street below, I sighed. We'd never make it through the sheer number of the undead littering the road.

And that was before we even considered any roaming around *inside* the club.

Far away, down an alleyway running adjacent to Armageddon, a figure darted from one alcove to the next, catching my eye. Whoever they were, they were fast, never stopping for long enough to get spotted by the shambling creatures around them.

It was a human. Spindly legs carried a billowing overcoat with the collar drawn high up against their neck. A cloak of white-blonde hair trailed behind the figure, like a veil. It was a girl.

Briefly, my mind pondered over why the figure seemed so familiar. Then it hit me. She was the ghost. The girl that left the apartment the moment I stepped out of my room at the beginning of the night. The same girl my dad had cornered in the kitchen. It seemed like a lifetime ago now, but it was definitely her.

"Help!" I shouted, the word echoing like a shotgun blast.

Monty clamped a hand over my mouth. "What the devil do you think you're doing?" he demanded. Below us, an audible shuffle told me I had attracted some unwanted attention. "If enough of those chaps downstairs realise we're up here, those glass doors aren't going to last very long," he scolded me. "Now, shut your mouth before I shove a boot in it! We need every second we can get."

I nodded and gestured that he could remove his hands. My call had done its job. Across the street, the girl's doe eyes flashed in our direction. She almost seemed more skittish at the sight of a human than she did the undead.

And I thought I had social anxiety, I thought, as she avoided my gaze from across the road.

A moment later, she darted away in the opposite direction. I had no idea where she was headed, but I hoped she planned to send back help when she got there.

"I saw a girl," I said.

"No time for ladies now, Romeo."

"No," I frowned. "Across the street. She could have helped us."

"Was she alone?" he asked.

"Yeah."

"Well, in that case, she's useless. We need muscle to get us out." He glanced over the railing. "The stairs are blocked now. Our only chance of leaving is if we climb over the edge, and in this wind, I don't fancy our chances without someone at the bottom to catch us if we fall."

"You wanna climb down?" I asked, my heart rate racing at the prospect of hanging off a balcony railing twenty feet in the air.

"Of course. Just think of it as rock climbing." He glanced at Sophia for unlikely support.

She raised her eyebrows and shrugged. "Classic gap year stuff," she said. "It's actually quite fun, once you get over the altitude sickness and the idea of peeing in a bush. Dangerous, though."

"More dangerous than this?" I demanded.

I pointed at the garden of arms below the balcony. They followed my movement like plants following the sun.

"Don't get frantic, old sport. I'm sure even you can manage it, once–"

"Manage it!" I exploded. "I can't hold my own bodyweight, you two are half-drunk, Wyatt's talking to a patio heater, and there's a mad bloke crying in the corner. What part of scaling a building over a pit of zombies seems *manageable* to you?"

I fumbled in my pockets for my asthma pump then remembered, yet again, I'd left it in my room. In a moment of desperation, I even looked to Wyatt for something that could relax me. Luckily, he was still engrossed in conversation with the heater.

"It could be worse," said Sophia.

"How could it possibly be worse?"

"I don't know. I guess there could be zombies up here with us," she said.

A rumbling *clang* made me jump, and I wondered if the universe was threatening to demonstrate her point. As a hot tsunami of shock rolled through my stomach, I looked up at a large vent set in the wall above the double doors. Three more clangs followed the first.

Suddenly, everyone took notice.

"They're in the vents." The coarse whisper came from Monty's throat like a rope threatening to choke him from the inside.

The commotion sounded close. Terrified, I glanced around in a desperate attempt to find anything I could use to protect myself when the undead inevitably forced the vent off the wall and spewed onto the balcony. There was nothing. No weapon, and no time to react.

As though it had been lying in wait for some time, the vent burst above me with explosive force, and a figure clambered out of the dark.

PART ELEVEN
SECRETS AND LARSSONY

The first thing I noticed was the pair of bug-like, yellow eyes emerging from the shadows. It didn't take long, however, to realise they were anything but natural. *Lenses?* The night-vision goggles glinted as black, rubber-clad hands came up and lifted them away from a darkened face.

"Oh, it's you," said a sarcastic voice. "And I thought the apocalypse couldn't get any worse."

"Amelia?" I asked, remembering the abrasive girl in the black uniform from a few hours ago.

"Sadly, yes," she replied, sweeping a strand of black fringe out of her eyes. "And you are?"

"Milo Callaghan. We've already met… in the flat. We live together."

She swivelled her legs so they hung over the edge of the vent, and then lowered herself onto the balcony with a rope.

"Oh, yeah. Back at the house. That's where I saw your face. Now I remember."

"You two know each other?" Monty asked. I nodded, and he continued, "Great! God, are we glad to see you right now! You see, we're in something of a pickle."

"I noticed."

"Nice climbing equipment you've got there, Rubber Girl." Wyatt sauntered over, apparently having lost interest in the heater. "You think we could go climbing some time?"

Amelia rolled her eyes. "Buy me a drink first. Besides, I'm kind of a lone wolf."

"But you're going to help us get down from here, right?" said Monty. "We really could do with the help."

"I wish I could." She sighed, watching the growing mass of bodies in the road below. "The truth is, I can't. I've been all around the building and there's no way out. This was the last place I could check, and I don't fancy our chances here, either. Anyone know what's going on? Why's everyone rioting?"

"Rioting? They're zombies," I said.

Amelia snorted. "And I'm a part-time billionaire."

I eyed her quizzically. Misinterpreting sarcasm had burned me in the past, so I was slow to respond.

"You're not too bright, are you?" she said.

"I'm telling the truth," I insisted. "We've come from the flats. Everyone there's dead. They're *eating* people in the streets. And those that get bitten and die are coming back as one of them."

"I'm not sure I believe that."

"You remember Chloe?" Sophia asked her.

"The skinny, orange girl?"

"Er…" Sophia looked awkward. "Yeah… Well, we saw her die. She got bitten and turned. Then she ate her friend."

"Really?"

Her poker face told me she didn't believe any of it. Darting her gaze between us, she paused, as though waiting for one of us to crack. Me, Monty, and Sophia were stoic. Wyatt drooled, petting the rope hanging from the vent, and Theo remained in the corner, avoiding eye contact with everyone.

When she realised we were serious, she leaned against the glass door and inspected the squirming bodies on the other side. Finally, she relented. "Woah."

"Woah, indeed," Monty confirmed.

"Well, that explains a lot. Has the government's fingerprints all over it. Looks like I had a lucky escape, being in the top floor of the student union."

I narrowed my eyes. Something about Amelia seemed familiar – like I had seen her somewhere else, in a different context. It happened to me a lot – like with old teachers. You see them five days a week in school for years, and then, when you end up bumping into them once on a trip to Italy, you have no idea who they are. You know them, but the context's all wrong.

"What were you doing on the top floor of the student union?" Monty asked her. "An odd place to be on the first night of Freshers', isn't it?"

Amelia smirked. "Partying isn't really my scene. Not much of a drinker. I'd rather focus on something a little more... worthwhile." Standing back, she leapt up, grabbing the edge of the vent and pulling herself back inside. "I'll be right back," she said. "Just going to unhook the rope. You sit tight, and we'll work out a plan when I'm done."

"Do any of you guys recognise her?" I asked the others when she left.

Monty shook his head. "Not at all."

"Nope," said Sophia.

Theo whimpered, which I assumed meant he didn't know her, either. He had calmed down a lot, which was good. I caught him peeking through the railing at the bodies below us.

"You okay, man?" I asked.

"Yeah," he croaked. "S-sorry about earlier. I get panic attacks. I was in the army for a year after my degree. Bad experience. My therapist says it'll pass."

"Say no more, sweetie," Sophia smiled. "Just take a few seconds to catch your breath. We can wait."

"Yeah, take your time, old sport." Monty's smirk was tinged with an ulterior motive as he saw Theo gaining clarity. "Mind you, it won't be long before this door can't take the pressure. You know anything about what's going on? That sort of information would probably be useful right now."

"Nothing." Theo looked sheepish. "It's just my condition. The flashbacks, you know? I wasn't there long, but I guess war wasn't my strong suit." Sweat developed on his top lip even as he spoke about his trauma. He ran a hand through his hair. "Basically, I see violence and it sparks something. It's like everyone around me is a dead body. I can still see their eyes…"

"That must be hard," Sophia assured him.

"It is. Therapists tell me the visions aren't real, but that doesn't make them any less real to me. Two have quit so far, and it looks like the third one won't last much longer."

"So, you… don't know what's going on?" Monty asked after a pause.

"No."

"Great!" He turned to me. "Yet again, we're stuck with a nutcase."

Sophia's whole head recoiled. "I'd rather be with a psychologically challenged person than a bigot! You know, not everyone can be an emotionless rock. We're not all detached from the world, living in an ivory tower, eating caviar from a silver spoon."

Monty growled. "For Christ's sake, think about what you're saying, woman! You're rich. You go on gap years. You're a rock who eats caviar just like me! Pull that stick out of your rear end and think like a rational human being. Political correctness won't get us out of this hole. We need to be real for a second."

"Ugh!" Sophia looked disgusted. "You're a moron, you know that? I can't believe you think…"

"Um, guys. Amelia's been in there a while. I'll just go check on her," I said, but quickly realised nobody was listening. *Whatever.*

Hauling myself into the vent, I ambled along a square tunnel. She'd been gone longer than I expected.

Please don't be eaten. Please don't be eaten, I repeated internally.

It was warmer than outside, and my clammy hands slid on the metal panels that surrounded me. At the end of the shaft, the system split into a fork and the rope trailed away into the dark. A strange, white glow exposed a corner bend, and I followed it.

As I got closer, I heard a voice. It was female, but sounded as though it had been fed through some sort of artificial filter.

"Hello?" I whispered, not sure whether I wanted the owner of the voice to hear me.

"…cover-ups are everywhere. You just have to know how to look for them. Finally, we've reached a discovery that will go down in history. Remember who exposed the secret life of..."

"There you are," I sighed, spotting Amelia as I peered around the corner.

Sat in the dark with her legs crossed and the rope end tied around a pipe, Amelia's eyes were fixated on a glowing screen. She was watching something on the flip screen of her camcorder. It sounded like her voice in the video.

She's watching herself?

In the ventilation shaft, the narrator was tinny but serious. Noticing me for the first time, Amelia jumped, slapping the camcorder closed.

"Don't do that!" she shouted. "There are dead people everywhere, and you decided now's a good time to sneak up on someone. Creep."

"What? I wasn't sneaking!" I said.

She huffed and forced the camcorder into a slot on her utility belt. Then she fiddled with a knot she used to fasten her climbing rope. It occurred to me all of her gear was authentic. I remembered making a joke earlier about her being some sort of spy or jewel thief. Now I saw the extent of her outfit, I wondered how close I might be to the truth.

"What were you watching?"

"None of your business. But, if you must know, I was updating my video diary."

"Oh, you're a vlogger?"

"Yeah," she said, revealing the straight-lipped smirk of a fanatic whose favourite topic had just cropped up in conversation. "I make videos and upload them to my site every week."

"Cool! Got many followers?"

"Not many, but the ones I do have are quite keen."

"Well, I bet they're about to get keener. This whole thing's gonna go viral. I mean, if we survive."

She rolled her eyes. "Views aren't really my goal."

"Oh, okay."

I realised I'd hit a nerve and hoped my disinterested response would close down the conversation before it got away from me. Amelia seemed to have other ideas.

"It's more about sending a message," she said, as I turned away. I could immediately tell she wasn't finished. "I go deep in my vlogs. People live every day in the dark, with no idea what forces actually shape their lives. I've spent years directing a spotlight on those forces – government departments, companies, people. I'm telling you, the truth lives among us."

The truth lives among us.

The words resonated with me. I'd heard them before. *But, where?* My eyes rested on the camcorder. Then they flicked up to Amelia's face, and the thought clicked.

"It's you!" I blurted. "You're that girl. I've got one of your videos on my to-watch list. You're the one who travels all over the place, breaking into businesses and chaining yourself to building sites. Your channel is what's-it-called…"

"'Secrets and Larssony' – yeah. It's funny because it sounds like larceny."

"I knew it!" My face brightened. "You're a maniac!"

Amelia bristled. "I prefer the term activist."

I faltered. "Yeah, I meant it in a cool way, of course."

Good save, Callaghan.

"So, you're like a prank channel, right? There's no way all of those officials can be corrupt."

"A prank channel! No! It's all real. I expose corporations and defend the public."

"Like Batman?"

"No. Not like Batman. Batman wears a mask. I'm not afraid if people know me. The truth needs a face and I'm prepared to offer mine."

"But, you commit crimes, film yourself, and upload them to the internet for everyone to see. Including the police. Hey, weren't you arrested a while back?"

Amelia rolled her eyes.

"Great. Another sheep," she said, more to herself than me. "You clearly don't understand, so don't try. Just go ahead and live in the dark, like everyone else, while I go down in history as someone who *really* lived."

"Erm… okay." I shifted uneasily. "Sorry."

"It's fine." She exhaled. "Not many people understand. I don't expect you to, either."

Noticing she'd untied the rope, I said, "Ready? We should really get back to the others before they send a search party."

"I thought *you* were the search party."

"I suppose, in a way, I am."

Colleting the rope into a loop, she watched me with languid eyes, but didn't move. Being strangers, the intimacy of her silence took me by surprise. However, I decided to go with it, wondering what might happen next.

Moments passed, and her pupils probed mine. The wind outside howled but in the vent it was quiet and warm. Was her façade crumbling? That was my first thought, but as time dragged on I began to squirm under her microscope.

"So, are you gonna move first, or do I need to force my way past you?" she asked.

"What?"

Oh God.

Realisation dawned on me. I glanced around. The dark, square passage locked us into single file. Amelia was trapped. I had completely covered her way out.

"Oh, sorry," I mumbled again. "I was – I mean, I…"

Molten embarrassment rose to my cheeks and I turned away to hide my red face. Even as we clambered back to the others in absolute silence, I knew she could sense my awkwardness. It followed me like a tail.

"And another thing…!" Sophia shouted at Monty as we entered the biting wind. "Oh, you're back. Where've you two been?"

"The knot was pretty tight. Took ages to get it loose," I lied.

"What's the plan?"

"Well," Monty said, clearing his throat. "The truth is, we don't know. You see, it's getting worse."

Sweeping my eyes over the street far below, I saw what he meant. In the few short minutes Amelia and I had been away, the crowd gathering beside the building had almost doubled in size. The bodies were at least four deep along the whole front wall of the Armageddon nightclub, and a much bigger horde had collected under our ledge.

There were so many now their faces had become almost indistinguishable from one another. Male and female, large and small – all were a mass of arms and teeth. Behind them, new recruits stumbled into the road, drawn by the beacon we had become. I found my eyes roaming on autopilot when my vision snagged on something that made the gears of my brain jam.

Amidst the field of shambling bodies, one individual stood out on a raised brick structure. The figure waved.

I did a double-take to confirm I wasn't imagining it. The waving body was carrying a crate of beer. It was a man. His lumberjack beard and lopsided grin were a dead giveaway. What's more, I knew him.

Robbie?

It was impossible, but then again, so was everything else that had happened over the past few hours. When he spotted me, Robbie wolf-whistled and waved again, ruffling the hair of a gnarled corpse as it ambled past him. Confused, I grimaced.

"Well, that's odd," I found myself saying. "Guys, I think I might be going mad."

PART TWELVE
LET'S GET MORTAL

It was the only possible explanation I could imagine.

Shutting my eyes tight, I pressed my fingers into them and shook my head until I saw the whole world under a blue film.

It got me, I thought. *The madness finally got me.*

Flicking my gaze up to where I'd seen him, I sighed. He was gone. I'd managed to fight it off, at least for a little while longer.

"You okay, Milo?" asked Sophia. "You're looking a little... Wyatt-y."

Wyatt smiled up at her with the mild curiosity of a simpleton.

"No," I said. "I'll be fine. I just thought I saw something... strange. I think I need a drink."

"Sshpeaking of drinks!" a jovial voice bellowed. "I have something to tell you guys! Are you going to throw me that... ropey thing?"

Oh, God! It's back!

Hanging my head over the balcony railing, I blinked. "What the...?"

Impossible! I frowned, speechless.

Monty's head appeared next to mine.

"Jesus Christ!" he said. "It's Robbie… and he's off his trolley!"

Robbie hiccupped, and poured a can of some questionable liquid down his throat. At first, I thought he'd been bitten, but it occurred to me the zombies wouldn't have stopped there. If they were going to attack him, he'd be torn to pieces already. They were all around him and yet none flinched, even when he staggered into them on his way to the bottom of the balcony. Discarding the empty can, he dipped his hand inside the cardboard box balanced on his shoulder and retrieved another.

"Look, guysss, I'm, like, not dead!" he laughed. "And look what I can do!"

He grabbed hold of the closest monster he could find and danced with it, swinging the poor creature high into the air. Other than scrambling to get away, like a bunny in the arms of a four-year-old, the corpse made no attempt to hurt him.

"How the hell are you still alive?" I called.

"Funnnny ssstory, actually." He belched.

"Someone pass him the rope!" Monty ordered.

"But, he's been bitten," yelled Sophia.

"No," I disagreed. "He hasn't."

Detaching the grappling hook from the vent pipe, we tied the end into a loop and dropped it to ground level. Between us, we hauled Robbie's hefty body up from the infested street. Hooking his arms onto the balcony, he swung one leg over the railing and toppled onto his back, cackling like a tourist stumbling off a rollercoaster.

"That would have been so much easier if you'd put down the beer," I moaned.

Robbie propped himself onto one elbow and pointed at me with an unsteady finger. "Ffunny you should sssay that. I'll explain in a moment. Bear with." He toppled back and reached for another can. Everyone lay for a moment panting as we recovered from the exertion. Eventually, after cracking open another beverage, he said, "This is the reason I'm still here."

"Sorry?"

"Thisss." He tapped the can. "This is how I'm alive. Remember earlier? How you guysss left me after I fell... in a busssh?" I didn't remember, but I nodded in the hope this story had a point to it. "Well, I managed to get into someone's apartment. It was empty. The zombiesss... were outside, tryin' to get in. I was all alone, and I knew it wasss the end. Anywayss, I found beer in the fridge. Lotsss of beer! So, I decided – hey, what the hell? And I drank it all!"

He toasted as he said the last line, drawing a long swig from a fresh can. Then he became sombre again. "Dutch courage for death, ain't it? Anyways, I got good 'n' pickled and then, I... opened the front door to let th-them have their way."

"Wow," said Sophia.

"Yeah," he agreed. "But, guesss what happened... Nothing. They didn't touch me. I wasss close to blackout drunk, lying at their feet, and they didn't even bother tryin'! What – ain't I tasty enough? It wasss like this prime meat didn't appeal to them?" He placed an offended hand over his belly to demonstrate his point, then hung over the balcony railing and shouted, "Uppity swinesss! You don't know good meat, you lot!"

All of us dived to anchor him, as his feet swung up off the floor and he threatened to roll over the balustrade. When we steadied him again, I looked at Monty. He frowned thoughtfully.

"Let me get this straight, old sport," he said. "You were being chased by those monsters, and you got drunk. And then what?"

Robbie rocked on his heels but kept a straight expression.

"They left me alone. It was like they didn't even s...see me."

"And then what happened?"

"Well it was cold outsssside."

"Yeah?"

"So, I invited 'em in, and poured myself another drink."

"Right?"

"And then, when I was sure they definitely weren't going to eat me, I left the flat and went for a walk."

"A walk, you say?"

"A walk."

"And then what happened?"

"Well, then I got here." Robbie hit his chest with a closed fist and belched again, taking another long swig. "And they ssstill haven't eaten me." He tapped the empty can. "I'm smart, sssee. I picked up this box o' beer and took it with me, becaussse I figured out, as long as I don't run out o' booze, they won't toussch me... oh!" Lifting the cardboard box to his head and turning it so it resembled a telescope, he grimaced. "I've run out."

Sophia grinned. "I think we've just found our way out."

"Hang on. Don't be too hasty," Monty argued. "I don't think any of this counts as evidence. And anyway–"

"How much more evidence do you want?" she bit back. "We all saw it. Robbie was down there and they didn't even look at him. Look! He's never looked more alive."

To back up her point, Robbie chose that exact moment to pass out. Drool worked its way down his cheek from his slack mouth.

"Yes, but he's one case study," Monty argued, seeming not to notice him either. "What works for one person might not work for another. And how do we even know it's the alcohol? Just because he's drunk, it doesn't mean that's what's kept him alive. There could be another factor –

something we don't even know about. He was drunk before, wasn't he?"

"Yeah, he was," Sophia reasoned. "But, not like this. This is another level of drunk – even for him! I'm telling you, it's the alcohol. Maybe it's the smell of it, or maybe it's something to do with brain functionality – I don't know. What I do know is, it's our way out of here."

"You're insufferable! Honestly, there are a thousand things it could be, and you believe–"

"Guys, there's no point arguing over this," I interjected. "We're stuck up here and Robbie's beer is all gone. It's not like we can test the theory or anything."

"Well, there is one way." A mischievous voice caught my attention and I glanced at Amelia, who was swinging her grappling hook. I didn't like the expression on her face. "One of us could sneak into the bar downstairs and get some booze."

The proposal was so ludicrous, I laughed. "And how do you suggest we do that?"

I pointed at the set of glass doors we had barred. Behind the panes, the zombies were now in double figures.

"I know a way in," she explained. "The blueprint for this club is kept in an archive at the student union next door."

"And you know that, how?"

"Not important. The ventilation shaft which brought me this far is shaped like a spider's web. It goes through the whole building. One part of it runs by the main bar, next to the dance floor. If one of us could be lowered down there, we could grab some booze and be lifted to safety before the zombies even know we're there."

A moment passed and we all let Amelia's plan sink in. Then she added, "So who's it gonna be?"

"I'm not sure about this," I said.

Unlike me, Monty appeared to be considering the idea.

"I mean, I could do it, if..." Amelia tried.

"Absolutely not!" he cut her off. "If we're going to do this, it'll have to be one of the lads. There's no way we're letting you girls go down there."

"Agreed," said Sophia. "Good plan."

So much for feminism, I thought. Monty had already taken issue with my cowardice, so I didn't bring it up.

Glancing at those of us who were left, my mind ran through the possible candidates. Robbie snuggled the concrete floor like a memory foam mattress. A soft whistle indicated he was fast asleep.

Obviously not him.

Next, there was Theo – the new recruit. He had unfurled his arms and legs and stopped quivering now, but just glancing at him made him shudder. It was obvious he'd bolt at the first sign of trouble.

Not him either.

Wyatt, I thought. He had stopped talking to inanimate objects now, and was even nodding along to the conversation. It was almost as if he was paying attention. That was a good sign.

Maybe, I thought.

Smiling dopily, he licked the back of his hand like a cat.

Maybe not.

Monty seemed to come to the same conclusion. Tousling his hair and sitting back, he threw me an option, turning my insides to mush.

"Looks like it's you or me, old sport."

"Then, it has to be you," I replied, quicker than I intended. "You're stronger and faster. If anything kicks off, whoever's down there will need to fight their way back to the rope."

"Don't forget someone has to pull them to safety, with an armful of booze," Amelia said. She gestured to the vent. "It's single file in there, so whoever's at the end will have to be strong enough to lift whoever's down there."

"Good point," Sophia agreed.

No, that's not a good point at all! That's a very bad point! is what I wanted to say, seeing the way this conversation was headed. I was as much a fan of logic as the next guy, but not when it got me dropped into a warzone to fetch drink for the troops.

I gulped. All eyes trained on me.

"Looks like it's unanimous," Monty said with a smile.

"Oh no it's not!" I said, practically stamping my foot. "This is ridiculous. I won't do it, and you can't make me!"

PART THIRTEEN
A LITTLE TIED UP

"Ow!"

The rope rode up in places I never knew existed.

"Stop complaining. I wouldn't have to tie it around you if you could lift your own bodyweight. I mean, you're not even fat! How've you survived life this long, never mind zombies?"

Monty pulled the rope tighter, and I squirmed. We were nestled in the ventilation shaft, one of us on either side of a removed tile leading to the club's main dance floor. I eyed the slick tiles far below. The twenty-something-foot drop was eye-watering. I was just thankful the shaft skirted around the main dome, instead of following it up even higher.

"Remember," said Amelia from behind Monty. We'd left Sophia behind to babysit Robbie and Wyatt. "You're small. Use that to your advantage. Don't try to bruise your way in, all guns blazing. Stay low and do whatever you can to keep out of sight."

"Noted," I said, without sincerity.

"Oh, and go for the hard stuff," she added. "Vodka, whiskey, gin. You won't have to carry as much, and they'll get us drunk faster."

"I'll have a *pinot noir*, old sport, if it's not too much trouble," said Monty. Sticking his head down into the hole, he surveyed the situation. "Alright, chaps. The coast is clear."

"Nobody cares about the coast. What about the nightclub?" I snapped. Nobody laughed.

Dangling my legs into the abyss, I waited for Monty to apply tension. Then I sucked in a few deep breaths and lowered my trembling body into thin air.

The rope tightened uncomfortably around my groin and lower back. I stayed steady, hoping it didn't slip. Then I breathed a sigh of relief, swinging gently in mid-air. The makeshift harness Amelia made from the grappling hook did its job.

Small miracles, I thought, as Monty slowly lowered me into the void, one hand over the other.

It took me a moment to calm down enough to take in my environment. The music was still as deafening. Obviously, the DJ had been mowed down before he had a chance to lower the volume. I found myself tapping my forearm to the rhythm as I descended – a nervous tick but it kept my mind off the fact I was horribly exposed.

The room itself was huge. The main wall lights were still out, leaving the club's lasers to provide most of the light. As terrifying as it sounded, I actually found myself relieved. The relative darkness and brain-mulching bass provided cover as I was lowered, like bait, into what I saw as a teeming fishpond.

To add to that, the cavernous space was almost completely devoid of life. I guessed most of the horde must have followed the survivors through the doors as they fled for their lives, because there weren't many around. The only signs of activity came from small bundles of carnivores squatted over unmoving casualties.

After what seemed like half a lifespan of silence, my toes touched hard flooring and Monty stopped feeding more rope. Looking up, I saw him flash me an 'okay' hand gesture. I flipped him off in return, and loosened the knots around my thighs.

My eyes barely strayed from the pack of living corpses hunkering like wolves over their spoils. They didn't turn my way. Even with the music booming, I was sure I could hear their loose jaws chewing raw flesh.

Using sweaty fingers, I fumbled with the rope.

Way too tight! I thought, straining to untie myself.

Digging my fingers into the hemp, I eventually got it to give. Finally, it came apart. I stepped out of the loops and raced for the bar. Dropping behind it with my back against a shelf of plastic cups, I ran through my plan of action.

Get in. Find heavy liquor. Try not to die. Get out.

The cellar door opposite me radiated temptation. A short run though the dark to the hydraulic lift. That's all it would take to get me to safety – at least, in the short term. The thought raced through my mind but left without me. I couldn't abandon the others.

"Okay, Milo, think," I said, scanning a row of illuminated chillers.

There was no telling how long I had before one of the undead dragged its feet over to the bar and spotted me, so I had to work fast. Bypassing the chillers and their glass windows, I headed straight for a sweeping curve at the edge of the bar, where two rows of heavy liquor bottles were slotted into optics.

I peered over the bar for any signs of discovery. The top shelf where I'd have to unhook the bottles was in full view of the zombies. Should they turn around, I'd be spotted immediately. Breathing hard, I dropped lower, psyching myself up for what I was about to do.

Man, I wish I had my asthma pump, I thought, craving its blend of mild steroids and other nameless ingredients more than ever.

Rocking slightly, I donned my game face and got to work. Unhooking the first bottle was easy. I chose an expensive vodka. *Why go for the house brand when you can have whatever you want, right?* Slipping the optic out of its slot, I upturned the bottle and screwed on its original cap, which I found in a plastic tumbler on the bar.

Next, I moved onto a whiskey. Screwing on the bottle top, my focus wandered to a mirror covering the bar's back wall. From my current angle, I could see the dance floor behind me. None of the predators had moved.

Two bottles down, I trailed my finger along the remaining options, already deciding any more than three would be too difficult to carry. My eye settled on a large vial of gin. Taking it down and fastening the cap, I kept one eye on the mirror. Still no sign of movement.

Once I was done, I dropped into a crouch, breathing a sigh of relief. Tucking two bottles under one arm, I grabbed the third, before heading back. My stomach fluttered with anticipation. Finally, an end was in sight.

That exhilaration didn't last long, though. Lifting my head as I neared the end of the bar, I shrieked like a seven-year-old girl and fell onto my back. The bottles clinked and rolled in all directions.

"Hehehe."

A boy stared at me from the edge of the bar. His panting almost mimicked laughter. Black mucus lined his eyes and soaked the Armageddon uniform he wore. The same oily fluid also greased his mop of curly hair. Judging by his unexpected arrival, I guessed he must have died in the cellar and reanimated in his own vomit.

He stood in the small channel behind the bar, blocking my only exit. All that time spent watching my back in the mirror had left me open to a side attack. As realisation dawned on his face, I scrambled to my feet and collected the lost booze.

My mind galloped, and I was left screaming internally as I struggled to keep hold of the reins.

The Armageddon bartender didn't hesitate. His lips were already curled back in a grotesque snarl before his feet started shambling in my direction.

I panicked. Locking my arm around the bottles, I flung open one of the chiller doors, hoping to slow down the monster. Little did I expect it to bounce on its hinges and hurtle back at my face.

Clang!

I stumbled backwards and slipped, catching myself on the side of the bar before hitting the floor. In an instant, the barman was on me, thrashing as I held him back with a forearm to his throat. He was heavier than me, and a few inches taller, but I had one critical advantage: balance.

His ankle was broken – possibly in a tousle that happened before he had hid down the cellar. I could tell by the lopsided way he carried his weight.

Managing to place one of the bottles on the bar behind me, I forced my free hand up beside his body and grabbed a handful of slick hair. Pulling him sharply to the right, I watched as he barrelled into a block of recycling boxes at the open end of the bar. The impact busted them open, and empty beer cans and broken glasses spilled around him.

A manic howl from behind me told me the crash had attracted unwanted attention. Grabbing the bottle, I froze. My gaze darted from the bartender to the packs of feeding zombies on the far side of the hall. A handful had peeled away from the rest of the pack and were now ambling across the dance floor.

With the bartender still blocking my exit, I grabbed the third bottle and jumped, rolling over the bar itself. On the other side, I thankfully landed feet-first, and tucked the gin under my arm with the vodka and whiskey, before making a dash for the rope.

"Milo! Run!"

Monty's words echoed from the vent high in the ceiling. I assumed he'd seen the barman long before me, but warning me would have alerted the feeding zombies. If only I'd paid him more attention, I might not have gotten in trouble.

Slipping and sliding, I approach the rope all too fast and found my legs sailing past it while my free hand grasped the hemp. With no time to tie the harness, I slipped my foot into a noose-like loop, using it as a foothold. The monsters arrived seconds later.

"Lift me up!" I screamed.

Far above, a whirlwind of hands and feet churned as Monty struggled to gain purchase in the smooth tunnel. Eventually, the line became taut.

Leaning into the rope for balance, I wrapped one arm around it and grabbed the neck of the gin bottle with my free hand. It felt fragile and unbalanced. As much as I didn't want to smash it on a zombie's skull and waste it, I realised it might be my only chance at survival.

"Now'd be a good time!" I reminded Monty.

Beside me, the barman thrashed like a lunatic. Somehow, he had managed to get himself wrapped up in a burst plastic bin liner, and was unable to get to his feet without the use of his arms.

The others, however, were more mobile. There were four of them – three male and a female, dressed in fake school uniforms, which seemed oddly out of place in the nightclub.

In about five seconds, they would get to me, and it would all be over. Realising the rope wasn't going anywhere, I knew I had to do something fast. Taking the taut line with me, I began to travel, moving in an arc to buy myself vital seconds.

It's working! I thought as I danced around them, sweeping along the edge of the bar.

Monty chose that exact instant to gain his footing and tug hard on the rope. Caught off guard, the foot I kept in the noose was lifted off the dance floor. I lost all stability and yelped. Had I not kept my grip, I would have been sent sprawling along the shiny tiles.

It was too late to readjust. My forward momentum carried me along the arc and I found myself leaving the ground.

"Aaaaahhh!" I screamed as I hit the highest point of the swing, stopped in mid-air for a moment, then swung back in the opposite direction.

The closest zombie – a petite, redhead girl in a short, pleated school girl skirt and too much make-up – never stood a chance. Facing backwards, I punched into her like a wrecking ball. Her arms flailed as I swooped onwards, knocked slightly off course.

Reaching the wall nearest the bar, I kicked off the sweat-glazed paint, deciding a moving target was more likely to survive than a hanging one. I felt the rope inch upwards as I closed in on the remaining three corpses.

Lashing out with my dangling leg, I drove my foot into the knee of one monster. The strike sent him spinning into the bar and opened up a gap for me to swoop between the two remaining attackers. After that, they became frantic.

This time, my swing was much more powerful, and the point at which the arc reached its peak was expected. Shifting my body, I pivoted in mid-air and found myself facing the right way this time. The rope inched a little higher. I guessed the others were also helping with my ascent. Within seconds, I would be out of reach.

Gotcha! I thought with a smirk, training my eye on the smaller of the two remaining zombies. Preparing to swoop in for a flying kick to the chest, I counted down for impact.

Three.

Two.

One.

A ragged shape darted out from behind a brick pillar separating the dance floor from a seated area. I had no time to react as the zombie – a chubby girl with a face caked in glitter and blood – clamped onto my knee.

Screaming, I swung like a pendulum, driving the butt of the gin bottle between her mouth and my leg. Her feet slid uselessly along the floor but she made no attempt to steady herself. Her only goal was to bite into my flesh.

Having been knocked off-course yet again, I crashed clumsily into the larger of the two corpses on the dance floor. There was a sickly moment in which he also gained purchase on my body, pinning my free arm to my side. I wondered how much longer I could fight to stay alive when the nightmare got worse.

The rope slipped.

Startled by the sudden jolt, my muscles constricted. Even then, they couldn't keep a tight grip on everything. The first thing to fall was the whiskey. Hitting the ground at high speed, it shattered, spilling its muggy contents all over the dance floor.

Next to give way was me. In a moment of idiocy, I tried to redistribute my weight and free my arm. What actually happened was I lost my grip on the rope for a second, just as one of the girl's legs clipped another brick pillar.

"Aaahh!"

I screamed for what I assumed would be the last time as the rope vanished between my fingers. For a moment, the whole world seemed to slow down to a fraction of its usual speed. I heard the smash and watched the vodka bottle explode before I hit the deck myself. Landing on my back, I smelled the pungent smell of alcohol. I was winded an instant later as the gin torpedoed into my chest.

My head bounced off the floor and white lights flashed in front of my eyes.

"Ow," I moaned.

Gleeful snarls rumbled all around me. Our plan had unravelled. Separated from the rope and my only chance of escape, I was completely alone. Nobody could help me now.

PART FOURTEEN
FOR SCIENCE

Wheezing, I assessed my limbs to make sure they were all intact. They were. How long they would stay that way, I wasn't sure.

The impact had changed things dramatically. In what I could assume was a case of mistaken identity, the two zombies let go at the same time and grappled amongst themselves, covered in a cocktail of whiskey and vodka. From my position, laying upside down, they appeared to be sliding away while remaining completely still. Either that, or the room was getting longer. Confusion contorted my face.

A second passed before I realised what had really happened. Glancing at my foot, I saw it was still stuck in the noose and I was being dragged along the floor with one legged propped up in the air. Ahead of me, in a place I was rapidly approaching against my will, lay the zombie in the bin liner.

"Aaaaaahhhhh!" I screamed.

"Aaaaaahhhhh!" the zombie hissed back, with very different motivations.

The inevitable collision happened. Just as the zombie managed to clamber to his feet, I hit him like a gangly missile, throwing him into an awkward summersault. His head cracked as it hit the floor and, running out of rope, I came to a resounding stop. For a moment, I lay breathless with the barman next to me, his eyes closed.

Good, I thought. *He's dead.*

But that had never stopped him before, and it wouldn't this time. We were face to face. Opening his eyes, he snorted and coughed. Then he lunged.

"Get off!" I yelled, bludgeoning him with my elbow as I tried to scoot away with the other.

My foot was still stuck in the noose. Fighting to free it, I winced as the rope tightened around my ankle, and I was suddenly dragged skywards. It would have been helpful had I not been in the process of being mauled.

Dangling by one leg, I parried the barman. It must have become apparent I was escaping because, with one feverish effort to claim his meal, he grabbed my shirt. Thankfully, I was too far away for him to sink his teeth into my skin.

I heard a tear, and a sudden jolt ran through me. Glancing up, I inspected the rope, terrified to see it threadbare and frayed. Luckily, it was fine. Another jolt sent the bartender tumbling away from me, fragments of my shirt sleeve clutched in his fist.

"Don't worry, Milo! We've got you!"

The voice sounded like Amelia or Sophia. Unless I'd hit my head harder than I thought, it definitely wasn't Monty. A much stronger tug than before pulled me up out of the zombie's grasp, and before I knew it, I was approaching the ceiling. Pressure built up in my head but I didn't care.

When a strong hand clamped around my leg, I sighed, still fighting to reclaim my breath. Another grabbed the scruff of my shirt and I was hauled into the warm ventilation shaft. Pushing me away from the hole, Monty replaced the missing panel and slapped me on the back.

"Jolly good show, old sport! Glad to have you back."

"I'm never drinking again," I said, barely able to breathe.

Pausing, our eyes met and we laughed. My chest was scorched, and blood pulsed in my head, but I laughed through it. Behind Monty, the others whooped and cheered. Then, when the thrill of the chase was over, we settled, and the mood became grave.

"Sorry I messed up, guys," I said.

"What are you talking about?" Monty asked.

"I dropped it all," I explained.

"Look in your hand, you spanner." Amelia called from the dark tunnel behind Monty. Shadows indicated the others had joined her.

Frowning, I glanced down at my hands. They were shaking, knuckles white, clutching a large, frosted bottle.

Gin!

I must have held onto it when I fell off the rope and it slammed into my chest. With all of the pandemonium, I hadn't even noticed it was still in my hand.

"That's gin," I said.

"You're a bright one," Amelia noted.

Punching me playfully in the shoulder, Monty said, "You did well, mate." Then, turning to the others, he added, "Alright, chaps! Show's over. Let's get back to the balcony and start drinking. After all that, I think we can agree, this experiment better work."

"Of course it will!" Wyatt's voice resonated sarcastically in the vent. Obviously, he had reached a moment of clarity in between waves of delusion. I'd seen it happen countless times before.

"For science!" he cheered.

"For science!" everyone agreed.

It didn't take long to get back to the balcony. By now, most of the road was teaming with bodies, and the smoking area's glass door resembled an exhibit in an overstuffed zoo. Bodies in the first throws of decay had built up behind it.

When they saw us drop out of the vent, the bodies pressed into the glass together. A groaning sound worried me. One fracture was all it would take to bring down the entire thing.

"Okay, so who wants to go first?" Sophia asked, eyeing the doors with concern.

"Well, it was your idea, so surely it should be you," Monty suggested.

"I'm not stepping in there with them! Are you crazy?"

"So, are you saying you were wrong and I was right?"

Narrowing her eyes, Sophia took the bottle and swigged it. Her cheeks puffed as she drew a second mouthful, and she heaved.

"You have no idea how disgusting that is," she moaned.

"Just keep drinking," Amelia urged. "For science, remember?"

Looking hurt, Sophia took another swig, and then another. Waiting a few minutes, she swigged twice more, and then stopped.

"Alright, if I have any more, I'm gonna throw up," she said.

"Sounds like you're right where you need to be," Monty suggested. "If we're to get out of here, we all need to drink just enough to slow down our brains and make us invisible to the zombies, but not so much that we black out or chunder."

"Ssso, a regular night out then?" Sophia giggled. "I think I'm clossse, guys." She pushed a closed fist to her lips and belched rancid air into her hand. "Ooo, danger burp. That was clossse."

Monty laughed. "You're ready."

Swaying as she stood, Sophia staggered over to the doors and pressed her nose against the glass. A girl with savage features and feathers hanging from between her teeth stared back at her. She growled softly, but made no attempt to attack her through the door.

"You think it'sss gonna work?" Sophia asked.

"There's only one way to find out," Amelia responded.

Monty arrived at her side, and the zombies crowded the area of glass near him, completely ignoring Sophia.

"It seems to be working," he said. "You ready?"

Sophia shook her head. "No, but open the door anyway."

"Okay."

Monty gestured for me to join him. Positioning ourselves on either side, we each bore the weight of a door. Counting down from three under his breath, he finally slid the bar out of its groove.

The door pressed up against me with unexpected weight as the bodies behind it pushed in my direction. Puffing, I held it tight, while Monty slacked his side ever so slightly. A seam of arms erupted through the gap like volcanic seepage.

Gulping, Sophia rubbed her right arm, holding it just out of range of the writhing faces. When they didn't take the bait, she inched forward. The zombies slavered and gnashed their teeth, but not at her. Their primary targets were me and Monty, neither of which they could reach.

"It'sss working!" Sophia yelled with relief. "It's actually working."

Allowing the gap to open a touch more, Monty instructed her to push her way into the build-up. More confident now – possibly because of her success, and possibly because the alcohol was kicking in – Sophia waded her way in amongst the bodies, clambering through them without difficulty.

One bedraggled individual almost slipped through our funnel, but we managed to close it behind her. A sharp kick from Monty sent the boy tumbling onto his back, creating a divide. Seizing the opportunity, Sophia slipped through the gap and bounded back onto the balcony, almost tripping over her own feet as she arrived.

"It works!" she announced.

"Yeah, it does," I said.

Monty and I pushed the doors closed again, and Amelia slid the bar back into place. Allowing it to take the strain, we all slumped, pulses racing.

"Well, that was quite a result," said Monty.

"What did I tell you?" Robbie asked rhetorically.

His expression looked woozy after his short nap, but I assumed it was intended to be smug. Rolling onto his side, he picked up the gin by its neck.

"Not my preference, but needs must, I suppose."

"Hold your horses, old sport," said Monty. "You can handle your drink. If you're let loose on that first, there might not be enough left to get the rest of us up to speed."

Snatching it from Robbie, he took a swig and grimaced. "You weren't lying, Soph. This is diabolical!"

"Can I have some?" The voice was unexpected. Glancing at Theo, I smiled. He looked more relaxed now. "I mean, I can wait for the rest of you to go first, but I'd really like to get out of here with you guys."

Monty tossed him the bottle – a reckless move in my opinion, but Theo didn't appear to be a butterfingers like me.

Catching it, he took a swig, and grinned. "I haven't had gin since I was a Fresher myself," he said. "And that was a while ago."

Under the gaze of the zombie horde, we drank, passing the bottle between us like a gang of kids with their first taste of alcohol. Conversations started, stories were shared, and I felt my face getting warmer, despite the freezing wind. For a few minutes, I realised I was slurring, but as the others caught up, the speech impediment became undetectable.

"Hey, Milo, so what's with the kitten?" Amelia said after a while.

My stomach did a barrel roll. Glancing at my right shoulder, I saw my tattoo for the first time that night. Apparently, so did everyone else. When the Armageddon bartender tore my shirt, he had – for want of a better expression – let the cat out of the bag.

Wyatt snorted, briefly distracted from a conversation with Sophia. I ignored him, hoping he didn't bring up my old school nickname. A zombie apocalypse was bad enough, without also having to endure a cutesy name.

"Long story," I said, drawing a short sip from the bottle and handing it to her. "It was meant to be a tiger but the tattoo artist messed it up. I went through a phase."

"Oh," she leaned closer, looking intrigued. "So, you were a rebel?"

"Yeah, well... sort of."

In my peripheral vision, Wyatt fidgeted. His desire to abandon his conversation with Sophia and intervene was almost palpable.

"Oh?" Amelia asked, with a spark of intrigue. "Ever do anything really bad?"

"Well." A smile crept onto my face. "There was this one time, when–"

"Ha!"

Oh no.

"Milo never did anything wrong," said Wyatt. "He once almost pulled a muscle in his brain agreeing too hard with a teacher. Wasn't exactly known for being cool. Until he got that tattoo, his most memorable moment was the time he had an asthma attack in the school swimming pool. We called him Puff Daddy for weeks."

"Puff Daddy?" Amelia giggled.

Shrinking into myself, I felt heat rush to my face. "That's not true," I lied. "He's lying. It's all the drugs. They make him... imagine things."

Wyatt brushed off the insult. "It was so funny!" he blurted. "And just when everyone started to forget about it, he went and got that tattoo, and a new nickname was born."

"That's enough, Wyatt!"

There was a bullish quality to my voice I had never heard before. I didn't like it. But, given the situation and the smug grin on Wyatt's face, I just couldn't hold back any longer. My hands trembled with rage, and I heard my voice crack.

"Woah, looks like someone's had too much to drink," he said. "Calm down, Tiger. Or should I call you Kitten?"

There it was – a taunt. A red flag to my bull.

"No, Wyatt." I said. "I've had it! You've always done this – pretended to be my friend, and rolled your eyes every time I've done something you claim is dweebish. I'm sensible. I don't take risks. I'm quiet. I stroll into life early and prepared. That's not uncool – it's reliable.

"You, on the other hand!" I jabbed an accusing finger at his chest. "You always do this! You sneer and make jokes from this high tower in your fantasy land, like I need you to show me the way. But, you know what, Wyatt? I don't!

"I mean, look at you! You're a mess. You almost got us all killed, and we've spent half the night dragging you around while you struggle not to drool on yourself. You're pathetic!"

"Hey, I–"

"I'm not finished! You know why I think you make fun of me? It's because you know, deep down, you're coasting, and pretty soon, you're gonna be all grown up and run out of track. Your dream world won't help you anymore. Call me Kitten all you want, but it won't make reality any less painful for you."

My teeth were gritted. Feeling my shoulders rise and fall with my breath, I stood back. Everyone was silent. I glanced at Amelia, a little uncertain of everything I'd just said. She looked away.

Glaring back at Wyatt, I watched tears well in his eyes. Immediately, I knew I'd gone too far.

I sighed. "Wyatt," I tried, my voice softer than before.

"No," he said. "You've said enough." With a whimper, he added, "Bro."

"Guys." Theo was learning against the railing, holding the empty gin bottle between his thumb and forefinger. His popstar hair had become unruly. "I hate to interrupt such rich drama, but we've run out of booze."

"Ah!" Monty exclaimed, a little too eager to pretend like my rant never happened. "Then that means we're ready!"

Jumping to his feet with the sprightly energy of a mad genius, he inspected the bodies behind the glass. There were well over a dozen, but thankfully the horde hadn't grown in vast enough numbers to overwhelm and shatter the doors.

"Alright, chaps. Everyone drunk as lords?"

A hearty cheer confirmed everyone was. I joined in, hoping it would help blow social dust into the enormous chasm I had created between me and the rest of the group.

"Good!" Monty continued. "Now, we should probably do this in a methodical fashion. Chances are, some of us are drunker than others."

"You're not wrong there!" cheered Robbie.

Monty nodded. "That's precisely why we should dive in one-by-one – test the waters. Only then can we be sure we can all make it to the next checkpoint – the pub!"

Another cheer. It became apparent to me how quickly emotions changed when alcohol was involved. Evidently, however this played out, we were in for a rollercoaster ride.

"So," Monty concluded. "Who wants to go first?"

There was a shuffle of activity and chatter, then Sophia volunteered.

"Done it once before, so why not show you boys how it's done again." She threw up a gang sign ironically, and said, "Feminism."

Steadying the doors as before, Monty and I removed the bar and let Sophia slip through the gap. Shortly after, she was followed by Robbie, who was still coasting on the astounding alcohol content in his blood. Wyatt and Amelia went through next, silent as they entered the wall of sweating bodies. The corpses sniffed them and pawed at their shoulders as they slid between them, but made no effort to attack.

Next was Theo.

"It's okay, old sport. They won't hurt you," said Monty, with a prizewinning smirk. "In fact, you might even have fun."

Wringing his hands, Theo accepted his fate and waded into the danger. Then only two of us remained.

"How drunk do you feel?" I asked.

"Not nearly as much as I'd like to be," Monty replied. "Our next pit stop better be nearby."

"That's what I thought."

There was a pause.

"This is it," he said, and then threw open the doors.

Holding up his arms like a conductor, Monty took a deep breath as the bodies piled onto the balcony, meandering around us like water around jagged rocks. The balcony became flooded with moans and shambling corpses. My breath trembled as I locked eyes with a girl's vacant stare.

There was no going back now. Our only sanctuary had been swallowed by death.

PART FIFTEEN
SOBRIETY CAN KILL YOU

"What's the plan again?"

All thought drained from my head the moment zombies entered the equation. Monty hurried his pace, dragging me along to catch up with the others, who were already on the stairs. Moving slowly, so not to attract too much attention, he explained.

"Our first port-of-call is the bar. If we can grab some drinks there before we leave, we'll have more chance of getting to the next pub without sobering up on the way. After that, all we have to do is hop from bar to bar until we hit the main gate."

"Just like a pub crawl?" I asked.

"Exactly like a pub crawl."

We joined the back of the gang and edged slowly in a procession between autonomous bodies. Dipping ahead of Monty and Amelia, I loped next to Wyatt.

"Hey, man," I said, guilt eating away at me. "You know – about what I said earlier…"

"Forget it, dude."

"I'm sorry. I didn't mean to–"

"It's fine. Consider it forgotten."

I studied his face, hoping it would crack one of those over-the-top ecstasy smiles I knew so well. It didn't.

"But, mate. What I said was way out of–"

Tripping over my own shoes, I stumbled and slung out a hand to steady myself. My palm struck something soft but firm, and I drew it back as a pair of piercing, yellow eyes got too close to my face. The creature's gullet reverberated with a growl.

"Hey! Eyes forward!" Wyatt scolded me. "You're too drunk. Stay focused."

Oh, the irony, I thought.

If I hadn't been quite so intoxicated, I would have noticed the hypocrisy in my previous rant now Wyatt had become my guide.

Straightening up, I cleared my throat, and watched with a warm, fuzzy head as blurred figures made of blood and pale flesh floated past. Turning a corner, we approached a fork in the corridor. Whispers came from Sophia and Robbie at the front, but I couldn't make out what they were saying. It was unclear whether loud noises and sudden movements would make any difference to the undead, but none of us seemed willing to take that risk.

A firm hand clamped on my shoulder when we neared a corner, and hot breath condensed on my neck. I flinched, willing the zombie to reconsider. That's when I heard Monty's voice in my ear.

"I think if we turn right, it'll take us back to the main dance floor. We should pick up some stuff before we leave. If we've got time, I might even look at their wine menu."

"Okay," I responded, not wanting to disagree, despite being plenty drunk enough already.

Turning the corner, we almost bumped into Theo. His body was frozen, as were Robbie and Sophia. A right turn did indeed lead to the main dance floor. What lay in the way, however, was a scene for which none of us were prepared.

Up until this point, I had imagined the corridors becoming gauntlets as freshers fled the building, but I'd never really envisioned the true extent of the carnage. The short corridor was teaming with bodies. Dozens were dead on the carpet, their blood soaking like red wine into the fronds.

Like hyenas, zombies swarmed over them, hackles raised, mouths grumbling with satisfaction as they buried their faces into open chest cavities and abdomens. There was barely an open patch of floor to place your foot. Getting through would mean drunkenly ambling over corpses, stepping on fingers, and using faces with open eye sockets as handholds.

It was unstable ground, even for a sober person. And with all of us already struggling with our balance, it was unlikely we'd get through without someone taking a tumble.

"Maybe not," I said. The joke wasn't funny, but it closed off my mind from the horrors I couldn't un-see.

"Yeah," Monty replied. Then he turned to the others. "Okay, change of plan. Let's head straight out into the street."

"But, the drink!" The protest came from Robbie.

"Are you drunk?"

"Mate, I'm always drunk."

"Then you have nothing to worry about. Let's move."

Nobody argued with Monty after that. Continuing on our glacial march through the crowded corridors, we eventually hit a wall of fresh air and wandered down a stretch of stone steps to the road. It was raining outside. Vortexes of white drizzle whirled out of the dark sky. All around, zombies glistened, their hair and clothes soiled.

Passing a corpse, so picked-clean it hadn't even had a chance to reanimate, I shuddered. The folds of a large, black pea coat, pinned open like moth wings in a museum, told me it was one of Armageddon's bouncers. His brute strength couldn't help him.

"We're gonna make it!" Sophia whispered between gritted teeth.

I also felt a rush as we passed through the shoal of zombies unnoticed, but I didn't show it. Too many horror films had warned me that the moment you get complacent, you get killed. It appeared the others had come to the same conclusion. With wooden movements, we powered onwards, ignoring any horrifying details which could distract us from our goal.

Rounding Armageddon, we carved a channel in the throng, entering a narrow alleyway. It was unclear when the outbreak had started but I could already see signs of rot. When a girl with grit-speckled eyeballs and a face marred by lacerations wandered towards me, I almost heaved. The stench of death already hung over her like a cape.

Meandering round our fragile fellowship, she stopped without warning, barring Monty's path. He and Sophia stopped dead. The corpse's lungs crackled as her lips moved with what I could only assume was a trace of vacant thought. Halting, I watched, paralysed, as she reached out and wrapped her grey fingers around Monty's wrist.

"Uh, guys?" His voice slipped.

"Oh, looks like someone's pulled," Robbie jibed.

Caught off guard, a laugh exploded from my mouth. The girl's sliced head snapped in my direction, and my face fell.

"Chaps, stop messing around. This is serious," Monty whined, struggling to shake her off.

She pulled him closer, until their noses were almost touching. Other monsters slowed their pace around us, creating a bottleneck in the alleyway. Opening her mouth, the girl breathed heavily, as if assessing whether Monty would make a good meal.

Nobody moved. Stuck in a standoff of nerves, we waited, hoping the decrepit girl would get bored and move on. Monty let out a quiet squeak. Her black saliva dripped onto his arm but he didn't wrench it away.

Finally, she let go. Panning her vacant stare away, she ambled past, bumping him with her shoulder as if forgetting he even existed.

"Ugh, her breath stunk like something died in there."

"Something did," Amelia said. "Her."

"You okay?" I asked him. He nodded, rubbing his wrist as we regained our pace. "Talk about sobering! After that, you could probably do with another drink."

"Yeah, keep yourself topped up, bro. Sobriety can kill you," Robbie added from behind.

I hated to admit it but Robbie was right. The need to get more drink was ever-present, especially for Monty. He was too sober, and there was no telling how much longer he would go undetected.

My pulse throbbed in my temples and the cold wind weaved its fingers under my shirt. I wasn't sure whether the alcohol was wearing off or the adrenaline had heightened my senses. Either way, I felt horribly exposed in the packed alley.

Thankfully, it widened into a full-blown street as we moved further away from Armageddon. I relaxed a little as the monsters became sparser, guessing that most had been distracted and hadn't made it this far yet. Nestled in a curve in the road, a pub beckoned us. Warm light spilled from its windows onto a seated beer garden.

"There's our next checkpoint," Monty whispered. "A bit touch-and-go there, chaps – not gonna lie – but it looks like we've made–"

A gnarled hand shot past my face and grabbed Monty by the ear. Wrenched off course, he yelled out, and hit the deck. The zombie had darted out of nowhere and was left staring at its fist, a clump of Monty's loose hairs protruding between its fingers. I recoiled, scrambling to get out of the way, totally unprepared. Thankfully, someone else saw the attack coming.

Turning my head, I caught a glimpse of the monster's grizzled head. A second later, Robbie thundered past me and drove a clubbed fist into its face. I heard a gut-churning crunch and saw the creature stumble away, its jaw hanging crooked under the rest of its face.

"Quick!" Amelia shouted, taking the reins. "Everyone get around him. He's too sober, but maybe we can hide him with our own bodies."

We did as she said, but it immediately became apparent the plan wasn't going to work. Robbie's outburst had set off a chain reaction of hisses. The zombies were sparser here but we were still heavily outnumbered.

Arching around, dozens of bodies gravitated towards us. I closed the space between me and Monty, along with the others. Crouching low, he ducked and we hastily shuffled forward, forming a protective shell.

The creatures ignored us like we weren't even there. The first to react was an ashen figure with an exposed ribcage. It was unclear whether he was a student or a member of staff, but he had definitely seen Monty. Butting him with the heel of my palm, I watched as he spun and face planted the ground. His skin was oily, so I wiped my trembling hands on my shirt.

"We need weapons!" I squawked.

"There'll be stuff at the bar we can use!" said Sophia.

Another zombie shuffled into our path. By now, we had built up momentum, huddled around Monty like secret service agents around a president. His eyes briefly locked with mine as it approached, and I could tell he was scared.

Splitting off from the shell, Wyatt clotheslined it, but a second one grabbed him from behind. Squealing, he whirled and managed to dislodge his attacker. The zombie thrashed but all it got as a reward was his fairly mangled, plastic hat.

"You bit?" I asked him.

Breathing heavily, he shook his head.

"No, but I'm compromised! They've seen me." A short girl charged him, and he deflected her with a backhanded slap to the face.

"Get in the circle!" I screamed, and he stepped inside.

More assailants peeled out of the dark and blocked our path.

"I'm up," I said regretfully, being the only one who wasn't preparing for attacks from both sides. My first enemy was short and skinny, not unlike me. Using my superior reflexes, I ducked under his grasp and kicked his ankles with as much force as I could muster.

His legs buckled and he went down. Next, I drove a foot into the side of his head and he fell still. His mouth chomped and he growled, but his body remained stationary. I could only assume his neck was broken.

Preparing myself for the next confrontation, I gasped. He was huge – at least six foot six – with broad shoulders and a reach that rivalled an albatross.

"Um..."

My mind searched for a plan of attack. Glancing around, I saw Robbie grappling with two girls on one side, and Theo busy with a zombie in a headlock on the other. Sophia and Amelia protected the boys from behind. There was no one to help me deal with this Ent of a man.

"Fine."

Dashing forward, I bounded once, twice, three times, then leapt high into the air. My knuckles made contact with the guy's Adam's apple but he didn't even flinch. Instead, he lunged, grabbing me awkwardly from the side.

Squealing, I felt the weight of his huge fingers curling around my upper arms. I tried to throw him off like a backpack but he didn't budge, offering only an alligator snarl as a reaction.

"Help!" I shouted.

Hot drool trickled from above. Arching my neck, I peered up, expecting to see jaws. The reality was quite different, and frankly confusing. His face had been obliterated, smashed open like an egg. Buried deep into his cranium was a heavy, four-pointed hook. The rope attached to it became taut, and it was wrenched free, showering me with gore.

"Get out of the way, idiot!" Amelia yelled, reeling in her grappling hook.

Her warning came too late. The giant crumpled, buckling my legs under his collapsing body. I landed on my back, the wind pushed out of my lungs. My legs kicked but my arms were pinned by his torso.

Gazing up at the others, I bellowed for help, but they were all locked in their own battles for survival. Now fully exposed, Monty and Wyatt covered each other's backs, swiping out at attackers whose open jaws were full of black bile. Amelia was busy, too, pushing her knee into a pinned zombie's nape while she snapped its head back with her rope. Sophia, Robbie, and Theo were nowhere to be seen. We were getting separated.

There were more zombies now. Our escape from Armageddon, and the fuss we were causing, had alerted dozens more. They formed a net, closing in from all directions.

"Robbie!" I screamed, spotting him in the middle of a cluster. Distracted by a trio of gnarled girls in football jerseys, who had gotten too close, he hadn't realised a fourth crept up behind him.

"Robbie!"

It was unclear whether he heard me, and it didn't really matter. Even if he had, there was little chance of him getting out of the scrape unscathed. Mowing the girls down would only open enough space for more to fortify his exit path. His options were dire, and so were mine.

I didn't see what he chose. Momentarily forgetting him, I yelped as a bulky leg stopped in front of my face. Grit splashed where its foot landed. Looking up, I saw the monster approach me upside down. It was a fat boy with broken spectacles hanging off his nose.

"Help!"

I needed it, fast. Dropping on all fours, the corpse knocked more earth in my face as I squirmed away from his gaping mouth. With the others indisposed, and me unable to move, I experienced what I could only assume was my life flashing before my eyes. Though, it didn't go exactly how I expected.

I'd admit, I didn't expect an action movie, but I hoped there'd be a little more excitement. What I got instead was a lot of spluttering as the dirt up my nose caused me to relive every time I'd ever sneezed simultaneously, like a nasal machine gun.

"Hel – achoo!"

The boy's pudgy hands closed around my throat. His mouth dropped open and a cloud of noxious stink filled my nostrils. Not even my friends could save me this time.

I'd always assumed we'd make it. That was what happened in all of the books and movies. The good guys won. The world was saved.

But, this was real life.

There was no shining knight. No caped crusader to save the day. We were a bunch of drunk kids, barely old enough to be away from home. And we were all about to die.

PART SIXTEEN
THE MINISTRY OF MYTHS

"Eat my blaster, noob!"

The words echoed through my head just a moment before the fat zombie's right eye popped like a red blister. Blood dribbled from the open socket onto my face, followed by the boy's hefty body, which added to the dogpile.

"Ooof!" I wheezed.

My hands wriggled uselessly under the bodies of the man-tree and my tubby attacker.

"Help, guys! Anyone!"

Screams and whoops boomed from somewhere in the crowd, but I was too preoccupied to think about who or what made them. All of my energy was focused on trying to get free before something ate me alive.

Still, nobody came to my aid. I went unnoticed as a corpse shambled past. The bottoms of his jeans were feathered, having caught under his shoes. They brushed against my cheek as he headed towards Theo. The young lecturer was hemmed in on all sides, but I couldn't warn him. My vocal chords strained as I tried to call him but the lack of breath in my lungs restricted the sound.

It was hopeless. Nothing I did would alert him to the oncoming danger, but I knew I had to do something to save him otherwise I'd never get out of my fix. My mind raced, wondering what I could do to help. It came to a disgusting conclusion.

Oh God, I thought as I arched my neck and opened my mouth.

Clamping my teeth on the bottom of the monster's jeans, I grimaced. The bitter taste of earth and wet denim flooded my taste buds. As the zombie took another step, I felt the weight of his body almost pull my teeth out by the roots. Then, pivoting like a lever, he tripped and hit the ground.

Arching around, he growled. He was a pale boy with blond, close-cropped hair. Fresh claw marks ran down the centre of his face. His nose was broken. Unfortunately for me, his jaw was still intact.

"I'm coming, Milo!" I heard Theo shout. He had finally noticed me, though I didn't hold out much hope. He was a tall, lean guy himself, but his muscle mass was no match for the horde surrounding him.

"Come on," I whispered, gritting my teeth.

My right arm wriggled free, sending a pulse of exhilaration through me. Pushing off the slick tarmac, I dragged myself backwards, grinding the back of my shirt against the dirt. Several heads turned my way.

Come on, Milo. One arm left.

Time ran out as the blond zombie reached me on his hands and knees. I raised a palm, splaying my fingers, hoping to fend him off long enough for someone to jump in and rescue me.

Overcome with excitement, the monster leapt forward. At the same time, I saw a flash of red light wipe across my eyes. A red dot appeared on his forehead and exploded, rupturing like a crack in a wine barrel. He collapsed on top of the fat boy and fell still.

"Aww, seriously?" I complained, crushed by a third body.

I paused and glanced around as realisation hit me. That red flash had come from a gun.

The army! I thought. It was the only explanation. Nobody else would have a gun fitted with a laser scope. *They're here! We're saved!*

Two more bodies fell around me. It appeared somebody had my back. That gave me the determination I needed to continue the fight. Twisting like a slime-covered butterfly emerging from a cocoon, I dislodged my other arm and shimmied my legs free. Without wasting a second, I rolled to my feet and grabbed one of the nearest undead by the arm as he reached for me.

Wrenching him, I spun, causing his shambling legs to teeter under his unbalanced body. When I let him go he spread-eagled, taking down two others along the way. A small window opened up and I took full advantage of it, charging towards the pub at the end of the street.

"Guys, where are you?" I called.

"Over here!" responded Amelia's disembodied voice.

I inspected the mob. Their close ranks made it hard to spot her. Being at the front of the group, I considered powering onwards. After all, it was unlikely the others would make it but I still had a chance. Only a handful of ghouls lay between me and my next drink, and by the looks of it, I was still invisible to some of the less sensitive monsters.

The building with its glossy sign and beer garden was only a short run ahead. If I was lucky, I could make it there in under thirty seconds. It wasn't like I was abandoning the others on purpose. I had no weapon. Going back for them would only get me killed, too.

A call echoed from the crowd, but I forced myself to ignore it. It sounded like Monty.

"Don't white knight, Milo," I reasoned with myself. "It'll only get you killed."

Okay. I'd made up my mind. I was going.

Crouching low, I ferreted my way between two bodies, then scampered under the legs of another. What I was doing was cowardly – I knew that – but there was no way I could go back. The others wouldn't do the same for me. At least, I hoped that was true. They'd understand.

Bypassing the last of the horde, I scrambled to my feet.

"There you are!" shouted a short, plump boy I was almost certain I'd never met. He wore a cape, tights, and a helmet fitted with horns, so I assumed I would have remembered him. Hurling what looked like a javelin, he shouted, "Duck!"

I dropped to my knees as he lifted some sort of silver gun. A scarlet beam glittered from its muzzle in the drizzling rain. Pulling a trigger, he laughed, and I sensed a body drop behind me.

"What's your name?" he asked.

"Um... Milo."

"Well, Milo. Welcome to the Ministry of Myths. I'm Lord Augustus. That's Lord Jacob, Lady Kate, and Lady Alycia."

He gestured to a bunch of students who darted around him, working as one to bring down the zombies at the edge of the crowd. Each of them wore a similar cape or shroud, and sported some sort of homemade weapon which wouldn't have looked out of place in a low-budget fantasy movie.

Behind them, the road was littered with corpses that had strayed too far from the herd. Slotting his futuristic gun into a utility belt, Lord Augustus replaced it with a two-handed, wooden broadsword, and rushed into battle.

A small Asian girl with artificially white hair weaved between the writhing bodies, dodging before any zombies could grab her. She was clad head-to-toe in red spandex and had a satchel slung over her shoulder which held down a flowing cape. As she moved, she slipped bright red hats out of a bag and slapped them onto zombies' heads.

What the hell? I thought. Just when I thought the night couldn't get any more bizarre, someone managed to crank up the weird-ometer.

"What are you waiting for, Milo?" Augustus called back, seeing me hesitate. "Wield your spear like the titan you were born to be!"

"But…" I glanced at the javelin, wondering what was happening. It had landed near me so I snatched it from the ground.

"Don't waste time!" Augustus said. "The enemy are OP, and nobody respawns in this game. We need all the help we can get to save your friends."

"OP?" I asked.

"Argh!" Augustus spun and kicked a zombie in the chest. "It stands for 'over-powered.' Now, come on!"

The others weaved around him, seemingly speaking in a code I didn't understand. Everything was made up of acronyms and abbreviations. It was like I'd fallen into another world.

Processing what I'd seen, my mind came to the only conclusion that made sense. They were nerds. They had to be. Like, *real* nerds. The kind you see in movies at Comic-Con.

"Are you coming? We're going in!"

"You're going in?" I asked. "Are you nuts?"

I glanced back at the 'spear' in my hand, and then gazed at the pub. I was so close now, I could read the writing above the door. The Black Mile. *Do I have enough time to get in there and drink alone before the ghouls catch me?* It was impossible to tell.

Against my better judgement, and possibly driven by guilt, I resorted to the safety-in-numbers approach and joined Augustus. Screaming a war cry, I raised the spear over my head and plunged the shaft through a zombie at the edge of the horde. The spike drove through its abdomen and pinned it to the ground.

Augustus brought down his wooden sword like a guillotine, snapping the monster's head back and breaking its neck. As it became inanimate, I awkwardly dislodged the shaft and watched as the zombie's entrails left its body.

"Don't go in yet!" he ordered. "Let Lady Alycia do her work first."

"What's she doing?"

"She's a caster. Her incantation will keep us safe in there after we've found your friends."

Bonkers. All of them.

I decided to keep my opinion to myself, as the thin girl dipped into the crowd and disappeared completely. A nimble arm popped up intermittently, slapping hats on every zombie crossing its path. Moments later, she emerged.

"Now!"

A boy with a mop of auburn hair battered his way through the horde with a shield and we all followed. Swinging my javelin, I struggled to manoeuvre it in the close quarters of the mob.

"We need to go back," I said to Augustus. "There are more coming from the club. If we go in any further, we'll never get out."

Around us, the small girl continued to attach silly hats to any untouched zombies.

"Just trust us, Milo! We're all level forty mages on MOM."

"Mom?"

"Ministry of Myths. Keep up!"

"It's a game?"

"Only the biggest RPG in the world!"

"We're facing real zombies, you lunatic. We could all die! Do you realise that?" I bellowed.

Swinging his sword like a club, Augustus bludgeoned a fragile-looking cadaver before it had a chance to pounce on one of his friends.

Retreating from the group, he grabbed me by the shoulders, shouting, "BRB, guys! Cover me. AFK."

"K, Gus," was their collective response. None of them even broke their stride.

"Look, Milo. I know. Half our group has already been killed. But you know who died first? The sports students. They never saw it coming. But we knew what was happening the moment the violence broke out. We're nerds. We've been preparing for this for years. Relax. Oh, and get yourself a horned helmet ASAP. I mean, what are you wearing? You're embarrassing yourself."

Turning away, he joined the others, leaving me perplexed and exposed. Already too far in to turn back alone, and with no other option at my disposal, I joined the Ministry and their crazy, hat-applying 'caster.'

"Which way are your friends?" Gus yelled.

"That way," I said, pointing in the direction of the alleyway. Then I added, "If they're still alive."

"Have faith, my friend. The gods smile kindly on you this day!"

"If this is a smile, I'd hate to see a frown!" I replied.

We were six or seven monsters deep on every side now, and that number kept growing. Undeterred by the odds, the gang blasted their way through the throng, armed with nothing but fake weapons and silly hats.

I wielded my spear where I could, taking out the odd ghoul, but it wasn't easy. Close combat wasn't my strength. Admittedly, neither were running, climbing, or swimming, but I would have taken those over a street brawl any day.

Alycia pulled yet more hats out of the bag strapped over her shoulder and forced them onto zombies' heads. Her movements were astoundingly quick compared to the rest of us. And yet, I couldn't help but feel her talents were totally wasted. That surely a short sword would have been better... or even a brick.

"Over here, chaps!"

Monty!

His voice filled me with more relief than I thought possible for someone I'd met just a few hours ago. Pushing towards the call, we reached him just in time. Wyatt and Sophia were with him. Somehow, they had managed to work their way to a nearby wall which protected their backs. A heap of bodies was strewn around them like sandbags, but they were trapped.

Hacking into heads with their ridiculous weapons, Gus' friends cleared a perimeter for us to jump into the circle.

"Kitten! We have to stop bumping into each other like this. People are gonna start talking."

Wyatt's sarcasm didn't hide his relief. It was clear he was prepared for the worst.

"You have no idea how happy we are to see you," Sophia added. "It's hotter in here than that time I crowd-surfed at Gl–"

"Hey!"

Whirling around, I searched for the source of the yell and spotted a pair of hands waving below the glow of a streetlamp. Robbie, Theo, and Amelia had found themselves stuck against the same wall, not too far away. They were stationed atop an industrial recycling container, hemmed in by hands.

"That everyone?" Gus asked me, pointing with his sword.

"Yeah," I laughed, astonished everyone had survived.

"Good. Onwards, men!"

"Argh!"

Suddenly, Gus' friend, Jacob, was on the ground. At first, I didn't register what had happened. Then, I saw the grizzled head locked onto his arm. Blood pumped from him like a leaky fire hydrant as more monsters breached the chink in our defences and absorbed him. Unable to watch him get devoured, his friend, Kate, grabbed his hand.

"Jake! No, Jake!"

Without warning, a second attacker darted at her throat. She fell into a heap, her screams bubbling up from a bleeding hole in her neck.

Horrified, Gus burst into action. "I'll save you, my frien–"

Monty wrenched him back.

"Stop!" he bellowed. "Do that and you'll end up just like them. Our best chance is to join the others." He deflected an attack as a zombie flung its body at Gus. "See! Focus and keep moving!"

Gus gulped. "You're right."

Gus' plan was unravelling fast, and it took all of my energy just to hold back the panic in my brain.

Elbows and fists swung as we cleared a path along the outside wall. As more undead rushed past us to gorge on our fallen friends' bodies, a space opened up for us to move. Only the creatures closest to us made any effort to stop us escaping. Thankfully, Alycia moved swiftly, bamboozling their lagging minds with her speed.

Wyatt frowned when he saw her distributing hats, but didn't comment. It seemed even he prioritised not dying above wit. Besides, her skittish movements offered a useful distraction we could use to our advantage.

"Grab my arm!" shouted Robbie as we approached his large container.

Sophia was hoisted to safety first, followed by me, Gus, Wyatt, and Monty. Rising onto the lid, I shakily got to my feet and watched the undulating mass of bodies surrounding us.

There weren't as many as I expected. What appeared to be a vast lake of corpses from ground level was actually just somewhere closer to seventy or eighty. They had just moved along with us, swarming us in an ambling migration.

Still, there was no way out and we couldn't all stay on top of the dustbin forever. Already, some of the smaller ghouls were getting trampled by the blundering giants behind them. It was only a matter of time before they became steps for the others to reach us.

Alycia's path was evident from this vantage point. A river of garish, red hats snaked through the bodies. Seeing them reminded me we were missing someone.

"Where's Alycia?" I blurted.

Breathless beside me, Gus frowned.

"She'll be fine. She's a caster," he said. "Trust me."

I fired him an incredulous scowl but he held up a hand to silence me. Seeing him nod, I followed his gaze. She was still in in the tangle of bodies, darting between cadavers as she burrowed her way towards us.

"There she is – woah!"

"Hold still!" Amelia cried.

The thin lid creaked underneath us as Gus leaned forward. Without warning, it buckled, and I felt the whole platform tilt. Gravity took over from there, tipping the bin and crushing several zombies in the process. My stomach leapt sideways as we lost our footing and landed on a floor of broken bodies.

Rolling onto my knees, I cowered at the feet of the horde. As one, they sprung from all directions. There was no struggling. No screaming. No time to do anything. Just a sharp intake of breath.

PART SEVENTEEN
THIS GODFORSAKEN KINGDOM

Without warning, a waterfall of white hair swept in front of my face.

"Shield your eyes, mortal," Alycia whispered, not looking my way.

"What?"

Before I could process her words, she splayed her fingers and produced a soft bleeping sound. A microsecond later, it was like I had been taken to the underworld. First to react were the zombies next to us. Their heads exploded as though their brains were made of napalm. Then a chain reaction of mini supernovas rippled through the crowd.

A sea of phosphorous light blinded me and I fell backwards, covering my eyes. For whole seconds, an almighty crackle, like a molten sword thrust into ice-water, was the only thing I could hear. When yips and howls finally broke through, I knew something big had happened behind the light. The crackles eventually subsided but I waited to hear movements before I unfurled from my foetal position.

"Alycia, where'd you go?" I mumbled, squinting through a blue film that covered my vision.

At my feet, I noticed her body. Her face was scorched, and two zombies were on top of her, their bony shoulders smouldering as they gulped in her charred flesh. Tendrils of smoke wound up from her hair.

"Alycia!"

Gus arrived and clubbed one of her attackers onto its back. It hardly noticed, simply rolling back onto all fours to return to its meal. Jumping upright, I pulled him back while Monty helped the others to their feet.

"Come on!" He yanked Gus in the direction of a snaking pathway which had opened up as a result of the explosion. "She saved us. Don't waste her sacrifice."

Gus obliged, but his face told me he'd almost rather die. Together, we raced into a corpse-littered charcoal passageway. The ground was hot underfoot and the stench of burned flesh made me retch, but I powered through.

Around us, the rabble closed ranks, eating up the space as we sped towards freedom. I elbowed a zombie, nearing the exit, angry I hadn't reacted faster and picked up my javelin after tumbling off the dustbin.

I can't believe it, I thought as I turned a corner. The road ahead lay empty. *We're gonna make it!*

A sharp pain flashed in the back of my skull and one of the buttons on my shirt exploded. I lurched to a halt. Tumbling backwards, I slammed into the ground. A bolt of electric pain blasted up my arm from my elbow and I cried out.

Glancing back, I saw a zombie holding a few tufts of my hair. It had snagged me as I ran. Gaping in surprise, I watched as its eye bloomed scarlet and it fell. A moment later, a silvery gun swung over my head and clouted another attacker.

Gus grabbed the scruff of my shirt and yanked me upright. His face was glazed with sweat. For a portly guy, I was surprised by the speed with which he had reached me.

"Thanks!" I mouthed wordlessly, and together we plunged into open air.

"This way!" Amelia ordered.

Two glistening figures ambled out of the shadows ahead of her. She lashed out, and their mangled features ruptured shards of skull and brain matter, prised open by her grappling hook. A moment later, we emerged, sweaty and burning with lactic acid, despite the bristling rain.

There it was: The Black Mile.

Monty booted a swinging gate almost off its hinges, and we raced into the beer garden. Unsheathing a patio umbrella from a picnic table, he took the lead, opening it to its fullest extent and charging into The Black Mile.

Bodies bounced off the strong fabric as we entered the lounge. The umbrella acted like a plough, rebounding them into tables and chairs. Unsurprised as usual, the corpses only hissed and struggled to clamber back to their feet.

I kicked one hard in the face as I stepped over it, then carried on before it found an opportunity to retaliate. It was difficult to see past the massive umbrella, but I gauged from a quick glance that there couldn't be much more than a handful of monsters in the room. Presumably, the walled beer garden had kept out all but the most pioneering undead.

Inside, the room was bathed in a welcoming glow radiating from muted wall lamps. Closing the umbrella, Monty swung it hard, flooring a growling old man who I could only assume was the licensee. Just behind him, a dozen others staggered towards us.

We raced behind the bar. Ignoring the cups, Robbie unhooked a bell-shaped bottle of yellow fluid and tossed it to me. Then he went to work on the other bottles.

Monty flapped open the umbrella again, and formed a fort over us, which acted like a force field when combined with the bar itself. Shadows of hands reaching over the oak bar descended upon it like heavy rain on a tent, but none of the corpses on the other side showed the intuition to lift the fabric and grab us.

"Plug up that entrance!" I yelled, remembering my terrifying trapeze performance at Armageddon after I had neglected the gap at the edge of the bar.

Amelia raced past me and vanished into the room. Moments later, she came back carrying two bar stools, which she promptly fastened to the thick barrier with her grappling hook. The mess of rope and furniture blocked off the entrance.

"Done," she snapped. "Now, are you gonna drink that, or are you gonna just hug it?"

Eyeballing the honey-coloured liquor, I unscrewed the cap and chugged a mouthful.

"Ugh," I grunted. "Banana and aniseed. It's so bad."

"As bad as having your face ripped off?"

"Close."

I handed her the drink and she downed a portion of the bottle before passing it on to Wyatt. Circling it around the gang, we made sure everyone got a share. Then Robbie dived over me and plunged his arm into a chiller.

"Beer!" he rejoiced. "We meet again, old friend."

"Hey, chuck me one of those!" said Theo. It was the first time I'd heard him say anything that wasn't all shaky.

"Sure thing, mate."

"I can't believe they're gone."

My attention turned to Gus, who was whimpering, slumped under the bar. His face was wet with tears as he filled his gun from a polythene bag of ball bearings. He blew his nose on his cape. "Jake, Kate… Alycia. I just don't know anymore… She said she knew what she was doing. And she seemed so confident as the Scarlet Sorceress. Like she couldn't die. Even as my nemesis in MoM, she never died. Her and Warrior Chief just grappled at Hades' Gate and fell into the hellfire together. I should never have let her use the fireworks... I knew something like this would happen. Why didn't I say anything?"

Breaking down, he plunged his head into my shoulder and sobbed.

"My mother was right. Gaming's for kids. I'm no hero. I'm just a fat loser who couldn't save anyone."

I was never good at consoling people. Just the thought of being a shoulder to cry on made my insides freeze with anxiety. Glancing around at the others, I pulled a face, hoping someone would rescue me. Only Sophia noticed my silent plea. And all she did was pass me a half-empty bottle of vodka, as if that would help. At a loss, I offered it to Gus. He pushed it away.

"Thanks, but no thanks," he mumbled. "I don't drink."

"It'll slow down your brain and make you invisible to the zombies," I said. "Or, at least, that's what we think it does. Robbie over there found out earlier tonight."

Robbie cracked open a fresh beer and toasted me as he heard his name. Gus shot me a dubious glance and wiped the snot from his face with the back of his forearm.

"What?" he said. "Surely that can't be true."

"Trust me." I passed him the bottle. "Or try it and find out for yourself, bro."

Taking the bottle, he shrugged. "What's the worst that can happen, I guess? We're gonna die anyway."

Patting him on the shoulder, I grinned. "That's the spirit."

I considered leaving him to swig from the bottle, sobbing quietly to himself. It would have been easy to turn and join a conversation between the others at that point, but I knew I couldn't leave it there. The poor guy had just lost his friends while saving mine. No matter how delusional I thought they were, it didn't change the fact they'd sacrificed themselves for us.

"Gus, you know what?" I heard myself saying.

"Yeah?"

"About your hero thing... You *are* a hero. I've only known you about an hour, and I have no idea what you're like normally. Though, I think I can guess." I gestured to his horned hat. "Anyway, what I've seen of you has been nothing but heroic. I almost died tonight. Quite a few times, actually. But the closest I came to death was just now.

"Believe it or not, I was about to abandon the others and head off on my own, because I thought it was too dangerous to head back. And then, some guy called Lord Augustus showed up with his moral compass and stopped me."

I waited for Gus to look me in the eye and offered him a winning smile.

"Yeah, it's true," I assured him. "And my point is, I'm not a brave person. I know that, and I'm trying to change. But *you* are. You might not think yourself a hero because you don't have a thirty-eight pack, and you're not able to save everyone, but that doesn't make you any less of one. It just makes you human. And that's a lot more than I can say for a lot of the cowards around here, like me, who probably lost their humanity the instant the zombies arrived."

Gus didn't respond immediately. So, unsure what else to do, I held up my fist to bump his. With a sad smile, he raised his bottle and clinked it against my knuckles.

That'll do, I thought.

Narrowing his eyes, he said, "Wise words... for a peasant." He grinned. "Now, let's drink this tavern dry and get out of this godforsaken kingdom."

"Yeeeaahh, boy!" Wyatt chimed in, learning over us and offering more drinks. "Apocalypse paaartay!"

Over the next half an hour, we all drank heavily. Theo and Robbie cheered and sang show tunes – much to everyone's surprise. Amelia and Sophia talked about the best ways to escape. And I discussed the next course of action with Monty and Wyatt. Monty explained his first intention was to get more acquainted with the booze, while Wyatt's was to get me to loosen up.

"Hey, it's the end of the world," Wyatt said, after what had to be our fourth drink at The Black Mile. "The least you can do is enjoy it. Anyway, I'll be right back. Need to find the little boys' room."

I almost stopped him to warn him about the danger as he left. That changed, though, when I saw the shambolic way he tried to scale the stools at the end of the bar. There was no way anyone that drunk would alert the zombies.

Speaking of which, the hands slapping on our umbrella roof had all but vanished. I stood up to inspect the rest of the room. The ghouls had moved away, disinterested, and were shambling around the lounge without purpose.

I wonder.

I headed to Amelia's barricade and un-looped the rope, propelled by a cocktail of curiosity and Dutch courage. I kept a hand on the bar for balance while I built up the nerve to try what was to become my next experiment of the night. Coughing into my hand to attract attention, I waited as several bodies turned my way. None seemed particularly interested.

I cracked a knowing smile. *We're ready.*

Pushing off the bar, like a child swimming into open water, I approached a pale girl in a short, glittery dress. With large, clear eyes, a rosebud mouth, and dainty features, she would have been attractive if she were still alive.

Now, however, her shark-like presence was impossible to ignore. A sting of adrenaline fired through me as she floated nearby. Like a diver, I couldn't help but feel compelled to place my hand on the thing filling me with so much dread.

It's a terrible paradox, the human mind – drawn to hideousness, with a morbid attraction. Its effect was evident all over the world, in thrill seekers and horror lovers. I was feeling it right then.

I had already resolved to tell the others we were drunk enough to make the next leg of our journey. But, first, I wanted to be absolutely certain we were invisible before we set off.

Raising a hand, I tentatively touched her arm with trembling fingers. Then, sliding it higher, I worked my way to her face.

"Phew."

She didn't react. My experiment was waterproof. With hazy eyes, she stared into mine as I contemplated the next move.

"Hmm," I said. "Guys, I think we're –"

A loud bang made my whole body shudder. At the same time, the zombie-girl lashed out.

PART EIGHTEEN
BLACKOUT

Sweeping me out of the way, the girl with the large eyes froze, staring at a jukebox that had blared into life with a heavy metal drum solo. In front of it, Wyatt stood with his back to me, feeding money into the coin slot.

"Hey there, Romeo," he called over his shoulder. "Thought I'd offer you some mood music. 'Rock My Chariot' sounded like a love song. Obviously not. Don't worry, I've put on something a bit dancier next."

"Wyatt, you scared me half to death!"

He grinned. "Better a scare than a bite, right? Still, anything with a pulse, I guess." He eyed the dead girl who, I realised, had now waded way too far into my personal space. "Or anything with no pulse, if that's what you're into."

"I'm not."

"Hey." He held up his hands. "I don't judge. Whatever floats your boat, dude."

"I was conducting an experiment," I insisted, shoving her away with a palm to the face. The fact my drunken tongue had trouble working its way around the word 'conducting' didn't help my argument.

"Whatever you say, Kitten. Another drink? My round."

I felt anger rise to my face but held my tongue, remembering the drunken apology I'd had to battle through earlier that night.

"No. No more drinks. We're ready to go. Guys! I think we're drunk enough now."

Gus and Amelia popped their heads over the bar, then strode into full view when they realised the coast was clear.

"Woah. It *does* work," Gus cooed, entering the main lounge area. Stifling a belch, he put his arm around a bewildered zombie and forced it to sit in one of the pub's plush booths with him. "Look at this!"

"Oh, my legs," Sophia complained, following behind him. "Great idea, Gus! I could do with a proper chair. That floor's awful."

Cantering next to him, she bopped along to the jukebox's music and perched at the table with half a bottle of brandy. "Move over, will you?"

Swinging her hips, she bumped Gus' new dead friend further into the booth to make room for herself.

"Oh, look! A pack of cards," said Robbie. "We should play Ring of Fire!"

"What's Ring of Fire?" Amelia asked, joining them.

"Oh, you're in for a treat!" Theo interrupted. "Robbie, deal 'em out, will you? I'll get some glasses. After that, we can play Arrogance and Chase the Queen."

"I take offence to that!" said Monty, putting on a voice even posher than usual. "The Queen is my fifth cousin, twice removed."

"Woah, really?" Robbie gaped.

Monty belly laughed. "No, you cretin. Just deal."

"Haha, you got me! Now, there's no dealing in Ring of Fire. How you play is, you start with a pint glass in the middle of the table, and then you spread the deck around it in a circle. Then one person picks a card from…"

"Guys, shouldn't we get going?" I mumbled. "You know, before the world ends and there's no one left to warn people about the zombie outbreak?"

Realising there was no room left for him in the booth, Monty dragged a chair to the head of the table.

"Not just yet. I'm not *that* drunk, old sport. If we're gonna get out of here, we all need to be near blackout. Don't you agree?"

"Um, I guess so."

"Then, what are you doing standing around? Pull up a chair, my good man!"

Giving in to peer pressure, I accepted a beer from Robbie and dragged a chair over to the booth. Theo arrived seconds later with an armful of clinking glasses. A pack of cards was set around a pint glass plonked in the middle of the table. As we all filled our glasses with a drink of our choice, Robbie explained the rules, and we began what I could only describe as the most complicated drinking game ever conceived. Even sober, I would have been confused.

An hour passed with rambunctious banter and high spirits. We only noticed a while into the game that nobody had closed The Black Mile's front door, so zombies ambled in at will, completely oblivious to us. As the game progressed, it all became a bit of a blur, and I stopped insisting we should leave.

"Milo, you're last again!"

I looked up from my drink after some time and was greeted by a council of woozy, grinning faces. Noticing each of the others had a thumb pressed against the table, I slammed mine down, too, almost knocking over my drink.

"Too late, buddy. As Thumb Master, I decree you down your freakin' pint!" said Robbie.

"Ugh, you're starting to sound like Lord Gus now," I groaned.

"Hey! I might be a fake lord, but I can hold my drink better than you, lightweight. And I don't even drink!"

"Hey, Kitten. I think you've pulled."

Wyatt nudged me and pointed in the direction of the dead girl from earlier. She was gawping at the table, her dumb stare trained on me.

"Pfffffftt!" I howled with laughter, only vaguely registering that Wyatt had come back from another toilet break with black moons for eyes.

"Maybe," I cried, between tears of laughter. "But, I wouldn't go there. I'm pretty sure she'd eat me alive."

Everyone fell about laughing. Despite my jokes, the beer goggles were having an obvious effect. At a certain angle, and with the right lighting, the girl actually looked… kinda hot.

I shuddered.

"Refill?" Wyatt asked, offering me a beer.

I covered the top of the glass with my hand. "I think I've had enough for now, bro. I'll just nip to the loo. Back in a bit."

With that, I clambered to my feet and stumbled to a door marked "Gentlemen." Amelia crossed my path on my way in, wiping her mouth.

"Amelia? You've got the wrong room. I think the Ladies is over there."

"I just threw up," she said.

"Tactical chunder. Good plan." I winked and shouldered my way past.

Inside, I paused for a moment, allowing my laddish façade to slip. The white porcelain of the bathroom urinals and the green ceiling bathed in sickly tube lighting spun around me. A pulse blared in my head as though my heart had climbed into my throat. My lips felt like rubber and my skin was hot to touch.

"Let's just sit down for a minute," I said to myself, pushing open a cubicle door and slumping onto a toilet without bothering to check if the lid was closed.

Sitting there for a few moments, I made a chamming sound with my lips. It felt like all that alcohol had curdled in my stomach. Placing my hands on the cold partition walls, I steadied myself.

My eyelids were heavy, but at the same time I knew I couldn't fall asleep. My guts wouldn't let me. They squirmed inside my abdomen, like an eel in river silt.

"Oh."

Retching, I dropped to my knees and swung up the toilet lid. A pang of sharp pressure rose in my throat as the first wave of vomit got stuck in my oesophagus. Just when it felt like my head might explode, my body emptied itself in hideous convulsions.

The sheer shock of the pressure caused me to slip. I moaned as the toilet lid hit me on the head, but lay there, breathlessly spitting deposits of regurgitated food from my mouth, with the porcelain pressing against my skull. If someone were to walk in, they would have discovered me half-eaten by the ceramic beast. Finally, I slumped onto the cold tiles of the cubicle floor, too hot and uncomfortable to even consider the germs pressed against my face.

"I knew Ring of Fire was a bad idea," I moaned, glad I was alone in the bathroom.

Whining softly, I closed my eyes, determined to get up and return to the others in just a minute. Convincing myself of this, I continued to lay face down on the hard tiles, as if sleep were a weapon that had struck me from behind.

PART NINETEEN:
LOST

The drawn-out creak of a door swinging open told me someone had entered the Gents. Mumbling and confused, I got up a little too quickly and smashed my head on the cubicle wall.

"Oooh!" I moaned. I bit my lip and clamped my hands over the back of my skull.

Footsteps shuffled past the stall. Scrambling up onto the toilet, I grabbed some tissue paper from a roll behind the tank and dabbed the corners of my mouth. Whoever had entered was clumsy. Bumping into what sounded like a metal container, they set off a loud hum, which I realised was the hand dryer.

Drunk, I thought.

I steadied myself by grabbing a coat hook on the back of the cubicle door and hoisted myself to my feet. *That makes two of us.*

"Robbie?" My voice sounded thin in the hollow room.

There was no answer. "Monty?"

A grunt confirmed it was him.

"Okay," I said. "I'll just be a minute."

Flushing the toilet, I unspooled the toilet roll and bunged a wad into my pocket just in case I needed it later.

Swinging open the door, I ambled into the sickly light.

"Aright, I'm here. What's the plan for – argh!"

A hefty boy, with a cavernous hole for a nose, stared back at me, his head tilted to the side. Blood and black vomit layered his chest like pond scum on a rock.

"Oh," I said. "You're not Monty."

Ducking past the ghoul, I searched the Gents for familiar faces. Finding us alone, I washed my hands, rinsed my gore-speckled face in the mirror, and vacated through the swing door. The sight greeting me in the lounge made me hesitate for the first time.

The pub itself was probably at half its capacity, just with the zombies, and yet, its volume had simmered to an unsettling hush. The jukebox playlist had come to an end, allowing room for an eerie silence to clamber out of the vacuum it created. That monster now hovered like a giant mosquito over me. Fear and an odd sense of stage fright sedated me as every face turned my way.

They were all dead. None of my friends were present. The table they had used to play Ring of Fire was strewn with abandoned playing cards and a city skyline of empty glasses and bottles.

How long was I out?

The question galloped through my mind, but I knew there was no way to tell. I'd left my phone in my room, there was no clock in the pub, and nobody wore a watch anymore. Besides, even if I did, I hadn't been keeping track of the time all night, so I had no idea how long I'd been lying unconscious. I was convinced I'd only closed my eyes for a minute or two, but evidently that wasn't the case.

"Jesus Christ!"

Something must have happened for them to abandon me. I ran my hands through my hair and paced the carpet for a second, unsure which way to turn. I'd heard of people getting left behind on nights out all the time – it was easy enough to forget someone when your entire gang is legless – but I'd hoped they would have remembered me, given the circumstances.

Thinking perhaps they weren't too far away, I headed for the door and dashed into the windy beer garden. Zombies loitered, staring into space all along the street, lost in their own solitary worlds. The rain was heavier now than it had ever been. Needles of icy water tore into my skin, but I didn't care. My only thought was to find the others.

"Monty! Wyatt!"

Still no answer.

Knowing the direction they were going, I staggered into the road and headed towards the main gate. Turning a corner, I passed a metal staircase running along one side of what I assumed was some sort of sports hall. It was the tallest building in the vicinity. I dipped back and climbed the steps three at a time, hoping the greater height would enable me to spot the others over the shorter buildings lining the rest of the street.

"Please don't be far, please don't be far."

Scanning the skyline, I urged under my breath for fate to reveal them. A mesh of streets and plazas opened ahead of me. Lamplight showed me the extent of the zombie spread. I must have been out longer than I thought because the next three or four open spaces were filled with the undead. Tall blocks of student accommodation stopped me from seeing any farther.

"Damn."

They were nowhere in sight. Desperate to get a grasp on something which could give me hope, I leaned over the railing at the top of the stairs and arched my neck around the corner of the building's brickwork. Had I been watching anybody else leaning treacherously on the edge of the slippery metal structure, having just woken up from a drunken coma, I would have cringed. Luckily, safety never crossed my mind, and my stupidity payed dividends.

The south portion of the student village was still being constructed. Although put on hold, with all of the machinery moved out of the area for Freshers' Week, the skeletons of buildings revealed something beyond them I hadn't anticipated.

There was a gap in the main village wall. Behind it, the wide moat, illuminated by streetlight, shimmered like oil in the dark. Better yet, I saw a figure moving swiftly along the pavement, flitting from spot to spot.

Ellie, I thought.

The ghost girl wasn't someone I hoped to find, but at least I knew someone else had survived the spread of the zombie infestation. I contemplated following her example and fleeing in that direction. All I had to do was reach the gap in the wall. After that, I could swim across the short stretch to freedom and I'd be home dry, figuratively speaking.

"Ghost Girl, you little, genius recluse, you!"

Drumming the railing with my palms, I spun, slipped down several steps on my back, and then remembered just how drunk I was. Groaning, I lifted myself off the ground, using the metal bannister, and cantered after my elusive flatmate.

If it weren't for the wind, the streets would have been eerily quiet. Skipping along as fast as I could without losing my balance, I weaved between corpses until my chest burned and I was forced to slow my pace.

At the roadside, I gasped as I entered a plaza bordered with high-rise accommodation. Under the shelter of a bending tree, a boy lay sprawled in the mesh carcass of a wheel-less shopping trolley. His head was wilted and his legs hung over the end. To my horror, I immediately recognised him. His shabby t-shirt and loose jeans gave him away.

"Wyatt?"

Inside, my stomach erupted with butterflies. I never thought I'd be so glad to see him.

Grunting, he raised his head, eyes still closed, as though he were coming around from an anaesthetic. When his head turned in my direction, I noticed the streak of black slime slithering down his chin.

"No," I gasped. "Oh God, Wyatt!"

My voice wavered unexpectedly, and my vision became glassy as tears welled in my eyes.

"Wyatt!"

Grunting again, he moved with the slow precision of a sloth, struggling to get out of the aluminium cart.

He's dead.

I couldn't believe it. Dead and already reanimating. *How much have I missed?* Forcing back the tears, I scanned the area for the others. *Are they dead, too?*

"Wyatt," I repeated, realising none of them were in sight.

I dropped to my knees. Either that, or my legs gave way. I wasn't sure which. My mind couldn't process what was intended and what was a reflex reaction. Slumping under the tree next to the cart, I groaned.

Snot dribbled from my nose, and I wiped my face with the back of my hand. Not that it made much difference. Everything was drenched in rainwater, anyway. The snot would have been washed away, diluted in the relentless downpour, had I not wiped it. Thunder grumbled like a monster behind the clouds.

"You've always been a pain," I said, feeling that maybe talking to Wyatt's reanimating corpse would be in some way cathartic. Soon, I knew, I would have to leave, but I couldn't go without saying anything. It didn't seem right. "I never realised seeing you like this would hurt quite so much, though."

I sniffed, and found one of the trolley's broken wheels. Fiddling with it, I continued. "I'm sorry I shouted at you earlier. You're not all that bad. I was just angry. I kind of liked having you around, you now? Like, a lot. If only I hadn't passed out... I would do anything..." My voice wobbled and I paused.

"Could you start by getting me out of this trolley? I'm stuck," said a familiar voice.

"What?"

Startled, my eyes flicked up to the corpse. Wyatt stared back at me, his face screwed up like a salted slug. Rolling the trolley, he toppled onto his side, and I pulled him out of the wreckage.

"You're not dead!" I said.

"Not yet, no. Are you here to take me home? You won't believe how bad I feel right now."

"But, the black sick..."

Wyatt touched his chin. "Oh? Jägerbombs, bro. They disagree with me. Do you hear that?" Listening, I shook my head. "The clouds are talking to us."

For a moment, I frowned. Then I saw his eyes and rolled mine. "You're still high." I palmed my forehead. "Obviously. Never mind. Where are the others? Are they okay?"

"The others?"

"The others."

"Who?"

I closed my eyes and sighed. Even with the alcohol to numb me, Wyatt was giving me a migraine.

"You know... the people you were just playing drinking games with. The ones who left both of us to get eaten while they sauntered off on their merry way. Those guys, remember? Or are you so off your face even simple thought escapes you?"

"Hey, man. Don't get shirty with me. You know I don't even like shirts. Look, I went out of my way tonight to wear a nice comfortable t-shirt."

"Moron."

"What ever happened to you telling me how much you loved having me around?"

My eyes widened in shock. *He heard everything!*

"I never said that!" I lied.

"You did, and you were gonna cry and everything."

"I was just being polite! Those were polite tears! You have to say nice things and cry when people die. It's the rules. Anyway," I backpedalled, trying to pick up some of the man points I'd dropped, "back to the guys – the ones we've had with us all night. You know 'em, right?"

"Oh, I'm with you. Those guys. The guys we know. Yeah… they're gone, man. Sophia and Monty got into a fight. They were still arguing when I decided to take a nap."

"In the rain?"

"People can argue in the rain, you know."

"No. I meant you decided to take a nap in the rain?"

"Yeah, if you relax hard enough, it feels a bit like a massage therapist with tiny hands. Man, I wish I had tiny hands so I could–"

"Wyatt, focus." I grabbed his face. "Which way did they go?"

"That way, bro. Probably… ten minutes ago?"

He pointed down a street leading to the gap in the wall. Judging by my own time lapse, I doubted Wyatt's accuracy. During a particularly heavy trip, he had once told me he'd been running down a corridor for seven years. Grabbing him by the collar, I tugged him along behind me, determined to catch the others.

"You're insufferable!"

We had only travelled to the next street when I heard Sophia's shrill voice cut through the storm. She didn't sound far away. Trailing Wyatt behind me, I turned a corner and saw my first glimpse of the others. Monty and Sophia were arguing like pit bulls. The others were several paces ahead, distancing themselves from the drama.

"I've had it!" Monty spat. "You're constantly on the attack, looking for some way to be offended. I have to watch everything I say – everything! We can't have a single conversation without you flying off the handle."

"Well, if you didn't assume everyone had the same privilege you had growing up, maybe I wouldn't be so offended by everything you say and do."

"I didn't have as much privilege as you think. My parents sent me off to boarding school when I was eleven. And even when I was home, they had the butler look after me. Not the good butler, either – the reserve one! Practically a stranger. Being wealthy doesn't guarantee a good childhood. All it really means is your parents can afford to outsource their responsibilities to someone who doesn't care as much as they should!"

"Oh, boo hoo! You had to hang around with your backup butler. Do you know what it's like for your family to go bankrupt? Because I do! We were in the same boarding school, you oaf! Not that you'd remember. I was a straight-A student. Then my father's company went under and I saw *exactly* what you multi-millionaires are like when the cash stops. We were shunned by friends, and I got kicked out of school because my dad missed a fee. Yeah, he clawed it back, and now he's worth ten times as much, but I hated him for the amount of brown-nosing he had to do to people we used to think were friends. People like *you*!"

Monty recoiled. "We were in school together for a few months when we were eleven, and you expect me to remember you? You have dreadlocks and face piercings now! I wouldn't remember you even if we were best friends back then. You probably look completely different."

Sophia covered her nose piercing defensively. "That's not the point! The point is, you look down your nose at us. Every time you try to help, it's patronising."

"I was trying to be nice!"

"Well, you failed. Go cry to your new butler."

"You know what? Fine! Forget coming to me next time you need something because I won't be there. I'm done with you."

Spinning on his heels, Monty stormed on ahead towards the others.

"Oh yeah?" Sophia called after him. "A posh kid turning his back on me? Well, that's nothing I haven't seen before! Good riddance."

"Hi, Soph," I said, pretending I hadn't heard any of what just went down as me and a rather starry-eyed Wyatt arrived.

"Oh, great," she scowled. Her words were slurred. "Come to defend Angel-Prince Montgomery, have you?"

"Hold that thought," I said, and then I made an excuse to catch up to the others where it was safer. Skirting past Monty, who barely acknowledged we were even there, I coughed to alert the others of my presence.

"Hey, dudes! We wondered where you two'd got to." Robbie wrapped me in a bone-crushing bear hug, and the others greeted us with warmth. Realising that none of them even seemed to notice we had been abandoned, I decided to let the topic slide.

"It's been quite a night," I said, glancing at Wyatt.

Behind us, Sophia was still ranting, quiet enough so it sounded like she was speaking to herself, but loud enough for Monty to hear every word.

"Honestly, who does he think he is? It's not like anyone really needs him here. The minute I get out, I'm never gonna look at his stupid face again."

"You think she's gonna be okay?" I asked the others.

"She'll be fine," Gus said, sloping towards me. "If there's one thing I know, it's girls." I begged to differ, but he continued before I had time. "They rant and rave, and spout all of these problems, but they don't *really* want anything fixed. All they want is for someone to listen to them. It's how they're wired. All the forums say it."

"Right," I humoured him. "Good talk, buddy."

"Anytime."

In the background, I heard Sophia kicking a tin can, blasting, "He's an idiot. Ugh! Like, get off my back, you freak! Argh! I'm so done with this place!"

Glancing over my shoulder, I caught sight of her. She had loitered while we moved forward, and now tailed quite far behind.

"Uh… Oh, Jesus Christ, Sophia!" I called.

Despite her drunken state, her thundering temper had attracted unwanted attention. Several ghouls had turned her way. Others had slithered out of hedges, and ambled along the edges of buildings, drawn to the commotion. One was only feet away, arms outstretched, honing in on the quick movements by instinct.

She didn't hear me, so I tried another tactic.

"Monty!"

He had his hands in his pockets and his head down, powering into the wind, his black mood following him like a raincloud. It was difficult to tell whether or not he could hear me. Either way, he was the only person who could get to her in time.

"Monty!" I tried again. The others turned and saw what I saw.

"Monty, go back!"

"Sophia! Behind you!"

"Sophiiiiiiiiaaaa!"

"Monty, do something!"

Each of us tried, one by one, until eventually Monty raised his head. He was scowling.

"Go back! Sophia's in danger!" I signalled to him.

"She's a big girl! I'm sure she'll be fine!" he shouted back, not realising the gravity of the situation.

Moron.

I bolted back in the direction I'd come, deciding that nobody else was going to save her so I had to intervene. With no plan, I moved on pure adrenaline. Stupidity and heroism didn't come into it. All I knew was, if I didn't make a move, Sophia would die.

Bounding into the dark, I left the safety of the group, watching as Sophia spiralled ever closer to death.

PART TWENTY
REGRET

"Sophia! Look behind you!"

"What?" She turned and was immediately knocked onto her back by a hulking creature.

As I reached Monty, I grabbed his shoulder and spun him. At first, he responded with a snarl. Then he finally saw what I was trying to tell him.

"Good Lord!" he yelled, and followed my example.

Sophia screamed as another corpse – a ragged girl whose hair was slick with mud – squatted and tore into her leg. Her face was obscured but I could tell it hurt because her voice cracked mid-scream. Her hands slipped from the zombie she was holding at arm's length. In an instant, its head snapped around and chomped at her slim fingers. I heard the bones crack as we arrived.

Being fitter than me, Monty hit the scene first and booted the monster's head with enough force to snap its neck. Not waiting for it to fall, he moved onto the next attacker, flipping the girl onto her back and pummelling her face until her hands twitched but stopped struggling.

More ghouls piled in, dropping to their knees to gorge on Sophia's squirming body. I grabbed one by the foot, as it landed on all fours, and dragged it away from her.

Narrowly avoiding a set of ravenous jaws myself, I dipped back to avoid further attacks. Screams from further up the road told me the others were on their way.

"Monty!" I called. He shoved a monster's chest, ignoring me. "Monty, it's useless. There are too many of them. They're coming for us now!"

"We can still save her!" he insisted.

"We can't, Monty."

"I can save her!"

I clamped a hand on his shoulder to steady him as he took a drunken swing at a mottled head. Turning his anger on me, he held up a fist.

"It's just me, bro," I said, fear flashing in my eyes.

Staggering silhouettes surrounded us. They were coming from every direction. Ducking under a grey boy whose outstretched arms were draped in barbed nettles, I shouldered him in the ribs and sent him sprawling

"We have to leave. Nothing we do can save her now," I said.

Our cavalry arrived. Coming to the same awareness as me, Gus ushered Monty away from the crowd. Already Sophia was buried under a dogpile of slimy limbs and faces. As we retreated, their clothed torsos resembled a mound of hessian sacks, wriggling above a vast rodent nest.

"Come on! We have to get off the street," said Amelia. "There are too many, and they're attracted by all the noise we're making."

Monty tried to disagree. As Robbie and Gus hauled him away from the site of Sophia's death, he wrestled to get free. His face told me he was angry but his wobbling voice and screams of anguish assured me the anger was entirely directed at himself.

"I'm not leaving!" he cried.

We had to disagree. Practically lifting him off his feet, Robbie and Gus carried him away. Sophia was gone, and if we hung around for much longer, we would be, too.

"He won't make it to the next bar in that state!" said Theo. "Follow me. I know a safe place to get him cleaned up. It's just around the corner."

Struggling against the sheer rage Monty had become, we all worked together to get him to the end of the street. There, we pinned him against a wall outside an ornate doorway. Above the door were the words, 'Little Shakespeare Theatre.' Theo pulled a set of keys out of his pocket and jingled them in the lock.

"You're sure this place is safe?" I asked him.

"Absolutely. Now, let's see – house, car... Oh, here we are: theatre! I haven't been in here for a while, being a drama *theory* lecturer, but I still get a set of keys."

Pushing open the door, he ushered us inside. Bursting into a quaint foyer and reception area, we worked together like a SWAT team, scoping the area for threats. When we were certain the place was empty, we swept past a visitor counter and entered a much larger space.

The main theatre auditorium was small when compared to others, possibly maxing out at around three hundred spectators in its tiered seating space. Having said that, it was just as beautifully crafted as any grand theatre I'd visited to watch pantomimes as a child. A deep semi-circle of suede seats, broken in two by steps, led down to a raised platform for a small orchestra. Overhead, harnesses hung from the lights' rigging frame, presumably so actors could fly over the crowd during shows. Right at the back sat the main stage. When Theo saw it, I noticed him pause.

"It's happening again," he whispered.

"What?" I asked, glancing around. "Where are they?"

"No." His throat sounded dry. "No zombies."

Allowing the rest of us to brush past him, he descended the stairs and approached the main stage with tentative footsteps. The others took the opportunity to rest up, slumping into chairs in the front row.

"Your students hide any drink in here, bro?" asked Robbie.

When Theo didn't respond, he shrugged and waltzed through one of the doors leading backstage with Wyatt. I guessed their intention was to loot any cupboards they could find for hidden stashes.

The others chatted amongst themselves. Tortured by the loss of Sophia, and mumbling regrets about how he could have prevented her death, Monty sat on the floor. Amelia and Gus stooped beside him, reassuring him with kind lies about how there was nothing he could have done differently.

"You okay?" I asked Theo.

Having clambered onto the high stage, he was slumped in a stylised mock-up of a set. The backdrop was an Elizabethan hamlet, painted onto thin plywood. There was a tavern, two houses, and a small chapel. Whoever had worked in the room last had carelessly left the footlights switched on. They radiated an ominous shade of nuclear green on the painted backdrop.

Turning my way, Theo shook his head. A tear streaked his face. "It's so lifelike," he said. "Just like I remember."

"The theatre?"

"No. The village. Bleakmoor. Next to Necroville."

Furrowing my brow, I asked, "What are you talking about?"

The question visibly jolted Theo. It was only then I notice he wasn't looking at me. His face was turned towards me, but his eyes were looking straight through my head, his vision lost in some nightmare.

"They said I shouldn't say."

This again, I thought. His riddles were really starting to get on my nerves.

"Just tell me," I said. "Whatever it is, spit it out. This isn't the time to keep secrets. Theo, holding stuff back will get people killed. Tell me what's on your mind."

Breathing deeply, he paused and leaned towards me with a conspiratorial air. "Okay. But, you won't believe what I'm about to tell you. No one does."

"Try me."

"This isn't..." he began in hushed tones. Then, reconsidering, he shook his head. "My therapists said this never happened. They said I should just stop trying. I imagined the whole thing."

"Just tell me, Theo. Tell all of us. We're all ears."

"Okay," he tried again, crossing his legs. "Guys, I've got a confession to make. I've been lying to you this whole time."

"Okay..." said Amelia. Leaving Monty's side, she leaned on the edge of the stage. "Explain."

Lost in his own world again, Theo sniffed, allowing himself a sad chuckle at something none of us could see. Finally, he raised his eyes.

"This goes way deeper than you think."

PART TWENTY-ONE
THE CONSPIRACY

"This isn't the first time I've been caught up in a zombie outbreak. It's happened once before. Seven years ago.

"Me and a group of mates from uni all decided to visit Necroville for a bonding session before we all moved away. It was a zombie survival park. You know – one of those places where they refurbish a patch of forest to make it look all post-apocalyptic. The owner, Amanda, gave us Nerf blasters and overalls."

"Sounds cool," said Gus.

Theo flashed him a sad glance. "I thought that, too, at first. Just me and the old crew. Will was a great lad. Sarcastic, but he meant well. Then there was Cathy. She was awesome, and her boyfriend Charlie was one of the chilliest guys I've ever met. Together, we planned to spend the night in the woods, have fun, and shoot foam bullets at a bunch of kids dressed as zombies on their gap years. That was it. No drama. Just good, messy fun.

"I was really into method acting at the time, so I jumped at the chance. Hired a Hummer and spent hours trawling the internet for a full US marine outfit. My American accent was flawless. Everything was perfect. It wasn't even raining! But the fun didn't last."

Amelia and Gus shuffled closer. I caught myself gawping, wondering what any of this had to do with us. Gulping, I closed my mouth self-consciously, not noticing it fall open again a moment later.

"We knew something was odd when one of the actors attacked Cathy," Theo continued. "We fought him off and threatened to report him. When he didn't go down like he was supposed to, we ran. That's when it got stranger."

"What happened?" asked Amelia.

"Cathy came down with a fever – like, really quickly. We carried her to a pub where an old woman attacked us. At first, we all thought she was part of the Necroville experience, too. But, when Will realised we'd accidentally passed Necroville's boundary and wandered into the nearby village, Bleakmoor, we all started to wonder exactly what was happening.

"Will was the first to suggest a real zombie outbreak. Of course, we laughed. We mocked him. If only I'd listened earlier."

Theo's throat tightened, and I watched him gulp. His eyes looked oily in the stage's dim light.

"Cathy turned first," he croaked. "Naturally, it came as a shock. Charlie fell to pieces, seeing his girlfriend reanimate, and me and Will were left to keep the team together. There were no phones. We'd left them in the car, so the three of us had no way to get help.

"It was a rural area, so we found a shed full of tools and even some hunting rifles. Not long after, Charlie was taken. Then Will and I got caught up in the woods. We stuck together for as long as possible, but I soon realised we had no other option but to split up. Either Will or I would have to provide a distraction for the other to live. When the time came, and I found myself stranded on top of a big rock, I knew what I had to do."

"But, how did…?" Gus murmured. A gesture from Theo silenced him.

"Keep your questions until the end," he said. The line came out like a scripted response, something he had probably said many times to his students. He picked his thumbnail. "Will didn't want to leave me. He said he could get me out, but I knew he needed cover to get through the woods, so I made him go.

"I killed a handful of zombies until my rifle jammed, and Will ran further than I could see in the dark. That was the last time I saw him.

"To be honest, I had problems of my own to think about. Even though I knew it was hopeless, I decided to fight my way out. One of the zombies climbed onto the rock but I was ready for it. I wasn't so ready for the next one, though. The blighter got a good hand on me and pulled me in. I can still see the hands and faces swarming me. I was convinced I'd die.

"Then a miracle happened. I saw a bright light. A Land Rover mowed through the crowd, bouncing bodies ten feet in the air. It swiped so close to me, I almost brained myself on the wing mirror.

"The details are a bit hazy after that. There was a lot of banging and shouting, and I was covered in so much blood I looked like that girl from *Carrie*. You know her? I forget her name. Anyway, the next thing I know, I was in hospital with my head between two foam blocks."

"So you were saved?" I asked. "The army came for you?"

Theo ignored my question.

"My therapists – the ones the military assigned me – tried to tell me I was lucky. They said everyone else within a two-mile radius was dead. They blamed the whole thing on an aggressive Ebola strain, saying one of the retirees at Bleakmoor had brought it back from a cruise in West

Africa – a killer strain that brought down victims within minutes of symptoms appearing. They said the whole place had been quarantined but I was the sole survivor."

"Woah," I mouthed. "That's awful."

There wasn't much more I could say. No point pretending I knew what he was going through, because I had no idea. Even now, the only people I had watched die were relative strangers, and most of us were still alive. It was impossible to imagine what was going on in Theo's head.

"I didn't believe them, of course," he assured me. "I told them they'd got it all wrong. That Necroville was the site of a zombie outbreak. I don't know whether my therapists played dumb, or whether they were paid by the army to help tie up any loose ends."

"No one believed you?" I asked.

Theo's eyes were hooded by shadow. "Before tonight, would you?"

I shook my head. He had a point.

"Reporters visited me," he continued. "The story hit national news at the time. The media called it the Necroville Tragedy. Over three hundred deaths were reported, and a further fifty people were never found. I told them exactly what had happened but they just mocked me. An article I read a week later described me as a delusional PTSD victim whose memories had been altered by trauma. My family were just as bad."

Now that he mentioned it, I recollected hearing something about Necroville during my childhood. It had been a huge story for months. Being eleven, I didn't take any notice.

"After a while, I gave in," Theo continued. "I started regurgitating what the doctors told me. I was ill. I'd taken a bump to the head after a traumatic experience. The two together caused me to hallucinate. My mind had imagined all the bleeding eyes and sweaty bodies as zombies trying to kill me.

"That was the only way I knew they'd let me go. After months of rehab and check-ups with doctors, I was finally allowed out on my own. Life started again. I went back to university and got an MFA. Then I started teaching. It always felt like there was something wrong– a void I only managed to fill with alcohol – but I've fought through it. I chose to believe my mind was broken. Until now."

"Wow," said Amelia. I pretended not to see her cover the LED recording light on her camcorder.

"Yeah," Theo continued. "I still get nightmares. Partying helps. It keeps me awake and makes me not care as much."

"That can't be good for you," I said. "Surely there's someone who can help. I mean, if we get out of this."

Theo shook his head. "No one I can trust. The government, or whoever put me in that psychiatric ward, will put me back. And this time I might not come out. Same goes for you. Even if we do survive this, we'll be split up and indoctrinated. They'll cover this up, just like last time. And you'll be haunted by the screams and explosions, too."

Absorbed in Theo's story, I gawped as it came to an end. I could almost hear the screams already. Then I glanced up at his starry-eyed face and realised he was making the sound effects with his mouth, staring into space.

"You alright, mate?" Gus asked him.

He didn't reply right away. When he finally dragged his gaze from an imaginary scene of death and destruction, he blinked at Gus. "I've seen some things in the military, man. You civilians don't know the half of it."

His voice came out gravelly. I wondered if he had something stuck in his throat, but when he didn't cough, I frowned, confused.

Was that an American accent?
"Oh-kay…"
Fantastic. Another looney, I thought. It seemed sanity was in short supply in our small group. I turned my back on Theo, choosing to brush over the weirdness we'd all just witnessed. Peering at the others, I waited for one of them to suggest what we should do next, knowing what we now knew. Amelia was the first to react.

"That's fascinating," she gushed, surreptitiously fiddling with the camcorder in her utility belt. "You must feel awful."

"Yeah…" Theo shrugged.

"Absolutely," she continued, a little too enthusiastically. "The world needs to know the truth. How about we–"

A sudden *bang* made us all jump as Robbie blasted into the room. His face was covered in sweat. With wide eyes, he said, "You guys won't believe this!"

PART TWENTY-TWO
AWAY WITH THE FAIRIES

"Look what we found!"

When we all paused, Robbie hesitated, but then his drunken mind ploughed through the wall of silence we had put in front of him.

"These drama students know how to have a good time!" he beamed and waved a bottle of green liquor in front of his face. "Oh, and there's cola on a desk back there, for the lightweights."

His eyes flicked playfully to me and Wyatt. Passing the bottle around, we all took an unpleasant swig. The snappy bite and explosive aftertaste of the drink was unlike anything I'd ever encountered. Washing down my throat like lava, it boiled in my stomach. Spluttering, I quickly passed it away.

Heat rushed to my face and I found myself leaning precariously. Moments after the bottle had gone, it still felt like I'd been kicked by a horse.

"Woah!" I said.

"Yeah, woah indeed, bro," Robbie laughed. "Absinthe. Half a bottle should be enough for all of us combined."

"Oh my God. Check out the ceiling, lads!" Wyatt exclaimed after swigging it himself. "Can you see that? Fairies. They're so... twinkly."

"They're stage lights," I reminded him.

He shook his head and turned to Monty. "You can see fairies, right?"

"Only the green kind," Monty quipped morosely, and grabbed the decanter. Tilting it on its end, he chugged a portion himself.

"I think you've had enough," Amelia told him, wrestling it out of his hands before he drained the whole thing. "Anyway," she gestured to Robbie and Wyatt, "you guys need to be brought up to speed. Theo has something more important to talk about than..." We followed her gaze to the stage to find a vacant patch of floor where Theo had been. "Where'd he get to now?"

A sudden crash drew our attention to the back of the auditorium where a dark figure came into view. The intruder was illuminated from below, having knocked over a projector facing the main stage. Its shambling movements gave it away as a zombie, even though it was covered in thick folds of dark curtain. A moment after it arrived, another appeared, and then another. As one, they saw us and began to clamber over the seats, not bothering to bypass them on the stairs.

"Who left the door unlocked?" Amelia demanded.

Snatching her grappling hook from the floor, she charged up the steps and waded into one of the aisles. Gus followed closely behind, passing her halfway up the stairs, presumably to lock the door. Knocking one body out of the way with his wooden sword, he disappeared through the doorway leading to the foyer.

"This might take a while!" he shouted from the reception area a moment later.

Weapons, I thought. *I need weapons.*

Too many times had I found myself heading into a confined space unarmed. This time would be different.

There had to be props backstage I could use to defend myself. Even a heavy club would do. Hell, I'd take anything as long as it kept those snapping jaws at arm's length.

Jogging into the wings, I left the stage and found myself in a dimly lit hallway. A single door led to a short set of steps. Taking them three at a time, I entered yet another passageway that split off behind a series of doors on either side.

Weapons, weapons, weapons, I pondered.

My legs throbbed, and a hollow feeling in my stomach reminded me I hadn't eaten in hours. Despite that, I forced my legs to hurry.

I poked my head around various doors as I raced forward. Each room was a compact dressing room, complete with bulb-bordered dressing tables and period drama costumes hanging on clothing rails.

"Hey," I said, encountering Theo in the third room I entered. "Any idea where the props are kept? We've got compan..."

My eyes drank in the curious sight with confusion.

The acting teacher was hunched over a stool, gazing into a mirror. One of the first things I noticed was that he had changed his clothes and now sported neutral cargo pants and a sand-coloured t-shirt. I understood the desire to get out of his sodden clothes, but my mind threw up questions I thought it best not to ask when I saw him powdering his face with a dusty sponge.

Having arrived mid-way through his metamorphosis, I spotted delicate features in the mirror's reflection. Had I not known it was Theo, I might have thought the figure was an actual woman in the dim theatre light. Not bothering to turn my way, he pointed down the hall. "Supply store. There's a sign on the door."

"Great," I said. "You coming to help?"

He didn't answer after that, instead reaching for a puffy jacket draped over the back of a chair.

Whatever.

I didn't have time to deal with his craziness. Following his instructions, I found the labelled door with an old-fashioned key left in the lock. Opening it, I grinned with murderous intent. The cupboard contained everything I wanted and more.

It was bigger than I expected. Plywood background scenery was stacked up against one wall, beside pieces of period furniture and racks of costumes. What interested me most, though, was a wall of old bookcases opposite the other junk.

Papier-mâché sticks and clubs, along with replica flintlock muskets and other guns from throughout history, lined the shelves. Bypassing the fake projectile weapons, I grabbed a heavy metal dagger about the length of my forearm. It had a long, ornate grip as big as the blade, and it was heavy.

Real metal, I thought.

The blade itself was relatively blunt, but that didn't mean it wouldn't penetrate a temple or stab through muscles. I'd just have to put extra force behind it to cause real damage.

Perfect.

There were no other blades in view, so I decided it would have to do. Grabbing a heavy candelabra on the way out as a backup weapon, I jogged past Theo's dressing room and joined the others in the auditorium. A shot from my asthma pump would have been a welcomed treat at this point, but, yet again, I reminded myself it wasn't available.

Gus wasn't present. That wasn't a good sign. Doing a quick headcount, I calculated that ten zombies had shambled into the room. Luckily, they'd split up in an attempt to scavenge on the survivors.

"Where the devil have you been?" Monty hollered when he spotted me. "I thought we'd lost you, old sport." He fended off an attacker with a right hook, and rolled up onto the stage to escape another two. Hurling him the candelabra, I explained where I'd been through heaving breaths.

"Went… to get weapons."

"Well, you're here now and that's the main thing." He swung the bronze ornament, clonking a ghoul on the head. It made an audible *crack* on impact. Snarling, the creature crumpled to the floor. "I'll be alright here," he said with a swashbuckling grin. "Go help the others."

I nodded and bounded off the stage. Amelia and Robbie seemed to be having more trouble, confronted by seven zombies and hemmed in amongst the chairs. To add to their concerns, new stragglers were trickling in through the doorway. Closing the space between me and the others, I prepared to make my first move.

"Eat blade!" I shouted, bounding after one ghoul shuffling along a row towards Amelia.

Grabbing it by the scruff of its t-shirt, I stabbed down hard with the dagger, aiming at its temple. After a moment of confusion, the beast spun and hissed.

"What?" I stepped back and saw the large blade emerge from inside its own handle.

Retractable!

"Ugh!" grunted the monster.

Squealing in shock, I fell backwards into the row. The air was pushed out of my lungs as I hit the floorboards. Staying down, I wheezed and wriggled, trying to free my arms which had become pinned between the chair legs. The monster descended, a clown's grin smeared across its bloodied face.

"Hold still, Milo!" I heard, and then I saw a rope swing over the monster's head. It tightened around his neck. If the zombie was at all surprised, it didn't show. Not even trying to escape the hold, it snarled, hands scrambling for me, fixed in single-minded determination as it was dragged backwards. Caving in the man's skull with her metal hook, Amelia offered me a hand up.

"Eat blade?" she said. "Really?"

I shrugged, embarrassed, but she had already turned the other way to rush into close combat with a gaunt, blonde girl who had no upper lip. Jumping to my feet, I sensed movement and anticipated a second attack. A girl in a beanie hat and sweatpants made her way towards us, hands outstretched. Dirt was ingrained under her nails and in the lines of her hands, as though she had been digging sometime earlier that night. Avoiding her fingers, I spun my dagger around, not bothering with the blade, and jabbed her with its heavy handle. Three clubbing blows to the head took her down.

Immediately, another took her place. There had to be upwards of twenty in the auditorium now. Battling my way past the second zombie, I dodged several others, using their lack of balance and the steep auditorium steps against them. When I reached the door, it swung open.

Holding his horned helmet in place, Gus appeared and slammed it behind him. I flinched, ready to lash out, but caught myself before I did him any damage.

"Door's locked," Gus hyperventilated. "Don't have an inhaler by any chance, do you?"

"Nope," I sighed.

"Shame." Whirling, he struck a zombie in the chest with his timber sword. I heard its collarbone crack as it tumbled into a curtained wall. Then he added, "I'm nearly OOP, and the lag is killing me."

"OOP?"

"Out of power," he said matter-of-factly. "Have you *never* played online games? These are common phrases, dude."

"Never," I said. "Candy Bash is the closest I get to gaming."

"Candy Bash!" He looked offended. "Heathen."

"Uh, boys!"

We both faced Amelia. She'd manoeuvred her way to the aisle now, and was busy pinning a flabby, shirtless corpse nearly double her size. Stunning it with a grappling hook to the back of the skull, she addressed us with unexpected anger.

"I hate to break up this little nerd-fest but I think Monty needs your help," she continued. "And God knows where Wyatt's gone!"

"Probably off with the fairies," Robbie jibed from the other side of the row. Losing his balance, he staggered, causing a zombie to misjudge its attack and swan dive down the stairs. "That absinthe blew my head off, and I'm me! He must be absolutely gazeeboed by now."

Dragging Gus along with me, I skirted past Amelia. On my way down the steps, I focused on Monty. He was an adept fighter, but even he struggled to concentrate his energy on so many targets. Almost a dozen ghouls had gathered around him, and he was backed up against the high stage.

"We're coming, Monty!" I shouted, eager to offer him hope.

A handful of the creatures turned on the stairs and staggered towards my voice. Stopping short, they arced their heads skyward and threw up their arms.

"WTF?" said Gus. For once, I understood the acronym.

Following their gazes, I gasped. High up in the rigging of the lights, Wyatt rested on a beam like a cat atop a garden fence. At that exact moment, he lost his balance.

"Wooooaah!"

Scrambling on the smooth metal bars, he tumbled sideways, swinging towards the pit of hands and teeth.

PART TWENTY-THREE
HOLD TIGHT

"Aaaaaah!"

Wyatt shrieked as his legs slid into open space. In a moment of pure good fortune, he hooked an elbow over the main bar and slammed onto the rigging. Though suspended in mid-air, his armpits kept their purchase, and his body swung upright.

"What the hell are you doing?" I shouted.

"The fairies. Couldn't see them, bro. I needed to get higher!" was his only defence. "Ahhhh!"

He retracted his legs into foetal position to avoid a lunge from a zombie trying to grab his feet. Not that it would have reached him. There were at least six feet of open air between them, so he was relatively safe – as long as his arms didn't give way. And that could happen at any moment.

His main problem was that he wouldn't stop screaming. It was attracting attention. Many of the undead abandoned their battles with the others, enticed by an easier meal squirming just beyond their reach.

"I'm slipping!" he yelped.

All drowsiness had left his voice, replaced by a panic so frantic it was as if his paper-thin dream world had suddenly torn open.

"Don't let 'em get me, Milo! Don't let 'em eat my face. I'm too pretty to die!" he cried.

"Argh!"

Distracted by the boy dangling from the framework, Monty dropped his guard for a second, and yelled as a monster barrelled into him. Together, they fell back into an on-stage piano tucked away in the wings. He grappled with a large boy whose hands were clamped around his throat.

Monty, Amelia, and Robbie were all too far away to help. That just left me and Gus. Two boys against ten zombies.

"Unhand me, villain!" Gus roared in his affected Lord Augustus voice.

A swift glance showed me he, too, was indisposed, trapped in a double-pronged attack from two monsters. A glancing blow of his sword sent it spinning out of his grip. He scrambled to draw his pellet gun from his belt as I raced towards Wyatt.

I halted only feet away from the predators, unsure whether to take down the monsters waiting on the lower orchestral stage or look for something soft to cushion Wyatt's fall. If we'd all just stayed calm in the first place, it occurred to me, this could all have been avoided. After all, we were drunk as lords. We would have gone unnoticed if we hadn't immediately rushed into action.

"Do something!" shouted Monty, disabling his attacker with a move resembling a judo throw. "Use this!"

He skimmed the bronze candelabra along the polished floorboards. It arrived at my feet with surprising accuracy. The interruption gave me the push I needed jump into action.

"Over here!" I shouted, and battered the first creature I encountered. Its skull compressed like a ball of soft clay under the weight of the heavy prop.

Immediately, several hands turned my way, and I found myself faced with an advancing wall of bodies. I lashed out instinctively, disabling a goth girl who wore deathly pale make-up to hide her deathly pale skin. As I stooped to brain her, powerful fingers clamped on my arm. Teeth followed closely behind, but I managed to avoid them.

I backed up until I bumped into a wall of warm flesh. I rotated, swinging the candle holder. It made contact, clanging something metallic like a gong, and I heard a startled scream.

"Sorry!" I shouted as Gus collapsed into a chair, his helmet crooked. I turned back to the zombies, but hesitantly added, "You dead?"

"Nearly!" came his furious reply.

"Sorry," I repeated.

Another three bodies broke from the herd, but it wasn't enough. Some lingered under Wyatt. Glancing up at him, a feverish energy roared through me like a gas explosion as he momentarily hung from the apparatus by one arm.

"I'm gonna slip!" he screamed.

This seemed to excite the predators. Despite me banging the candelabra on the back of a chair to focus their attention on me, one of them circled back and re-joined the forest of arms.

"Hey! Here, zombies, zombies, zombies!" I sung, as though they were cats.

It had little effect. I needed to get higher.

Edging back onto one of the steps in the main aisle, I placed my foot on something vaguely round and rolled an ankle. The object hissed, and I instantly knew I'd made a mistake as an ankle biter lashed out with grasping hands. As I fell, I realised I'd accidentally stepped on a moving head.

Screaming and on my back, I kicked out with one foot to distance myself, and rolled to safety just as three creatures joined me on the stairs. Suddenly, I found myself completely cut off.

"Wyatt, hold tight!" I called, seeing his legs flailing against the rigging.

"Hurry up!" he called back. "I can't hold on much longer."

My whole being lurched, as I saw him drop again and then save himself, holding on with just his hands. He was completely outstretched now, his sloppy jeans falling slowly down his legs, stealing away the last dregs of his dignity.

"Faster!" he yelped.

"I need a minute. Just hold tight!"

"What do you think I'm doing?"

"I SAID, HOLD TIGHT!"

Bashing one of my enemies in the temple, I watched it go down. On the other side of the auditorium, Robbie had managed to dislodge himself from combat and was racing down the stairs.

"Don't worry, bro! I've got you," he called, pile-driving into a corpse who clearly wasn't expecting him at the bottom of the steps. "Just hold tight!"

"I swear!" Wyatt ranted. "If one more person tells me to hold tight I'll – aaah!"

We were too late. Coming loose, Wyatt fell.

PART TWENTY-FOUR
REPORTING FOR DUTY

The next second was a blur. Following Wyatt's descent, my eyes lost him somewhere between the rigging and his plunge into the zombie horde. My brain struggled even harder to keep up when I saw him flying horizontally between them.

Swooping in a wide arc, his ragdoll body made contact with the ground back at the main stage. There, he skidded along the boards like a crash-landing paraglider. For the first time, I noticed a rope trailing from the rafters, hooked on the back of his collar.

Offering an explanation, Theo stepped out of the shadows, dressed head-to-toe in a US Marine costume, complete with aviator sunglasses and a thick, unlit cigar. In his hands were two ropes, each tipped with a hook, which I assumed was used to hoist equipment to the ceiling. Hurling them both, he watched as the heavy hooks found their targets. One smashed a zombie in the face, gouging out its eye, while the other caught the shirt of another, holding it in place like a toddler on a harness.

"Now *that's* what I'm talking 'bout!" he shouted in a bad American accent. "Oorah!"

Leaping from the stage, he reached back over his shoulder and took out a heavy-looking replica shotgun. Swinging it like a golf club, he swept the legs from under two bodies on the orchestral stage. They scrambled on their backs, bewildered, as he moved onwards. Already forgetting them, he struck out with a powerful roundhouse kick, catapulting his next victim six feet off the lip of the stage.

"Feel that?" he called after it. "That's freedom, brother!"

It was like Theo was a whole new person. Watching him take down more with the butt of his shotgun, I gawped, mesmerised – at least, until a zombie threatened to drag me down the stairs. He was a boy, dressed in a suit far too mature for his face. A business student, maybe. Grabbing him by the lapels, I rammed him into the chairs, inspired by Theo's rampage.

Amelia arrived at my side a moment later, bludgeoning a face zeroing in on me. ThenABmoveus, Monty, and Robbie also appeared near me, and together we rushed the stage.

"Good work, chaps!" Monty exclaimed as we approached.

"Keep some for the rest of us," Robbie joked

Theo walloped a dead girl so hard her jaw detached from her face and hung, cradled in the skin of her chin. He flashed Robbie a proud smirk as he punched the final zombie and sent it teetering off the stage.

It hit the floor hard and didn't get back up. After that, there was silence. The extermination was over.

"This ain't my first rodeo, soldier," Theo said. "When it comes to Zs, I take what I can. Now, step off! There's one more."

His accent was awful, but I chose not to poke the bear, having seen him unleashed. Instead, I followed his gaze to the door at the top of the auditorium. A sole, wiry figure had bumbled into the room. *One left.* Raising his shotgun, Theo slowly breathed out and then pulled the trigger.

Click.

Confusion appeared on his face. After an awkward silence, he tried again.

Click.

"Piece of junk!" he grumbled. "Must be jammed."

"Or fake," suggested Monty.

"I know a real firearm when I see one, boy."

Sighing, Amelia dropped from the stage and headed towards the lone zombie. "I'll get it," she said.

"No! Fall back. I got this."

"See here," Monty insisted. "For a start, you have the safety on. And, besides that, I can prove it's fake. My parents and I usually summer in South Africa where we hunt guinea fowl."

Snatching the weapon out of Theo's hands, he turned it onto its back. Before he even got to glance at it, Theo clawed it back.

As they argued, I diverted my attention to Amelia. My eyes were drawn to her swinging hips as she advanced carefully up the stairs. Clearly, the drink was having an effect. On any normal day, I would never risk staring like that in case she noticed me.

She advanced on the zombie slowly. It was caught between the rows of chairs, pinned back, hissing at her and fighting to get closer. At first, I thought she would swoop right in and put it out of its misery, but she didn't.

Flicking my eyes upwards, I realised she was holding something. I couldn't see what it was because she had her back to me. I craned my neck to get a better view. That's when I spotted the camera.

She's filming. Clever.

No doubt she'd keep quiet about it. If Theo's predictions about the government's involvement held up to scrutiny, then we'd need proof to back up our story. The last thing she wanted to do was tell the others. With the drunken states they were in, they'd blab about proof the moment they were told they couldn't go to the press, and then it would be all over.

Snapping the screen shut, Amelia spun on her heels unexpectedly to check on the argument that had broken out on stage. Startled, I tried to divert my eyes and act natural, but the cover-up came out awkward.

"Were you checking me out?" she said, just loud enough for the others to hear. Luckily, no one did. Robbie and Wyatt were busy wrestling to separate Monty and Theo.

"No!" I blurted, looking offended. "I was just wondering what you were doing. What's that in your hand?"

Phew! *Good diversion*, I complimented my drunken mind.

Sliding the camera into her belt, she said, "Just adjusting my hook." She swung it like an ice pick, lodging it in the zombie's forehead. "Anyway, don't try to distract me. I saw you eyeing up–"

BOOM!

I ducked as an avalanche of wood chippings and plaster board tumbled out of the roof. Monty and Theo froze. The others stepped away from the gun with tentative movements.

Clearing his throat awkwardly, Monty released the barrel, handing the shotgun back to Theo. He peered up at the gaping hole in the ceiling. Rain water dripped from broken roof tiles onto his face.

"Sorry, chaps," he floundered. "Apparently, it's realer than it looks."

"When they don't have enough props, the students borrow real guns from the hunting society, knucklehead," Theo chastised. He slung the gun over his shoulder and vented a disgusted, "Civilians." Then, reaching for extra shells from a carrier attached to his belt, he proceeded on a lopsided march to the main doors.

"Alcohol and powerful guns," I remarked. "And I thought this night couldn't get any more dangerous."

"Well, y'all comin'?" Theo barked when nobody moved. "Now Downton Abbey's alerted every zombie in the area we're here, we have to get moving before they trap us in the building." He turned to Gus. "Tights, bring your pea-shooter. You're with me."

Blasting the door open with his boot, he stormed into the reception area. Gus followed wordlessly behind him.

"I don't know about you," said Amelia, "but I'm sticking with him."

We all exchanged glances on the stage, silently communicating our thoughts. As one, we came to the same decision, and bounded after Theo. I'd take crazy over dead any day.

Entering the stormy street, I sidled up next to Amelia, making sure we couldn't be overheard. "I saw you filming," I whispered.

"Yeah?" she responded. "So what?"

"Don't worry. I won't tell the others you have proof."

"Good. You'd better not. Not if you want to survive this thing." Her nostrils flared angrily as she said the last part. Obviously, my words must have come out sounding more like a threat than I intended.

"I'm just saying I've got your back," I explained to clarify. "The world needs to know about what's happened here tonight – the sooner the better. If the police, or whoever, show up, I won't say anything about the camera."

"That might not matter. If they get to me before I get internet access, they'll probably find it anyway. I can try to hide the SD card, but there's only so much you can do when you're stripped naked and forced to squat and cough."

"Yeah..." I agreed with uncertainty, wondering exactly how seriously she had taken Theo's story.

Seeing what he'd become, I seriously doubted his accuracy. And I was pretty sure the only thing stopping me from disregarding his madness completely was my hopeless desire to ingratiate myself with the pack. As scary as the whole night had been, I realised fighting for our lives had somehow accelerated our pub crawl bonding process. By the university's standards, Freshers' was a success. I, for one, intended to keep it that way, at least, until we no longer needed each other to survive.

"So, when do you think we'll get back online?" I asked.

"Not sure." Amelia became weary as we sidled past a large swathe of shambling bodies which didn't look too dissimilar from drunk students staggering home from a night out. They didn't notice us. Obviously, without drawing attention to ourselves, the alcohol worked its magic.

When they were out of earshot, she continued. "I heard there were hotspots near the edges of the wall, but we haven't made it anywhere near one yet. I'll just have to keep checking."

"Well, we're not far from the wall now," I noted. "When I got split up from the rest of you guys, I climbed a fire escape to look for you. Part of the village is still being built just ahead of us on the next right. There's a gap in the wall there. I could see the moat through it.

"Yeah?" Her eyes brightened. "Awesome. In that case, we should tell the others before Theo takes us in the wrong direction."

She trotted ahead, leaving me to my thoughts. I lagged behind, not willing to risk speeding up with so many dead bodies nearby. Around me, two lines of four-storey tower blocks loomed. Dirty yellow lights were still on in a lot of the windows.

I dreaded to think how many creatures were locked inside, and whether there were any survivors curled up under their beds, or in wardrobes, waiting to be rescued. If only they knew the full extent of the outbreak, they'd know better than to stay put. Forever was a long time to go without food and water.

Sidling over to Monty, Wyatt, and Robbie, I said, "There's a gap in the main wall up ahead, just to let you guys know. Amelia's already gone to tell the others."

"About time," said Monty.

"Freedom!" Wyatt shouted, and then he was promptly cut off as Robbie clamped a grubby hand over his mouth.

"Shut your mouth, mate," he growled. "Don't ruin it. We're so close." He had developed a limp, and his beard was now looking more 'homeless person' than 'lumberjack.'

"You okay?" I asked, gesturing to his leg.

"I haven't been bitten, if that's what you're asking."

A cool wave of relief ran through me. "Good," I nodded.

He offered a painful smile. "I'll just be glad to get out of here. I love a pub crawl as much as the next bloke – more, in fact! – but this one… well, it's been something else."

"Yeah. If we get out of this, I think partying will be the last thing on my mind for a while. I'm quite happy to celebrate back home in the comfort of my own bed."

"You got that right," Robbie smiled. "Just me, a TV remote, and a smooth beer."

I rolled my eyes and we all laughed. It was impossible to tell if he was joking.

Hitting a crossroads, we all made a beeline for the gap in the wall. Thin metal fence panels set in breeze blocks marked the edge of a building site. At some point, they had been forced apart, possibly by other survivors, at a place where two panels were connected by a padlocked chain.

Ducking under the chain and squeezing between them, I joined Theo, Wyatt, and Amelia on the other side. Together, we waited for the heftier members of the group.

"It's even creepier here than back there," Amelia whispered.

"Proper post-apocalypse," Robbie agreed.

It was certainly quieter here. And darker. A lot darker. There were no functioning streetlights. Obviously, the installed ones hadn't been connected to the main grid yet. A handful of zombies had somehow managed to find themselves inside the construction site, but there were fewer than in the residential streets.

Wind whistled through the carcasses of half-made buildings, turning scaffolding poles into haunting panpipes. Although it was meant to be a new development, the combination of shambling corpses and exposed metalwork gave me a glimpse of what the world might look like if the monsters continued to spread.

Stop over-thinking, Callaghan, I reminded myself, stopping my mind from exploring the morbid possibilities of an apocalypse.

"Tread carefully, guys," Amelia said, gesturing to a fluorescent hazard sign. "It's dangerous in here. The last thing we want is a broken leg."

"Follow me, troops." Theo darted ahead, and dropped momentarily behind a wall of sand bags. When literally no one followed his example, he scampered in another direction. "Anybody smell that?"

"Petrol?" I guessed, sniffing the air.

"Exactly. It's all over the ground." He picked up some dirt, crushed it between his fingers, then licked them. "Still fresh. Mind your feet or you'll slip on the rocks. It's just like back in Nam."

"Vietnam ended in the seventies, mate," Monty corrected him. "You weren't even born."

"Yeah, that's kinda true, bro," Gus admitted. "You're talking through your–"

"Arson is a real risk here. Don't make any sparks, whatever you do. The whole place could blow, just like an apache chopper I saw once… in Nam."

"Seriously," Monty insisted. "You're, what? Like thirty-one?"

"Twenty-seven."

"So, you were born twenty years after Vietnam."

Theo hesitated as the penny dropped. Then, simply narrowing his eyes, he said in a huskier voice than usual, "War works in mysterious ways."

Monty frowned. "What does that even mean? Oh, great. There he goes again."

Theo vanished, scurrying like a bloodhound through the building site, without offering any more explanation.

"Let's just follow him," Amelia suggested. "He'll only roll on his gun and shoot himself if we don't."

We passed the skeletons of more buildings, our lowered voices gaining excitement as we felt ourselves nearing freedom. Even I had to curb my drunken tongue when I saw heads snapping in our direction.

The faded eyes of the dead were even more piercing in the dark. Their pupils were almost indistinguishable from the bloodshot whites of their eyeballs. It felt almost like we were trudging along the ocean floor – never able to see more than a few feet ahead, but constantly under the watchful gazes of hidden sub-surface dwellers and their pale, anglerfish eyes.

"You feeling okay, guys?" I asked.

"Never better," said Robbie. "Just a bit tired, bro."

That worried me.

Closing my eyes, I thought hard about the rain on my skin. A ripple of goose bumps confirmed my suspicions. I could feel the cold. That meant I was walking myself sober again – and so were the others, by the looks of it. Almost half an hour without alcohol had already started to sharpen our senses.

"You think the zombies got out of the complex yet?" I asked as we approached a final turn.

"Not sure," said Amelia. "I assume so. They must have started somewhere outside the uni, right? Like, in a lab, or... I don't know."

"Sound logic, but I hope you're wrong. Let's just hope there aren't any more outside h– uh-oh."

Rounding a naked structure, we stopped. At the front, Theo was stone still. Just ahead of us was the gap in the perimeter wall. He held his shotgun but seemed unsure what to do with it. Strolling next to him, I paused and scanned the gloom.

The blackness here was almost impenetrable. It took a moment for my eyes to adjust. However, as moving shapes materialised, and my ears compensated for my ineffective eyesight, I felt the familiar spider of anxiety crawl inside my brain.

"No."

This was bad. Worse than bad. It was catastrophic. Not only had we removed ourselves from any reasonable sources of light and alcohol – both of which we desperately needed – but we had also done so under false assumptions.

I stared at the glassy moat. A purple and green sheen glossed the top of the water. Something about those colours came across as unnatural, even in the gloom.

A trick of the light? I considered.

The sight was like a scene from a stylised movie. For a moment, the water's surface reflected the moon perfectly. It would have been impossible to tell which way the sky was located were I not rooted to the ground. Then, very gently, something breached the surface.

"There's something alive in there," Wyatt murmured, apparently hitting a moment of clarity in his drug-addled haze.

"Or dead," Theo suggested. "Probably dead."

PART TWENTY-FIVE
HAZARDOUS AREA

"What the devil's that?" said Monty. My gut told me he knew the answer but he wished his intuition was wrong.

"A fish?" said Amelia optimistically.

I gulped, struggling to stay rational. "I doubt it. Look at the water. Something's wrong with it."

"It's oil," Robbie explained. "A tanker overturned on the road into the village, remember? My parents were stuck in a traffic jam for ages this morning before they dropped me off. I assume the truck's been taken away now, but the oil's spilled into the moat."

"Ah," I acknowledged. "So, I guess anything living in there before tonight's probably long dead."

Begging to differ, another ripple radiated from the centre of the water and reached the shallow bank. Then, like the eyes of a Nile crocodile, two short stubs emerged from the depths. I frowned, confused, as they drifted towards us.

Getting nearer, the two stubs rose out of the black water, followed by a bigger mass. *Fingers.* A whole hand, and then an arm shot up from beneath them. Retracting, it vanished a moment later.

"Still think it's a fish?" I asked.

"It's *one* zombie," Robbie reasoned, already taking off his shirt for the swim. "They're slow on land, never mind in the water. I'm sure we can avoid it."

Amelia blocked him from moving any closer to the water's edge. "Wait."

"So, I guess plan B is – argh!"

Turning to her, I jolted with panic as a pair of giant eyes glinted next to my head. I stumbled back, my face contorted with terror, before I registered what I was actually seeing. Amelia's eyes flashed behind the night-vision goggles. Ignoring me, she scanned the still water.

"It's not one. There are more," she said.

"How many more?" Theo pumped his shotgun. Next to him, Robbie hastily pulled his shirt back into place.

"Too many to swim across. I think we're going to have to head back to the road. It's the only way out of..." Amelia's voice trailed off as she spun to look at the building site behind us. "Uh, guys. I think we should get moving."

"Why?" I asked. The hair on the back of my neck prickled, despite being doused in rainwater. I peered into the black veil of night, but saw nothing. "What's happening?"

"We're... uh, attracting attention."

Growls radiated from the dark. Its inhabitants had grown interested in us. I hoped mild curiosity was all it was, but I doubted it. Not when the surface of the moat erupted, and a hairless head rose into view, glistening in oil. Its eyes were twice the size of a normal human's, swollen by moisture. All traces of gender had been washed away by the murk.

Theo was the first to react. Orange flashed from the end of his gun and the creature's head disappeared. Its body slumped in the shallow water. Akin to a swarm of wasps, the nightmare creatures of the dark bristled as one, and rushed towards us.

On the other side of the moat, the water rippled like it was teaming with tadpoles. Then a sea of gnarled fingers and scalps broke the surface. Countless bodies surged towards dry land, emerging from the cold water.

"Alright! Time to move!" Amelia yelped, seeing something through her goggles moments before the rest of us.

Shapes shifted into my field of vision, jaws hanging slack, gore clinging to their teeth. Wielding my candelabra, I split open the head of an emaciated cadaver so we could escape.

"Just like back in Nam! Freakin' fish heads!" I heard Theo shout. His 1950s racism would have offended me, had I not immediately seen a zombie stagger out of the silt towards him, clutching an impressive catfish between its jaws.

"Where're we going?" I breathed.

"That way!" Amelia pointed into nothingness. "There's more space. We can't go back the way we came. It's infested!"

Thinking it best to trust her advice, I bolted in the direction she suggested with the others in tow.

"Anybody got booze?" Robbie shouted.

"No. It's gone. We're on our own now," said Monty.

A ragged hand shot out from behind a wall as we passed through a walkway, grabbing hold of his shirt. Before Monty even had time to react, Theo swooped in and smacked the corpse full-on in the face with the butt of his shotgun. It teetered backwards and fell into a hole left by the construction workers.

"Troops, move, move, move!" he shouted. "If we're quick, we can circle around and find a gap in the – argh"

Slimy bodies poured through an open doorframe between me and the others. The commotion we were causing was like a beacon, and true to form, the monsters had gathered to its call. My mind's initial reaction was to panic, watching my friends get closed off behind a wall of grey flesh. But I didn't let the shock take over.

"Keep going!" I shouted, knowing heroism would only get them killed. "I'll catch up!"

My breaths came in short bursts. Stumbling, I doubled back on myself, without leaving a moment to think. There were times for considering all the options but this wasn't one of them. My brain ran on autopilot as I navigated a maze of exposed brickwork in the dark, hoping my fingertips reached any obstacles before my head.

I wound further through empty rooms with concrete floors, searching for an exit. The evergreen hiss of the zombies simmered lower the further I travelled. Scampering along as fast as I could, I eventually saw open ground ahead of me. A doorway with no top beam looked to me like a portal to paradise.

Cool relief overcame me, and I bounded into an earthy clearing. I was so relieved, in fact, I didn't notice the dark body spring out of the shadows at blinding speed.

"Ugh!"

I would have screamed but the force with which the figure struck me pushed all the air out of my lungs. Falling to the ground, I tumbled onto my back and wheezed as the full bodyweight of my attacker landed on my chest.

I winced, my eyes closed, expecting to feel hot breath and burning lacerations. Shaking with my eyes shut tight, I was surprised when that moment never came. Opening them again, I gazed at the lithe outline of a girl in dark clothing.

"Don't scare me like that! I could have killed you," Amelia grumbled. She released her thighs' stranglehold on my ribcage, clambered to her feet, and offered me a hand.

"Where are the others?" I gulped. There was no time for pleasantries.

"Gone," she said. "I got cut off, like you."

Snarls from the brick labyrinth I'd just left behind reminded us to keep moving. I'd broken ahead of the undead for now, but that distance wouldn't last forever. Glancing around, I checked for a path back to the student streets and their lights.

There wasn't much to look at. No heavy machinery or tools. The workmen had obviously been thorough when packing up. It looked like the whole site had been cleared specifically for Freshers' Week, just in case drunken students broke into the compound. All I could see was a loose path made of soil and chippings. It led one way into complete darkness. An alternative path curved to the left.

"This way," said Amelia, pulling a pen-sized torch from her belt and igniting it with a click. It was for my benefit. She could already see, on account of her goggles. "That way goes back to the moat. I think we might still be able to team up with the others if we move fast enough."

"Okay." The single word was enough to send us on our way.

Bounding along the path, I did everything I could to keep myself upright. The terrain was bumpy, and muddy in places where the rain and footsteps had churned up the soil. Far ahead, a streetlamp glimmered, casting light like a UFO tractor beam onto a mesh fence at the end of the building site.

There were only a few half-built structures left. After that, we would emerge into a wide, bulldozed patch of land separating the edge of the development from the working university buildings. Seconds – that's all we needed. Twenty seconds would see us clear of the lightless void.

My eyes flicked to a highlighter yellow sign marking the hinterland.

Hazardous Area.

I read the bold, black font but the words didn't sink in until it was almost too late.

"Watch out!" Amelia yelled.

She flashed her torch at a girder jutting from a building like an exposed rib. Dipping to the right, I scraped by without injury.

That was too close.

I had to focus. Although a lack of fresh drinks, cold weather, and a rush of adrenaline had all subdued the alcohol's effects, that didn't mean I was totally cognisant. A mild buzz reminded me I was still drunk, if only slightly.

"Thanks!"

I grinned back in her direction, then slowed my pace to a complete stop. My stomach churned. Freedom was in sight, but Amelia was gone.

PART TWENTY-SIX
SACRIFICE

Jogging to a halt, I checked for the sound of moans amongst the scaffolding. There were none, so I began a feeble search attempt.

"Amelia?"

There was little I could do but squint. She had the torch, so I couldn't even use that to look for her.

"Amelia!" My call, barely audible, dripped with urgency. Anything more than a whisper could attract unwanted attention.

"Down here!" Her voiced sounded like it came from somewhere lower than me. Like she was lying on the ground. "Don't come any closer or you'll fall!"

A pinprick of light appeared in the dark. Its bright beam exposed a deep hole running from her to me. Exposed roots and clay-coloured soil told me it had been dug recently, probably as a foundation or a basement for an unbuilt structure. Amelia might have been covered in dirt from the fall but I couldn't tell. It was too dark, and we were all pretty disgusting already.

"What happened?" I asked.

"What the hell do you think happened, genius?"

"Fair point… Throw me your rope and I'll pull you up."

By a stroke of sheer good fortune, she still had the climbing gear looped over her shoulder. Uncoiling it, she swung the hook several times and tossed it high into the air. I ducked as the heavy metal spikes sailed right through a patch of air that had previously been home to my head.

"Good shot," I said, returning to the pit edge.

"Clearly not. I missed."

She laughed at her own joke, but a murmur in the dark pulled the axel right out of her banter bus. Whirling on the spot, I scanned the area for any signs of life. Although, it wasn't the life that concerned me.

"Everything okay up there?"

"Yeah, I think it was just the wind. The scaffolding's too far away for me to loop the hook onto, so I'll just stand on it, okay?"

"Yup. Just make sure you keep your footing. The last thing I want is to get stuck down here with you."

"Got it." I signalled for her to begin her reverse abseil.

Setting her feet on the incline, she formed a triangle between her body and the almost vertical surface, and began a slow trudge up the crumbling sidewall.

Come on... We're so close.

I eyed the light that stood far away across the deforested clearing. Like a spotlight in a trophy cabinet, it showed the freedom on offer. All I had to do was reach it.

"Arrrrrrggggh!

Amelia was about half-way up the steep slope, when the first grizzled body trudged out of the unfinished building closest to us. It was a stocky boy with wet clothes that seemed two sizes too small for his bulbous midriff.

Torn between steadying the rope and tackling the creature, I held my breath. When that didn't help, I let out a small yelp. It had spotted me. Spinning the candelabra in my hand to test its weight, I anticipated the inevitable lunge.

"Hissssss!"

Another body slithered out of the gloom. This time, it was a girl. Wiry with Roman features and bronze skin, she moved fast. Before I had time to shift my weight on the rope and face her, she ploughed into my side.

"Argh!" I swung the candelabra but only managed a glancing blow to her shoulder.

In the low light, her potbellied counterpart seemed shapeless, his grey flesh flashing white as it rushed towards me. Startled, I stumbled, and my body eased off the taut line.

Harrumph!

"Oww!" Amelia complained, hitting the deck.

Too distracted to take notice, I barely registered the metallic *clink* of the grappling hook sliding back into the pit. For a moment, I considered whether I should try to lead the monsters away and lose them before circling back to save Amelia. But I knew I couldn't leave her alone. She'd be trapped. Only one ghoul would need to discover her and my plan would fall apart. She'd be a packed lunch.

"Stay right there!" I shouted.

"Oh, don't worry. I will…" she said, not really having a choice.

Think, Milo!

I glanced around at the scenery. There was nothing I could use to help me. Cursing the builders for being so thorough when cleaning up, I dashed to the edge of the site and tried to grab the sign. It was a pole slotted into a solid stone slab. Heaving it until blood pressure rose hot in my face, I gave up. It was fixed in the concrete block.

Glancing back at the pit, I made out the vague outline of the Roman girl. She had found Amelia. Dropping to her hands and knees, she jabbered at the edge of the pit, then tumbled in head first. Fire erupted in my stomach and I forced myself to push harder. Still, the pole didn't wiggle free.

A third creature appeared. Another big guy, this time with a patchy beard and long hair. He didn't notice me, and the potbellied zombie wasn't looking my way, either. All attention was drawn to Amelia.

"Hiss!"

To my horror, a fourth creature arrived. It was a bald guy with a white t-shirt that was remarkably clean for a man with a blended, fleshy stump for a hand. It appeared the horde's scouts had arrived. I wasn't sure if the zombies were capable of coordinated plans, but it seemed they moved in groups. If we didn't head off fast, I had a feeling it wouldn't take long for the rest of the swarm to arrive.

Could I leave her?

The coward inside me was the loudest of all my internal voices. Just contemplating our diminishing odds of survival made me reach into my pocket for my abandoned inhaler.

I glanced at the zombie making a beeline for me. *Could I sacrifice Amelia to save myself?* If I did so, the act would cling to me like dirt for the rest of my life. It would be a messy existence, but I'd survive.

I could make it, I thought. *Alone.*

Taking a single step towards the bulldozed field, I thought about leaving. The distant light was only a street or two from the main gate. I could get there easily. And then…

I thought about Theo, and how he dealt with the guilt of leaving behind his old flatmates. He was a wreck.

"Milo, what in holy hell are you doing up there?" came Amelia's voice. When I didn't answer, she followed it up with a shaky, "Milo?"

My brain almost tore itself in half as my conscience fought for control. Finally, it won, and I changed tactics. The pole wasn't going to budge so I stopped trying to break it out of the concrete. Instead, I had another idea.

Tilting it on its side and dragging the heavy base with it, I forced my legs to push back into the heart of the action. I couldn't use it as a weapon, but that didn't matter. I had a better idea.

"Hey! Over here," I shouted, just as the pot-bellied beast stepped onto the unstable soil at the top of the pit.

Distracted, he struggled to steady himself as the earth crumbled under his weight. His zombie movements, though, were shambolic. As the mud fell away, his feet parted and he slid into the dark.

The second ghoul wasn't so easily incapacitated. Growling from thick vocal cords below his neckbeard, he moved away from the hole to face me. I raced at him, dragging the weighty hazard sign.

An instant before impact, I dropped the sign and it swung upright. The arc briefly distracted the creature, so I took my full opportunity. Leaping high and bringing down my whole weight behind the candelabra, I struck the unkempt boy clear on the forehead. His face imploded. From a standing start, he stumbled backwards at a full run and dropped dead on his back. Blood and pus leaked from the fracture left in his skull.

My face twisted into a victorious smirk. The celebration didn't last long, though. A solid form dived low into the back of my knees, causing me to sprawl on the moist soil. My weapon sailed into the distance and I called out in shock. As soon as I hit the ground, I rolled, hoping a moving target was less likely to get bitten.

In the confusion, I managed to gain a handhold on the bald man and wrenched his head sideways. My momentum swung me up onto his chest. There, I punched him over and over again. Snarling, he bit down hard, and I panicked, feeling his incisors clamp onto my shirt's fabric, dangerously close to my skin.

"Hurry up! It's getting crowded in here," Amelia shouted.

"Busy!" I replied, yanking my arm free of his teeth.

During what sounded like an arduous struggle, I heard quick footsteps and then a hard blow to a soft object. At first, I wondered if Amelia had fallen. Then her voice re-emerged.

"I can't hold them off forever! Are you killing it or giving it a massage?"

My concentration slipped for a second and the monster's hand immediately struck my throat. I heaved, feeling pressure build in my face. My windpipe screamed, crushed in a clamp-like grip. Searching the ground with feverish fingers, I located a hard object in the dirt, and pulled. It didn't budge.

Damn!

The candelabra wasn't far away. All of our rolling had moved us along the edge of the hole. Now my trusty weapon was only just out of reach.

I knew I had to make a move, and fast. Moans and hisses had emerged from the darkness, and unless buildings had evolved the ability to catch the flu, that mean only one thing – the horde had tracked us down.

Pushing off the ground, I scrambled for the candelabra. Whiplash struck me as the monster's grip tightened on my throat, and I slammed into the ground, just short of my target. The man's piercing eyes widened in delight and, certain he had me, he snorted like a pug.

I couldn't turn so I reached under my own body, all too aware of the familiar cockroach scuttle of the approaching crowd. I couldn't see them yet their stench and din were enough to tell me they weren't far away.

Pins and needles made my skin hazy as I stretched further. Finally, my fingertips rested on something hard. *So close!* I thought, fidgeting with the base of the ornament. One false move would have send it rolling in the opposite direction.

I hooked my fingers over the edge. There was a heart-wrenching wave of adrenaline when it hit a rock, and threated to rebound, undoing all of my hard work.

My vision blurred. Though I had managed to hold back the zombie with my free hand up until this moment, I was weakening. The creature's stranglehold was shutting down the air supply to my brain. In a few seconds, I'd be unconscious, and the last sounds I'd hear would be Amelia's struggle and the footsteps of the horde.

Come on, Milo. You can do this! You can do...

My vision dipped out completely, and I felt the tension release in my arm as everything went black.

PART TWENTY-SEVEN
FAST FOOD

The zombie dropped as my arms gave way, its iron fingers briefly sliding free of my Adam's apple. The jolt brought me back to reality and I awoke with a gasp.

Suddenly, I was presented with the opportunity I needed. Rolling free, I grabbed the metal prop with one hand and brought it down on my attacker's head like a hatchet. When the first blow didn't kill it, I kept going, pulverising its face until its nose and mouth became a tenderised flesh cave, bejewelled with bones and teeth. The creature fell still the moment I broke its skull and plunged the heavy candle holder into the soft tissue of its brain.

I glanced at where I assumed I'd see the horde. They were even closer than I anticipated. Breathing heavily, I scurried towards the edge of the embankment.

"Amelia! Throw me the hook. I've got a plan!"

"I'm a little busy at the moment!" she admitted, using it to prise off the lower jaw of one of her enemies. From above, they resembled gladiators in a Roman colosseum.

"I don't care!" I responded. "Just do it. If you don't move now, you'll die."

Staggering back, I waited to see the four-pronged hook fly over the lip of the gorge. True to form, Amelia hurled it with the grace of a prize-winning burglar. It ploughed into the earth at my feet. I wasted no time. Snatching it up, I sprinted to the signpost I had dragged closer to the pit. Pushing the pole's base behind a discarded girder, I ensured it was anchored in place then looped the rope around it. With a yank, I drew it taut.

"Hold on!" I warned her. "This is gonna be fast, so don't let go."

Keeping hold of the hook, I ran back towards the hole, dragging Amelia's full weight behind me. The crude pulley system worked perfectly.

"Woahohoh!" I heard Amelia say as she struggled to keep balance, scrambling up the steep dugout.

Her head crested the lip, where she used her arms and legs to claw herself onto solid ground. An instant later, the horde rushed to meet her. Letting go of the rope, she held out her hand. I passed her the hook, and together we fled to safety. Moments later, the deluge of bodies swamped the area. A fleshy waterfall of corpses toppled into the void Amelia had left behind.

Breathless, I crouched, resting my hands on my knees. My chest ached, and my feet were sore from the new leather shoes I'd bought specifically for Freshers'. Had I known there would be so much running involved, I might have gone for a sturdy pair of hiking boots.

I'd been running on empty for hours now, but Amelia wasn't content to let me rest, even though I'd earned it. Not when we were still in the danger zone. Grabbing my hand, she dragged me away from the stampede of grey bodies.

"Can't… breathe," I wheezed, trying to shake my hand out of her grip.

"We can't stop!"

"But–"

"Just keep moving!"

She tugged me closer to the light. My legs carried me, despite my protests. As we neared the regular roads, with their sparser zombies and yellow hue of electrical light, I saw a gang of what looked like survivors fighting in the pedestrianised street.

Theo? I wondered, noticing that one of them was holding a gun. When a second figure appeared, crowned with a horned helmet, a grin rose on my cheeks. Gus was with him, and the others weren't far behind.

Fuelled by adrenaline, I found a well of untapped energy and drove one leg in front of the other. Our pace wasn't a sprint, but it was fast enough to stay ahead of the monsters tailing us.

Watching the scene underneath the streetlight, I gasped as I heard glass smash. Bodies spilled through a broken door like sewerage from a burst pipe. Monty was the first to react. Seeing the carnage headed their way, he yelled an order, commanding the others to fall back.

To their left was a low-lying, circular building made entirely of glass. A neon sign – Greasy's – glowed above the doors. The inside was illuminated. Judging by the assortment of chairs and table tops I could see, it was some sort of fast food restaurant. It had two sets of double doors; one in the middle of the glass wall facing us and another on the opposite side. Both were open. Presumably, the staff had abandoned the place without stopping to lock up.

"Look. There they are!" I told Amelia, pointing at the others as they fled. "Monty!" My call was almost noiseless, starved of volume by a lack of oxygen in my lungs.

"Monty! Robbie!" Amelia tried.

We were close now. Under calmer circumstances, we would have been noticed. But a cocktail of wind and an army of groaning corpses drowned us out. Frustrated, I watched as they appeared and quickly circled around the perimeter of Greasy's, scaling the foot of a hill.

"Wyatt!" I tried one last time, knowing he wouldn't hear me.

After the state he had been in for the past few hours, I doubted he would even recognise the sound of my voice. I could only guess at how he saw the world around him.

Once again, we found ourselves distanced from our tribe. As they slipped away, heading up a tarmacked incline, I wondered if we could gain enough ground to regroup at all. My only consolation was that they were all alive.

Finally reaching the mesh fence, Amelia leapt as high as she could and clung to it like a cat on a curtain. Scaling the obstacle took very little effort for her. As a practiced climber, she commando crawled up the wire wall and dropped elegantly on the other side. On arrival, she scowled over her shoulder.

"Come on!" she screamed, watching me tackle the fence with all the grace of a hippo. The zombies were only feet behind me. I hadn't checked to see how many there were, but their moans suggested at least a hundred.

Come on, Milo. You can do this, I affirmed.

My arms and legs were burning, filled to bursting point with lactic acid. Never one for team sports – or exercise in general, now I came to think about it – I realised how embarrassingly unfit I was in comparison to Amelia. She had made it look easy, and was now fighting assailants on the other side. I forced my untoned excuse for a human body up the vertical climb. It was only about ten feet high, but might have been twenty if my arms were to be trusted.

"Milo! CLIMB!" Amelia screamed.

She took out two ghouls as they approached. Individually, they posed little challenge, but three were ambling closer in a coordinated attack. Pretty soon, we'd be surrounded. Scrambling hands grabbed the scraggy tails of denim at the bottom of my jeans. Kicking out, I lunged for the top of the fence and got my leg over the mesh.

Perched for a moment to catch my breath, I jolted. The horde hit the fence with the force of a river, snapping the chain holding it in place. It swung open, and Amelia dived out of the way, watching in disbelief as I wobbled at the top of what had become a gate. She fell back as dozens of bodies poured into the open street.

"Amelia!" I squealed, hoping she wasn't leaving me.

A portly creature with a blubbery face and a woollen jacket circled back on himself, clawing at the fence. Suddenly, there were zombies on both sides. I realised my only chance of survival was to drop into a small channel of open space and make a run for it.

Wobbling on the rickety top beam, I made the leap and sailed like a gangly tree frog ten feet through the air. Had I targeted open ground, I would probably have sprained my ankle, so I didn't do that. Instead, I did the unthinkable.

The fat zombie never saw it coming. As my feet landed on his shoulders, and his body broke my fall, he stumbled, carrying me to the edge of the crowd. He hit the deck like a sack of potatoes. Being only narrowly more composed, I tumbled, making sure to roll away from danger. Pain flared in my shoulder as it made contact with the mud, but the alcohol in my system numbed any lasting effects.

In an instant, I felt several pairs of hands on my back. I grabbed one and allowed it to help me up. Taken by surprise, the zombie collapsed in a heap, and was immediately trampled by others as I sprung over it to freedom.

"You're crazy! Absolutely mad," Amelia said as I joined her next to the glass restaurant. "And slow... But, mainly crazy!"

"Thanks!" I smirked. "You're not too sane yourself. Now, where are the others?"

"Just around the corner by the…"

Her voice trailed off as monsters severed us from the route the others had taken. Circling back, we made a bid to sprint around the building anticlockwise. That was when we discovered the horde had beaten us there, too.

"What now?" she asked.

"The doors!"

I pulled her through the open double doors. Spinning on my heels, I slammed them shut and barred them with a metal broom propped up against a nearby seat.

My plan was never to go through the restaurant. Its bright lights and glass walls made it a beacon, which would transform it into a trap at a moment's notice. Ensuring that didn't happen, I nudged Amelia onwards and we raced for the doors at the opposite end.

"We're not gonna make it!" she yelled.

Unfortunately, she was right. A wall of bodies, four deep, closed around the doors. Gangs from either side knitted together when they met in the middle, making them impassable. As we hit the doors, Amelia wrenched them closed and slid a bolt across to hold them in place. On the other side, the zombies pressed against the toughened glass. Drool hung from their chins as they tried to bury their teeth into the flat surface.

Just behind them, I spotted the others. Their outlines were little more than blurs through the wet glass. They were about half a street away, climbing the hill, too far away to hear us shout. The rain had died down but the wind was still too strong for sound to travel that far.

"Hey!" Amelia banged the glass with an open palm. "Heeeeeeey!" Monty's head briefly snapped in our direction, and my heart beat sideways. A second later, though, he spun to confront a zombie, then scurried up the hill after the others. It was unclear whether he registered we were even there. When Amelia realised she'd failed, she turned to me. "Alright, what options do we have?"

"Umm…"

I eyed the glass panes. About three quarters of the perimeter was made up of glass, with the only opaque part being the small section backing the kitchen and cash register.

As far as I could see, we were totally enclosed. A handful of the hundred or so zombies that had followed us from the construction site teetered up the hill after the others. The majority, however, zeroed in on our glass prison.

To one side of Greasy's, I spotted a second gap in the campus wall. A small pier protruded onto a moat. I vaguely remembered reading in the university prospectus that the campus had built a state-of-the-art boating facility the previous year. It wouldn't help us get out of Greasy's, though. Other than trivia, I had nothing.

Realising the outside world beyond the ring of ghouls offered no help whatsoever, my vision settled on the restaurant. Put simply, it was a pit stop for drunk students. Other than a collection of cheap, plastic chairs and wooden tables, there was little in the way of weapons. Behind the counter, deep fryers sizzled, having been abandoned by the workers, and a log of greasy kebab meat swivelled on a spit.

"There's nothing we can do," I said eventually. "Absolutely nothing."

"There has to be something," Amelia replied. She leaned on one foot and put her hands on her hips, as though stubbornness alone would save us. "A skylight? Weapons? Something we can use as a distraction?"

"No." I shook my head, feeling misery consume me. "Nothing. We're done, Amelia. The others have left and they're not coming back."

It was true. Bodies were mounting up behind the glass. Even now, safe behind the borders of our enclosure, we watched as the door's metal bolts creaked. I wondered what would give way first – the glass, or the fixtures. Either way, death was certain.

The moment the barrier broke, we would be overwhelmed, and our flesh would become indistinguishable from the kebab meat behind the counter. Just like the lamb, we'd be slaughtered. Fast food at the end of a hectic night.

PART TWENTY-EIGHT
IN COLD BLOOD

I turned my back on Amelia and eyed a small, concealed stock room behind the counter. As much as I wanted to clutch at straws and hope for a miracle, I knew it was unlikely to hold anything more than refrigerated boxes of burgers.

My hands had stopped shaking. Maybe it was the certainty of oblivion – the sense of finality that came with reaching the end of your road – or maybe it was just my body had drained all of its adrenaline reserves. All I was certain of was, for the first time that night, I felt nothing.

"Well, at least it can't get any worse," I said.

The restaurant's lights flickered and died. A major generator must have been taken out because the streetlights went next, darkness charging along the road like a tsunami.

"You had to say it," Amelia groaned.

"Ugh."

Dismissing the whole scenario, my mind turned to snacks. My stomach had been grumbling for hours now. Throwing up half your bodyweight in alcohol does that to a guy. I spotted the familiar cuboid outline of a fast food box on the counter. It was placed on a napkin-carpeted tray.

If I'm gonna die, at least I'll have a full stomach, I reasoned.

Grabbing the colourful box, I opened it and peered inside. The welcoming smell of fried chicken greeted me. Obviously, someone had left the food just after placing their order. It was relatively fresh. Taking it with me, I slouched into one of the plastic chairs and threw handfuls of popcorn chicken into my mouth. A soft groan of satisfaction escaped my lips.

"So, you're just gonna sit there?" Amelia grumbled. When I didn't answer, she added, "Fine. I'll have a root around. There has to be booze in here somewhere." She folded down her night vision goggles, and I heard a high-pitched hum as the tech booted into life.

"Go for it," I said, holding out the box for her to grab a piece as she passed. She ignored the gesture, dipping behind a sign that read 'Employees Only.'

I got in three more bites before I heard the clang of a metal container being overturned and reached for my candelabra. Weighing it in my hand, I begrudgingly put down the chicken.

What now?

Amelia emerged from the store room, backing away from some unseen attacker, with her grappling hook in her hand.

"Freakin' morons locked themselves in the freezer," she explained.

"How many?"

"Four. Two staff, two customers. I guess one of them got bitten, and when all hell broke loose, they all hid in the back. Must have shut the door by mistake."

"Horrible way to go, trapped in the cold with a corpse."

"I can think of worse ways," she quipped.

"Stuck in a chicken takeaway place with me?"

She laughed. "It's like you read my mind."

Clicking her pen-sized torch, she passed it to me, just as a familiar hiss entered the room. I flashed the torch's beam at the counter. In the circle of white light it created, a blue hand curled around the edge of the partition wall. A glove of frost covered its skin.

A girl emerged. She was dressed in a patchy onesie, with plush udders sewn onto the front, and a hood that sported cow ears and a pink nose. Blonde hair hung limp under her hood, cracking as she moved her head. White ice crystals covered every part of her body. Her hair must have been wet from the rain because it was now completely frozen.

"Wow, the food's really fresh here," said Amelia. "They kill the cows on site. You want the big ones or the small ones?"

"She a big one?"

"Yup."

"Then, I'll take the small ones. With help, of course."

"Fine." She swivelled the hook so it rested like a dagger in her palm. "Just follow my lead."

Striding into torch light, she approached the first zombie, and batted her flailing arms aside. As the creature recoiled, she struck her in the forehead. A guttural *click* told me she'd broken her nose. Sweeping a boot behind the girl's feet as she recovered, Amelia thumped her chest, and the cow-girl toppled. Then she drove home the kill strike, pummelling the creature until her limbs stopped thrashing.

The girl's counterparts hadn't emerged yet, so I approached with trepidation. Stepping over Amelia, my intention was to block the other bodies from approaching while she finished the job.

Probably half-frozen, bless 'em, I thought confidently, seeing how slowly Amelia's opponent had reacted.

A hunched shape, white as a polar bear, pounced with electric speed the moment I rounded the corner. In an instant, my confidence crumbled.

PART TWENTY-NINE
AMELIA'S CONFESSION

I saw the sheen of glasses in the murky moonlight as I stumbled backwards, but I couldn't discern any details beyond that. The torch spun violently out of my hand, temporarily blinding me before I was plunged into darkness.

"Argh!" I screamed. My throat cracked from the strain of overuse.

Crashing against something hot and soggy, I screamed as grease radiated through my shirt. I kicked out, sending the monster careering into the dark, and dropped to my knees amidst the shadows.

I glanced over my shoulder and grimaced. The kebab meat rested lopsided on its spit, having broken my fall. Already, the grease was cooling, and my shirt clung to my skin, cold and slimy.

"Thought you said this was a small one!" I hissed.

Amelia didn't respond. She had dropped out of sight. Meanwhile, the spectacled polar bear ambled closer. He sniffed the air but seemed to have lost my location. Bumping absentmindedly into a second monster, he grunted, snorting like a pig hunting for truffles.

So, that's two of them, I thought. The first one was sprawled on the floor, its oozing brain matter glittering in the moonlight. *Where's the third?*

To my question, a knee struck me in the ribcage and I collapsed, cold flesh falling on top of me. Somehow, the last one had left the freezer unnoticed while I was fighting the abominable snow zombie. Before it had a chance to process what it had just tripped over, I spun out of its clutches and backed into the middle of the room.

Stepping into the moonlight had an instant effect. All three zombies snarled and jumped at me. The windows rattled, as the ring of spectators also spotted my living form.

"Oh-kay." I clicked my tongue, searching for Amelia. She was still doing her Houdini act. "Amelia, now would be a good time to show up!"

There was no response. Realising I'd probably have to handle this one alone, at least for a while, I grabbed one of the restaurant's round tables and lifted.

"Nnnnngggg!"

It was fastened to the floor. Almost embarrassed under the watchful eyes of the crowd, I turned my attention to a chair. Swinging it, I deflected the first attack that came my way. It was from one of the workers – a wiry girl with long dark hair poking out, spider-like, from a dishevelled hairnet. I heard something crack inside her as she ploughed into a table.

Next, I turned my weapon on a customer. He wore dark clothing – a long sleeve shirt and trousers – making it hard to see his movements in the low light. As he lunched, I charged at him, using the seat as a battering ram. His natural instincts to brace himself as he fell didn't kick in, and he crashed wholeheartedly into the cash register. Jamming his arm between the chair leg and the hard surface of the counter, I twisted. There was a sharp *crack* and white bone protruded from his wrist.

"Amelia!" I yelled into the darkness. Part of me worried she'd found a way out and left me to distract the horde while she escaped.

As I struggled with one creature, pudgy hands grabbed my shoulders, and I ducked, releasing the chair. The fat polar bear of a man shunted me against the worktop. At the same time, the broken body next to me turned to join in with the attack. Suddenly overwhelmed, I screamed.

Hot breath warmed the back of my neck. I winced, expecting to feel a sharp bite, as another dark figure appeared over my shoulder. What happened instead, though, was a sudden whistling noise. Then, without warning, the fat zombie was wrenched away. Spinning, he arched backwards and halted with a thump, clamped face-up on the countertop.

Seizing the opportunity, I wrangled with the zombie with the broken hand. He gnashed angrily as I spun him out of my grasp and into the girl with the hairnet. She had just untangled herself from the wreckage of broken furniture but the impact sent her right back into the porcupine of metal legs. Hitting a leg at full speed, she plummeted, a red spire of metal and blood rising out of her back. She kept moving, but I knew there was no coming back from that.

The other one, however, recovered quickly, and returned with a nefarious look on his face. Fumbling for a chair, I swung it hard at his head. He crumpled in a heap and fell still, a tentacle of blood leaking from his ear.

I turned back to the fat zombie, registering a high-pitched sawing noise, and wondered if my ears were wringing. Searching, I located the torch and my candelabra. The creature writhed, arms clawing at thin air. His glasses had fallen off. Before approaching to offer a finishing blow, I hesitated.

"What the hell...?"

A bright red seam of flesh opened up between the boy's multiple chins. For an instant, I thought he'd developed a second mouth, and that this night was about to get a whole lot weirder. Only when I got closer did I realise what was actually happening.

Amelia was hunkered behind the counter, one foot on the floor, the other pushed against the wood itself for support. Each of her gloved hands held a small cylindrical object. An ultrathin wire glimmered, stretching from one hand to the other, curved taut around the zombie's gullet. As it coughed and gurgled its way to oblivion, Amelia's mouth was a thin line of concentration. Methodically, she sawed. Blood poured from the wound and dripped down the back of the counter with every pass.

When the wire finally bisected the zombie's spine, its head dropped, dangling short of her lap by a thin flap of skin. Even in death, the creature's jaw writhed, defying the laws of nature.

"Amelia?" I asked with trepidation as she lay on the floor. "You okay?"

"Yeah," she panted, flipping up her night-vision goggles to reveal a lioness' steely gaze. "Never better." She held up the cable in her hands. "Cheese wire. Who knew this dump would have something so fancy."

I gulped. "That was intense."

"Yeah."

"I could do with a drink."

"Me, too."

"Anything in the store room?"

She flashed me a grin, snapping out of her trance for the first time. "I never got a chance to look. But now..."

Bouncing upright, she headed for the door behind the counter, and rummaged through bags and boxes. Seconds later, she re-emerged. Her face had wilted.

"Nothing. Just a bunch of old candles and boxes of chilled food."

"No alcohol?"

She shook her head. "Looks like you were right." She browsed a slanting shelf holding customer orders and selected a burger with delicate fingers. "I guess there's nothing else we can do but get comfortable."

It was a morbid idea, but nothing I hadn't thought of myself. Instead of refuting it, I simply gestured for her to join me at a table. While she picked up the rest of a meal, I swept past the table I'd sat at next to the window, picking up my box of goodies. I chose a circular booth as our station. The padded seat was a more comfortable option, and the high back bordering it blocked out most of the ghoulish faces spoiling the view.

Bringing the candles and a box of matches she found nearby, Amelia sat opposite me, lighting the wicks. Together, we ate. Strangely, the subtle notes of iron I could smell in the air didn't turn my stomach. Neither did the girl with the hairnet. I ignored her efforts to make contact with us, harpooned in the broken bonfire of twisted furniture.

Was I in shock? I didn't think so. It was probably the comforting buzz of alcohol still in my system keeping me relaxed. The only things I noticed were the rich taste of fried chicken and the delicate method Amelia used to pick her way around a burger.

I laughed.

"What?" she asked. Her face wore a self-conscious smile.

"Nothing. It's just funny. You're trying not to get ketchup on your fingers but you're drenched in blood."

She paused, leaving me to wonder what witty insult she would brew up in response. Instead of saying the expected, she caught me off guard.

"Sorry. I get nervous on a date."

"What?"

My eyes widened. Then it was her time to laugh.

"Moron. I'm joking. I just don't want to get blood in the burger. If those things bite you, you die and come back as one of them. Who's to say the same thing doesn't happen if you eat part of them? I'm not gonna take that risk, are you?"

"Fair point," I mused. "You're smart, you know that?"

"Alright." She rolled her eyes. "This isn't a real date, Romeo. I was joking."

"No, I'm not flattering you. I mean it. If it weren't for you, I'd have died several times tonight. I bet if you *really* put your mind to it, you could get us out of here. You're braver and more resourceful than I'll ever be."

She snorted. "Bravery. Stupidity. Same thing really. Look where it got us."

She gestured to the windows all around. In the orange candlelight, the faces of the undead glowed like the residents of hell on the other side of the glass. The crowd seemed to have almost doubled in size since we locked the doors. My worst nightmare was to see one of our own group appear, ashen and bemused. Something told me it was only a matter of time.

"Looks like someone's having a better night than us." Amelia said, breaking the silence which had descended over us like a fog.

Following her sightline, I saw what she meant. Our booth was slightly raised, overlooking the heads of the zombies. Even in the dark, I could see the figure she was talking about flitting through the ruins of the student village. She was far away – too far to call for help. I guessed she must have got held up somewhere to still be inside the walls of the student village. Her spectre-white ponytail gave away her identity the instant she entered open ground.

"Ghost Girl," I said.

"Indeed. You think we should call her?"

"I doubt she'd answer even if she heard us."

"That's what I thought."

"You think she'll get out?" I asked Amelia.

After a pause, she said, "I hope so. It'd be nice to think someone made it. Don't you th–"

The wall yawned like a submarine on the ocean floor. Eyeing it dubiously, I wondered how long it would hold. I assumed the glass was toughened – it needed to be, with all the drunken students in the area – but that didn't mean it was indestructible. The bodies pilling up behind it were now five deep in places, and all of them were pressing inward, drawn to us like moths to a lightbulb in an old shed.

"We don't have much longer," I said. "That glass'll give way soon, and then it's all over. There's no getting out of something like that, is there?"

Amelia shrugged. "I don't know. Maybe we could…" Her eyes wavered as if browsing some invisible instruction manual for optimists. Obviously, she didn't find the passage she wanted. "No… If only we had more light, maybe we'd come up with something. It's so frustrating!"

"We'll figure it out," I said, deciding she could do with some false hope. "We're smart. Come on, think."

"Think? I can't think my way out of a paper bag! I couldn't even think of a legal way to get into university."

"Wait. What?" I frowned.

She signed. "I guess it's time to come clean. What's the worst that can happen, right? We're gonna die anyway."

"Yeah…" I paused, hoping she would elaborate. Eventually, she did.

"When I bumped into you guys at Armageddon, you all wondered what I was doing on the top floor of the student union when the outbreak started. Well, I was covering my tracks. That's what all this gear's for. When I applied to this uni, they rejected me. Not even an interview. Just a flat-out no. I got the grades, so I'm guessing my paperwork didn't hold up or something.

"Anyway, I had no second option, so I did the only thing I knew I could; I broke into the student union in the summer and changed the records. Only, I left some climbing equipment behind. If I didn't come back and steal the evidence on my first night here, I knew someone would eventually see the harness and look at the CCTV. Then I'd probably be carted out of here before we even finished the first semester."

I paused, allowing her words to sink in. "Right," I said finally. "That's okay. I bet lots of people cheat to get in. Rejecting you for missing something on the form is unfair. I know you're smart enough to be here."

"But not smart enough to get us out of this, clearly! And you know what the worst thing is?" She paused, but I didn't answer, realising it was a rhetorical question. "I've done everything in my power to get into this place, only for it to blow up in my face in the most ironic way possible!"

Pushing away the empty chicken box, I said, "What do you mean?"

"I'm an orphan."

There it was; the secret I'd sensed she was hiding. Now her dark clothes and standoffish attitude made more sense. They were a barrier.

"My mum was an immigrant, and a single mother," she explained. "She was intelligent, sweet, funny – everything I could ever want. She moved me here, aged eleven, hoping for a new life. After weeks of living in hostels, and begging at government buildings, she finally got a job doing admin work for a construction company, and moved me into safe, rented accommodation. The company was based not far from here, actually. She seemed to love it."

"Uh-huh." I nodded, unsure where this way going.

"Then she died."

My stomach tingled with butterflies. Knowing she was an orphan, I'd expected the twist but it still seemed too real – not like a story at all. More like I was there.

"With no other family left, here or back home, I was taken into care, where I stayed until just a few months ago. I was told my mum died because of an illness. I suspected a cover-up. After all, a lot of people died that day, so it couldn't be a disease. Not that quick. Still, I never expected to find out the truth tonight. Or for it to be so strange."

"You found out the truth?" I asked. What she said made no sense. *How could she possibly have found out the truth about her mother's death tonight?*

She smiled sadly. "I never told you where my mother was stationed when she died. I was in school a few miles away, staying with a neighbour, while Mum worked overtime. She was so excited. It was the break we needed to change our lives."

"Where?" I croaked, with a dry throat.

Amelia's eyes flicked up at me. "Necroville."

PART THIRTY
PRESSURE

It all made sense now – Amelia's passion for uncovering conspiracies, her hatred for the government; her brooding character, and reluctance to get close to people; her lies and fascination with Theo's Necroville account. Her entire life's work as a whistle-blower was just a façade – a secret crusade to seek out the truth behind the day her mother died. The day she became irreversibly damaged.

"Your mum was at Necroville?" I needed clarification, just in case I'd misheard.

She nodded. "Along with hundreds of others. My social worker told me it was a terrible act of God. I knew it wasn't true. Deadly strains of Ebola don't just spring up out of nowhere and kill hundreds of people. But I couldn't prove anything. I did a bit of digging, years ago. Managed to get myself on a day-trip with the other orphans. We were staying near Bleakmoor's closest police station.

"One night, I snuck out and broke into their file room. There wasn't much in the way of records, which surprised me. Only two slips of paper. One was an eye-witness account from an officer. He didn't describe it well, but he claimed the victims weren't diseased; they were possessed.

He reckoned they'd become monsters. The other sheet was just a psychological assessment."

"Of him?"

"Yeah."

"Woah, so Theo was telling the truth?"

"Looks that way."

"That's awful."

"What's worse is, I can't get more concrete proof. The officer was sectioned and there were no other records. It was hopeless. I've been alone ever since… It's easier if you don't care. When nobody has your back, you get used to it."

"I had your back," I whispered.

"When?"

"At the ditch. You fell in and I could have left you to catch up with the others. But I didn't do that. I turned back. Someone always has your back, Amelia. You just won't notice if you don't recognise kindness. I got stuck under a freakin' zombie just to get you out of that hole."

"Thanks," she said. "Worked out well for you, right?"

I shrugged. "It certainly made me feel a lot better in the short term. Now, I guess, not so much."

There was an awkward pause as our inevitable mortality dangled in front of our faces like a noose. The silence was only broken by the creaking wails of the windows as more bodies were crushed against them.

"Still, it could be worse," Amelia said finally.

"Yeah?"

"Yeah. We could *both* have a stupid kitten tattoo."

"It's a tiger!" I growled. And then I laughed, and she punched me in the shoulder.

"Can I show you something, Milo? It's something I keep hidden… Something else."

"You might as well. It's not like either of us are gonna survive to tell anyone."

Standing up, she lifted the dark t-shirt clinging to her stomach. When I saw pale flesh, I wondered just where this was headed, and shifted with anticipation. Then she stopped about half-way up her torso.

"Is that a duck?" I frowned.

"No, stupid! It's an eagle."

I laughed and poked the amateur tattoo with my index finger, making her flinch.

"Stop! That tickles."

"That's definitely a duck," I said.

Lowering her shirt, she slotted back into the booth next to me. "It's an eagle," she insisted, laughing again. "So, it looks like you're not the only one with a ridiculous tattoo after all."

"No," I said. "I'm not alone. And neither are you."

Orange candlelight flickered in the oily surface of Amelia's eyes. Call it the 'last minutes on Earth' effect, but, for a moment, I was lost in them. None of us said anything, leaning closer, as though the air around us had hands pressed against our backs. The air crackled with tension. I felt like it would snap at any second. And then it did.

Without warning, the window exploded, washing bodies, rainwater, and gore into the room. Our force field was broken. Our sanctuary had come to an end.

PART THIRTY-ONE
RESCUE MISSION

We leapt to our feet and grabbed the only weapons we had at hand. As much as I knew this was the end, that didn't mean I'd go down without a fight. Rest assured, there would be casualties on both sides.

"Woohoo! Let's do that again!"

It took a second for my mind to process what I was seeing. The edge of the booth had protected me and Amelia from the explosion of shattering glass, but it also stopped us from seeing what caused it.

In the centre of the floor, belly laughing on his back, lay Robbie. He was wrapped in what looked like a suede curtain. An overturned shopping trolley lay strewn next to him. It had created a trail of destruction akin to a miniature meteor in the small restaurant where he had blown through the wall.

"Now *that* was fun!" he said, picking his way over the broken glass.

"Robbie?" I heard Amelia say. "What are you doing here?"

"Teaching a horse to knit. What the hell does it look like I'm doing? I'm saving you!"

"This is a search and rescue mission. Now, move, soldiers!" Theo poked his head through the gaping wound in the side of the building.

We didn't need to be told twice. Bounding over the debris caused by Robbie's entrance, Amelia and I blasted through a hole that had opened up in the zombie wall. Hands clung to me like thorns from a hedge, but I unsnagged them with sheer force. On the other side, I paused. Amelia stopped beside me.

"Where's Robbie?" I asked her.

"Right behind us," she said. "He'll be fine. He's plastered. Don't know where he got the booze, but I wish there were more."

The undead closed ranks, but Robbie didn't seem to notice, barrelling through them like a Christmas shopper on Black Friday. When a more observant zombie seemed to notice he wasn't actually dead, and was just drunk, Monty swept in to save him. Wielding a metal bar with thick ends, he obliterated the creature's skull with one devastating swing.

"Is that a barbell?" I asked, confused.

I was far from a gym rat but I recognised a weightlifting bar when I saw one. There were no weights attached to the ends, but the bar itself was solid metal – probably way too weighty for me to wield in close combat. How Monty managed it, I had no idea.

Reassuring himself Robbie was free, Monty moved on, cleaving through a zombie's shins as it toddled towards Wyatt. Both lower limbs snapped instantly, jutting backwards like the legs of an ostrich. A tingle of pain-cringe vibrated in my lower extremities.

"We all good to go, chaps?" he asked, turning to the rest of the group.

Booting a corpse in the face, Theo said, "Wouldn't miss it for the world."

"Okay. Let's go!"

I followed without hesitation. Together, we crossed the small plaza. It separated the restaurant from residential apartments and stretched uphill.

"You're lucky we're here," Gus explained as the group moved. "I thought you were zombie snacks for sure. It's only because Monty noticed you we came back. It took a little while but we circled round."

"Thanks," I said. "We definitely weren't getting out of that one on our own."

"No problem. It was easy once we found the twenty-four-hour gym down that lane." He pointed at a narrow, slabbed footpath weaving between two apartment blocks. "Robbie found beers there, and came up with the rescue plan. Of course, there was only enough for him."

Well, that explains the barbell, I thought.

"Thanks, Rob!" Amelia beamed at him.

"T'was nothing." The beer pong legend bowed lower than a royal butler, then burped on his own feet. "Oh, danger burp. Almost wasted it, then."

I smirked, glad to be back.

"Nobody leaves a good man behind," Theo grunted in agreement, overhearing our conversation. Spotting Amelia, he added, "Or a good, err, woman."

The incline was steeper than it looked from the bottom. Already, I could feel my thighs burning. Being by far the least in-shape member of the team, Gus was particularly flushed. His lungs rattled as he breathed. I knew that as Lord Augustus, however, he'd be too proud to slow down the group by complaining, especially when slacking could get us killed.

There were far fewer ghouls on the hill than there were on the lower-lying land, but it had become apparent we were no longer heading up the herd. They were all around us, shambling absentmindedly in their lonely worlds. At least, they *were*, until our appearances triggered something inside them that translated into hunger.

A pale, shambling figure peeled away from the residential woodwork. Dissecting himself from the group, Theo battered the unsuspecting creature looking for a quick lunch and sent it tumbling down the slope. Blood from its open sores left scarlet skid marks on the tarmac. Black vomit bubbled from its mouth as it screamed in fury at him, but by the time it staggered to its feet, we had already moved on to the next target.

"There are so many!" I said.

It was true. Like scum, the zombies accumulated in clusters, teaming together in places where dirty bodies, too devoured to reanimate, could be found. They were stationed in mobile herds all the way up the hill. I hadn't seen any living victims in a while. There were no faraway screams. Just groans.

After what we'd survived over the past few hours, it was hard to imagine any other environment outside the spreading stain of the undead. The normality probably going on in the city – just a few miles away – seemed completely alien now. I struggled to comprehend people worrying about traffic and laundry when a massacre was happening within walking distance of their homes.

Progress was slow. Corpses gravitated to us like magnets. More were appearing by the second. For every one we lobotomised with a metal object, or disabled beyond repair, another three took their place.

One thing was apparent – while the zombie populations of the few roads ahead of us were sparser than the ones we'd left behind, they wouldn't stay that way for very long. Pretty soon, the dead's stain would spread right up to the borders of the student village and beyond.

Speed was critical. If we didn't get to the main gate and gain some ground soon, it would all be over. The world would never be prepared in time to stop the infection at its source.

"We're close to the main gate. It's just around that corner," said Monty. "I'm positive."

As we crested a plateau, we found ourselves surrounded by low-lying structures. A pizzeria, an ornate fountain, and a media centre, along with a collection of signposts for visitors. This was the face of the village – the place closest to the most expensive accommodation, and a hotspot for photos featured on the university's marketing materials.

The main gate still wasn't in sight, but I knew Monty was right. A sign marked 'Visitor Entrance' confirmed it wasn't far away. Following the line indicated on the sign, I saw a final curve in the road. I recognised it immediately because it was plastered on the home page of the university's website.

Just around the corner, we'd descend the other side of the slope to find a modern library and a giant clock face. A driveway bisecting a clipped lawn led to the carpark. That was where we'd find the cars and our ticket to freedom. It was so close, I could almost taste the cut grass and feel the driveway shingles under my feet.

Skidding around the final corner, we raced past a squat building, with two overturned boat hulls on the roof. *The boathouse.* I'd seen it in the prospectus.

We skirted it and headed back downhill. My lungs thanked me as they spluttered back to a more regular breathing rate. Together, we reached the last stretch of road and braced ourselves for the relief of seeing the finish line. I could sense the apprehension building as we rounded the final corner and emerged onto open hillside.

"Good Lord!" Monty yelped as he saw the gate.

I turned the corner with a relieved smile, but it faded as I took in the view from the top of the banking. The colour drained from my flushed face, and a sobering chill ran through me.

"No way," I whispered.

The others also slowed to a stop. One by one, they noticed the bombshell landing at our feet.

"This wasn't meant to happen," Amelia said.

Not even in my darkest nightmares had I encountered anything so terrifying. As I stood, dumbfounded at the crest of the hill, I considered our chances. They were microscopic given the scale of this new obstacle.

A ghostly moan reached us on the wind.

PART THIRTY-TWO
THE GATES OF HELL

"How?" I whispered.

The problem was bigger than we had realised. The emerald lawn I remembered from the university's open day no longer existed. In its current condition, the field more closely resembled a medieval warzone.

A patchwork of bodies lay strewn across each other in viscous mud, some moving, others deathly still. There were hundreds of figures – maybe a thousand – standing in the open pasture, all caked in gore and oily vomit, their hair layered wet across their faces, gouged meat visible through ripped clothing.

The haunting din of moans drifting from the colossal horde could probably be heard for miles around. Behind them, the gates themselves – giant steel monstrosities that held in student life like a zoo enclosure – were closed.

Locked? Why would they be locked? I wondered, searching the back of my mind for an answer. *Did the university lock them in the early hours of the morning for some reason?* I didn't remember any rule about that in the prospectus. Perhaps it was something to do with the outbreak. *Would the army have done it if they arrived?* It didn't look like that was the case. There were no fortifications. They were just shut.

"Okay, new plan," I said, hoping someone would finish my train of thought. "Err... Anyone got one?"

"Fall back!" Theo jumped in. "The boathouse doors were unlocked. We can wait them out there if we have to!"

There was no telling how long that might take. Judging by the size of the zombie herd, nothing was getting into the complex anytime soon. We were sitting ducks. Having said that, there was no other option. Theo was right; our best chance at survival was to hide and wait to see what happened next. If we were lucky, a gap might open up in the ranks of the undead.

We didn't even need to speak to know we had all come to a unanimous agreement. Our body language was enough. Not wasting a moment, we swivelled back on ourselves, and trudged up to the boathouse.

"Uphill?" I complained, through heaving breaths. "Why is it never easy?"

I wasn't the only one having a hard time. Glancing over my shoulder, I noticed Robbie and Wyatt panting just behind me. Even further back, was Gus. Several times he tried to break into a short jog to catch up to the rest of us but faltered, tangled in the suffocating folds of his cape.

"You okay, Gus?" I asked him.

"I think I'm gonna throw up," he wheezed.

He stopped and gazed at the sky. It appeared the moment I dreaded had come. He'd hit the wall. And then it got worse.

A wooden door near him swung open, and three figures lurched into his path. The others hadn't noticed. Robbie and Wyatt overtook me as I slowed my pace, urging Gus to fight through the fatigue. He didn't see the monsters skulk closer, circling on both sides.

"Gus!" I yelled.

His head snapped towards me, drenched in sweat. Taken off guard, panic flared in his eyes as he noticed the oncoming attack. He charged forward – an instinctive reaction – and bashed one of the attackers out of the way. The ghoul stumbled but didn't fall. Teetering for a moment, it dropped onto all fours, then climbed the hill after him.

Gus' legs were failing. Stumbling to a halt again, he drew his sword. As an afterthought, he also reached for his gun.

"Give me a minute!" he roared, shoving the next approaching monster.

This one didn't go down so easily. Deflecting it twice, he came to a halt. I saw a shift in his stance that worried me. It appeared he had come to the conclusion he couldn't make it up the hill fast enough, so he went on the attack.

"I'll smite thee, foul monster!"

He sliced an arc through the air with his wooden blade. The weapon missed its initial target by inches. Thrown off balance, Gus gasped as the second creature to approach him stepped on the weapon and fell into him.

"Get off me!" he squealed, breaking character. A sharp elbow to the face bought him a second, so he followed it up by arming his gun and firing. The metal pellet burrowed into the monster's eye socket at point-blank range. Wobbling like a new-born fawn, it collapsed. Still, Gus didn't move.

"Gus!" I screamed.

He obviously wasn't going to last much longer. The giant army of corpses had begun their ascent of the hill, but that wasn't our biggest problem. With Gus distracted, even more lone monsters had arrived, weaving out of the crevices between buildings like Saharan animals drawn to a watering hole. He was surrounded.

I didn't realise I was racing towards him until I felt my feet scuff on the wet road. Colliding with one of the creatures at high speed, I drove my candelabra into the back of its unsuspecting skull.

It fell, but not before I heard a strangled yelp. A withered arm had snagged on Gus' cape. I didn't see him fall, but it was obvious what had happened. He was sprawled on his back. Unfastening the Velcro holding it in place, he rolled onto his hands and knees, and began a hasty crawl towards me.

It was the fastest he had moved in some time, but still wasn't fast enough. A dark predator landed on his back as he passed by. It was a girl with feathery blonde hair, a blood-soaked jawline, and long nails painted black. Gus squirmed but you could tell his strength was waning. Like a buffalo under a lioness, he writhed, his horned helmet falling crooked over his eyes.

Trying to shake himself free, Gus whimpered as the monster refused to let go. Furious at not being able to bite her way through his heavy cape, she grabbed his utility belt and wrenched him closer.

"Argh!" he squealed.

Finally, a link broke, and the belt came free. Ball bearings from Gus' ammo bag rained down on top of him. In a bid to steady herself, the lioness-zombie trod on one. Her legs slid in separate directions. On her way to the ground, she barrelled into two approaching carnivores, and together, they buckled.

"I'm coming, Gus! Just hold on!" I shouted.

My voice sounded abnormally confident, like a different person altogether. There was no trace of the reedy quality normally defining it. Only a few hours ago, I would never have seen a fight to the death and thought to run *towards* it.

"Jesus Christ, Milo!" I heard Monty bellow. He sounded far away, probably already at the boathouse.

Two corpses blocked my path. As a pair of hands shot at me, I grabbed one wrist, and used the monster's own weight against it. It stumbled past me, and I drove my weapon into its cheek, sending it careening away at a diagonal. Bronze gleamed in the air as one of the candelabra's cups came off on impact.

Wielding the broken prop like a prison shank, I moved onto my next target. This one was more powerful; a tall boy, with aquiline features and baggy clothing. His right arm swung as he hobbled towards me. Ducking out of his reach, I circled around and hooked the crux of my elbow around his neck. A sharp blow to the temple stunned him. I didn't release him until his body went slack.

"Lady Alycia!"

I spun.

The joyful cry hit me with a wave of goose bumps. It was odd how something usually so pleasant could be completely turned on its head given the right conditions. Like a child's laughter; pleasant at a picnic. Not quite so endearing at three in the morning when you're home alone and you don't have kids.

Gus was stone still, an uneasy grin spread on his wet face. In front of him stood a spindly figure with long, white hair and pale features. Somehow she had pealed out of a crevice unseen. I thought I would have noticed her, given her outlandish cape and red spandex bodysuit.

Showing dramatic patience uncharacteristic of the undead, Alycia paused, seemingly bewildered, in front of her gaming buddy. She was above him on the hill. Her hands splayed, leaning backwards slightly, like a tarantula poised to strike.

Don't be stupid, Gus, I thought, forging a path towards him.

"Alycia, it's me."

Bonkers.

I knew Gus had always been a little unhinged from the moment I met him. After all, who tackles a zombie apocalypse with a wooden sword and a cape? But that didn't stop me from assuming he'd snap out of his delusions the moment he needed reality to stay alive.

"Gus!" I shouted as another corpse cut me off. I could already see his fallen attackers clambering to their feet in the background. Circling, I yelled, "Gus, behind you!" Getting closer would mean splitting off from the group a second time, and that wasn't a gamble I could to take again. When Gus didn't acknowledge me, I tried a different approach. "That's not Alycia, Gus. She's gone. You have to listen!"

He didn't.

"Alycia, can you hear me in there? I never thought I'd see you again." His eyes glimmered as he held out a gloved hand. Removing his Viking helmet, he pressed it respectfully to his chest. "M'lady. I swear, if you come back to this world, I'll find you a healer. I'll–"

"Tights, what the hell are you doing?" Theo appeared at my side, barking at Gus. "You can't reason with 'em. They're monsters. I've seen people try in the past, back in Necroville. It's not possible."

A zombie barred his path. Without hesitating, Theo snapped the barrel of his shotgun up and pulled the trigger. One moment the ghoul's head was there, the next moment, it wasn't, and the sky became brainier than Hitler's bunker.

"Shh!" Gus snapped at him, never taking his eyes off the girl in the red spandex. She staggered closer, so close they were almost touching. "I think I'm getting through to her. Look! She recognises my voice. Don't you, Alycia?"

"No, stop!" Theo retorted. "I've seen it before. You'll die."

Gus wrinkled his nose. "You don't know her like I do. We're good–"

"Just listen, Charlie! NO!"

I noticed Theo's slipup, but it wasn't the time to correct him. Without warning, Alycia lunged at Gus' jugular. There was no struggle. Her teeth sunk into his throat before he had time to recoil, and he dropped his helmet. It landed next to his sword. As he struggled, his pellet gun flew out of his grip and spiralled across the road.

The approaching battalion's groan had become omnipresent, drowning out almost all other sound. Despite that, Gus' gurgled scream pierced through it. It bubbled from a hole torn out of his neck.

I didn't see what happened next. Alycia covered Gus, obscuring him from view. Blood haloed him like a sacrifice as the swarm descended from all sides, ready to dismantle his still-breathing carcass.

PART THIRTY-THREE
IT LIVES IN THE DARK

"For Christ's sake!" Theo shouted. "Civilians! They never learn."

Leaping forward, I raised the candelabra above my head. A strong hand closed around my wrist and swivelled me on the spot before I could make a move.

"What do you think you're doing?" I screamed at Theo. That's when I noticed it wasn't him who'd grabbed me. Monty yanked me up the hill with more force than I could resist. Scrambling to keep balance, I had no choice but to follow.

"We can't save him now, old sport," he grunted. "I know what you're going through – I do – but we have to save ourselves."

My first instinct was to defy him, to break out of his grip and race back down the hill to avenge Gus. A second's consideration changed that. Admittedly, the thousand zombies pouring over Gus' dead body in our direction helped clear my mind.

"Quickly," Monty urged. "Some followed us up here from the other side. We've got to outpace them."

My eyes flicked up to the boathouse at the crest of the hill. Already corpses snarled at the top, yipping like hyenas.

Wyatt and Robbie held them off until we reached the main doors.

When we arrived, we all piled into boathouse courtyard. Luckily, Theo's keen eyes were right. The pair of heavy oak doors decorating its ornate frontage had been left unlocked. Slamming them behind us, we entered a large foyer. Most of the room was shrouded in darkness, but I could tell it was large because our footsteps echoed on the tiled floor.

"Help me with this!"

Monty hefted one end of a sofa into the air. It was the studded, leather kind, unbelievably heavy for its size. Just what we needed. Placing his shotgun to one side, Theo grabbed the other end while I supported the middle. Amelia ushered Wyatt inside and bolted the doors while we propped the sofa against them.

"Now what?" Monty asked.

"I don't know," I admitted.

It seemed as though everyone had moved on from the trauma of seeing Gus' life snuffed out pretty quickly. Perhaps it was the adrenaline, or the alcohol, or maybe we had just become monsters, desensitised by death. Whatever caused our blinkered focus, I couldn't help feeling guilt after leaving him dead in the road. Even now, I kept moving without sadness, stuck in a mind-set fixated on forward momentum.

It didn't look good for us. Despite having been trapped several times in the last few hours, this time was definitely the worst. The student village had become a prison. Most of the population had now joined the legion of monsters. With no cavalry to come to our rescue this time, and more predators circling than ever, our odds were dire.

"Come on. Let's look around," Amelia suggested. "Maybe there's drink here."

Booze!

"Awesome idea!" I said.

Robbie pushed past me with the grace of an elephant seal. "Now we're talking! Let's go, Wyatt. There's drink to be found."

"I could do with a jar or two myself," agreed Theo.

I had to admire their spirit. If anything could get us out of this, it was a boatload of beer. I just hoped rowers were as infamous when it came to drinking as other sports teams.

"Good idea, chaps." Monty headed for the darkness. "Jolly good idea, in fact."

Even though there was enthusiasm in his voice, it didn't reach his eyes. There, fear resided. Peeking around the seam of a thick curtain, he gazed through the window. His hands fidgeted with the barbell he had taken to using as a staff.

"You okay, bro?" Wyatt asked him. "You don't look so good."

"It's just… I wasn't there."

"Where?"

"There for Gus. We keep leaving people behind. People that could survive if I didn't keep pushing us so hard. I keep making rash decisions and it's getting people killed."

"Hey!" I locked eye-contact with him. "If it weren't for you pushing us, most of us would be out there with them right now."

I gestured to the blood-glazed hands slapping on the window pane. It was lucky the zombies couldn't see us behind the curtain because they would have made short work of the glass.

"I suppose you're right," Monty said. He shook his head. "I just need to bottle up my thoughts, at least until we get out of this. Stiff upper lip and all that, right?"

I sighed. "If that's what it takes."

It wasn't the answer I wanted to give, but it would have to do for now. The last thing I wanted was for Monty to fall apart on us just when we needed his strength most.

"Right!" Robbie clapped his hands together with finality. "Now that's sorted, let's make use of our lower lips and get swiggin'!"

"Sir, yes, sir!" Theo clacked his heals together and raced into the dark. Robbie and Wyatt thundered after him. The clatter of footsteps on floorboards told me they had reached a staircase and headed to the next floor.

"I guess that leaves the ground floor for us," said Amelia.

"Right," I said. "Oh, Theo left his gun behind."

Picking it up, I tested its weight in my hand. My arms tingled as though anticipating an explosive kick. I'd never seen a gun in the flesh before tonight, let alone touched one.

"I'll take that," Monty said. "Don't want you shooting yourself now, do we? Or someone else, for that matter."

For a moment, I scanned the weapon with dubious eyes. *Should I trust him with it?* His mood that night had been a rollercoaster ride to say the least.

Giving myself a nanosecond to consider the implications of weaponising Monty, I reluctantly handed it over. Immediately, the tingles in my arms stopped. I released a breath I didn't know I was holding. Monty set his unwieldy barbell aside and took the firearm.

"Alright, but stay close," I warned. "Who knows what we'll find in the dark."

We moved through the foyer, slipping through a dark doorway. It was eerily silent as we headed further into the building. Despite getting more accustomed to the undead now, the silence and darkness still set me on edge.

Sensing my disquiet, Amelia drew in close and slotted her torch into my hand. I could tell she'd been fondling it for some time by its warmth. Flicking it on, I pointed it into the shadows as we navigated the lower rooms, Amelia heading up the front with her night vision goggles lowered.

The first room we entered was a dining hall. A long table with twelve chairs acted as the centrepiece to an otherwise bland space. The walls only featured a single plasma screen TV. I fiddled with a light switch next to the door but found that the electricity was still out and probably would be for some time. Whatever had knocked out Greasy's energy supply had obviously devastated the lighting here, too.

The main thing we noticed was that there was absolutely no alcohol. Unerring, we moved onward.

Next came a cloakroom, complete with a tumble dryer, and a wall full of wetsuits on hooks. Long plastic oars were stacked in the corner of the room nearest the door. A few small weights and pieces of cabled exercise equipment were strewn sporadically along a bench. Bypassing it all, we shifted through to a much bigger space.

The first thing that struck me was the heat. Sliding into a curtain of warm air, I noticed a wall of stainless steel doors and the shine of a hob as the torchlight ran over it. A marble-topped island amidst a terracotta floor provided a centrepiece for the whole room.

A kitchen.

"Feels like someone's been cooking in here," I said, pushing the door wide open.

"If they were, they're not here now," Amelia stated.

"Well, were they cooking with wine?"

"This is a sports kitchen," Monty stated. "Rowers are serious athletes by nature, especially at uni level. I'm sure they wouldn't tarnish their physiques with alco–"

He picked a dark bottle off the countertop and held it up to the light. One bottle. Hardly enough to get us all wasted but it could come in handy if need be.

"You were saying?" I grinned.

Flashing me an indignant glare, Monty simply pointed the bottle in the direction of a refrigerator.

"Obviously, they're the deviant sort," he admonished. "Go check over there, would you? There could be more."

I crossed the floor and opened the fridge. Cool air that had been trapped inside doused me in an arctic front. There was no interior light to accompany it. I frowned.

"No. No more bottles. How about you, Amelia? Anything over there?"

Amelia wandered under a dark arch with a sign that read 'Pantry' above the door.

"I don't know," she said, clutching the handle of a freestanding cupboard. "Give me a minute and I'll have a better idea of…"

She kept talking but I stopped listening as her hand absentmindedly opened the door. My world had gone silent. Eyes wide, I spotted the black shape move out of the shadows long before she did.

The next few seconds were a complete blur. I threw myself across the room and struck the predator as it pounced. Pain exploded in my leg the moment our bodies entwined, and I tasted the toffee-flavoured blast of blunt trauma to my head.

Coiled together, we both slammed into the wall. Before I hit the floor the sound of smashing glass chimed in the dark. Then an earth-shattering *boom* erupted somewhere in the room, followed by a girl's scream. Woozy and convulsing in waves of agony, I writhed on the floor's warm tiles for a few seconds, sucking in lungfuls of sweltering air.

Then everything went dark.

PART THIRTY-FOUR
THE BAR

A scream was the alarm clock that brought me back to life.

My eyes opened and my stomach lurched as strong arms dragged me backwards along the floor, my head at chest height, my shoes sliding uselessly along the kitchen tiles. A slug trail of blood was left in my wake.

I couldn't see much, given the cavernous darkness of the room, and the fact the torch was now pointing in the opposite direction. A pale body lying on the floor next to the pantry door was the only evidence that anything had occurred. Its frizzy hair covered its face, but I could tell it was dead by the lack of movement.

"I can't believe it!" Monty's voice shook behind my head. "What have I done?"

I don't know, Monty. What have you done?

Dipping out of consciousness for a second, I shook my head. We were closer to the door now. In the handful of seconds it had taken to drag my limp body past the kitchen's island, my leg had gone completely cold. The feeling in my toes on my right foot felt like TV static to my brain.

Losing sight of the body as I was dragged into the cloakroom, I eyed my leg. *Woah!* My brain recoiled at an idea surfacing inside me. *Is it possible? Could that thing have bitten me during our short fight?*

I tried to scream but the words didn't come out. All that escaped my lips was a woozy jumble of groans that neither made sense, nor made Monty break his stride. Then I closed my eyes.

Amelia's voice sounded worried as I came to, though I couldn't make out exactly what she was saying. It was like listening under water. In the background, I heard distant banging. I felt myself rising off the floor, a stretcher of hands forming under my entire body.

Cold air hit me in the face just a few moments later. We were outside. It was windy, and fine, powdery rain speckled my cheeks. Something was constricting my leg.

For a moment, I wondered why the buildings around us had sunk into the bowels of the earth. Then my mind processed the information, and I got my bearings. They hadn't sunk at all. We had risen. We were high up, near the boathouse roof. A pair of familiar, glossy hulls, turned upside down, lay to either side of me. They were fixed in place, tethered next to the sloping roofs bordering what seemed to be a patio.

"Guys, I think he's coming round! Milo! Milo?"

My eyes opened a crack, for an instant, and I saw Amelia's raven features. Smiling, I tried to talk. Again, my words were slurred beyond recognition.

"Oh, hey, bro! Hold in there!" It was Robbie this time. He was leaning over Amelia's shoulder, shirtless.

There was another bang, and Robbie shot me a concerned glance. "Stay put," he said in a low voice. Then he vanished. Amelia went with him. The others sounded close by, but I realised I was alone.

Rolling onto my stomach, I winced at the pain in my leg. I brushed my fingers over a white sheet that had been wrapped around my upper thigh, cutting off the blood supply.

Robbie's shirt.

The thought crossed my mind to unravel the t-shirt and take a look at the wound, but I decided against it. If it was as bad as I imagined, seeing tooth marks and an infected hole in my leg wouldn't help my situation. It would only confirm my doom.

No. I'd rather not know.

"Guys?" I finally managed to say.

The word appeared, but it was small, shrunk by dehydration. When nobody answered, I fought to sit up. I'd been propped against a generator. The metal box was warm on my back. Dragging myself along the floor, I curled my fingers around a railing and pulled myself a few inches into the air to peek at the scene surrounding the building.

A sliver of early-morning sunlight had risen over the horizon, glowing like a far-off nuclear explosion that barely penetrated the cloud cover. The dingy light source was just bright enough to illuminate the scene below.

The ground was a cesspit of carnage right out of Dante's *Inferno*. Sweaty bodies covered in dark sludge and sticky blood had reached the walls.

The patio that held me above it all faced out from the back of the boathouse. One floor below, a long concrete ramp ran from the building, as the crow flies, to the open pontoon we had passed on our winding way up the hillside. During term time, I guessed it would offer easy access for the rowing team to carry their boats to the moat from the boathouse garage.

The entire stretch of open ground was populated with contaminated corpses. Their grimy bodies shifted with unnatural, jittery movements that more closely resembled insects than humans. Large subdivisions were covered head-to-toe in a glistening, tar-like sheen. Obviously, those nearest the jetty had emerged from the oil slick in the moat.

Ghouls nearest the wall paced the structure, clambering over discarded gas canisters and storage boxes. They had formed a current of heads patrolling the building, reminding me of the whirling River Styx. My only reassurance was they hadn't noticed me.

"Hey, Milo! Get back from there!" Amelia arrived at my side and helped shimmy me back into my original resting place.

"What's happening?" I croaked.

"Nothing," she said, too quickly for it to be true. "Nothing at all. We're gonna get out of this."

"What's wrong with my leg?" Again, the words came out slurred. I knew it was a bite but I had to hear the truth from her mouth. My mind wouldn't let go of its spark of denial any other way.

She must have thought my mumbling was delirious, because instead of answering, she placed a delicate finger on my lips and said, "Just rest, Milo. And drink this." She held my chin, while pouring a cold liquid into my mouth. "Wyatt got some water for you from the kitchen. Drink it slowly. And don't worry about anything. We'll sort out the rest."

Her face flushed, and I saw a hint of tears gathering in the waterlines of her eyes. Her chin wobbled. This wasn't the Amelia I knew. Leaving me to slouch in silence, breathing heavily, she paced the patio, meerkatting for anything that could help us. Eventually, her attention turned to the camera. Whipping it out, she muttered into the lens with a tremor in her throat.

The horde's moans had grown so loud now they resembled vuvuzelas at a sports match. So omnipresent was their din, it was almost difficult to listen to anything else around me.

"Why aren't we downstairs?" I asked her.

She didn't reply, but my question was answered by Theo.

"Damn Zs have taken the bottom floor!" he raged on the far side of the rooftop patio, to nobody in particular. "Downton Abbey, what in God's name are you snivelling about?"

"I killed him," Monty replied. His face was devoid of emotion as if its reserves had been exhausted. "First, Sophia, now this!"

Killed who? Seeing as I was injured, I assumed he meant me. *I'm not dead, am I? Not yet.*

Seeming not to notice my condition, Wyatt hunkered next to me on his knees, his eyes wide and alert. His hands were shaking, but he settled them by gripping the railings, watching the glowing horizon.

"Man, beautiful, isn't it?" he said. "Really majestic. I mean, we're so small, it's like…"

Craning my neck, and trying to drown him out, I settled on the argument between Theo and Monty.

"Man, it was kill, or be killed!" Theo continued. "That maniac was going after Paws and Cam Girl. If you didn't step in when you did, we'd have lost one of our own. I've killed plenty! You don't see me whimpering now, do ya?"

"Give it a rest, Theo! I don't think you *have* killed people!" Monty exploded. "This mental problem you've got," he gestured to the commando's attire, "is just an illness! Did you even survive a zombie outbreak before? Because I'm not sure even that's real. Everything else about you is fake. And, besides that, you do whimper. I've seen it! Just a few hours ago you were snivelling in Armageddon."

"How dare you!" Theo snatched his shotgun out of Monty's hands. "You don't know my life!"

"Neither do you, by the looks of it!"

"That may be so, but at least I know what's up when it comes to survival. And don't tell me you saw me cry, because you didn't. I just had dust in my eye. I ain't never cried! I don't even cry when I cut onions. In fact, I don't cut onions. I just yell at them, until they cut themselves. And then they cry. Now, suck it up and help me figure out our next move."

"Guys, stop arguing," Robbie intervened. "Did one of you say something about booze just now? Was there any in the kitchen?"

"One bottle," Monty moaned.

"One bottle? Of what?"

"Wine."

"Ugh... Oh well. Beggars can't be choosers, I guess. Where is it?"

"Dropped it."

"You what, mate?"

"Oh my freaking God!"

All faces turned towards Amelia. By this point she was perched precariously on the patio railing, with one foot on the roof. Her camera was thrust high into the air.

"What is it?" Robbie asked.

Amelia beamed at him. "I've got a bar!"

PART THIRTY-FIVE
LOST AT SEA

"A bar?" Robbie's eyes widened. "Shut the front door! I could do with a pint so hard right now."

"Not that kind of bar, you moron! A signal bar. 4G!"

The others rushed to her side.

"You have signal?" asked Monty.

"Where exactly did it happen?" Theo climbed up next to her. "Do you have the internet on that thing? What am I saying? Of course you do! Everything and the kitchen sink can get online these days. Post a status! Someone's bound to see it. They can send help."

"Already typed it, and I've attached a video. Argh! Get off!" Amelia cried, wobbling on the railing. "Oh, look what you've done now. Failed to send!"

"Give it here. You ain't as tall as me. I can reach the signal. Where was it?"

She handed it to him and pointed into open space. "There."

Waving his arm like a metal detector, Theo stared so hard at the screen I thought it might burst into flames. When nothing happened, he said, "I need to get further out."

"Okay." Amelia switched places with him, giving him free reign of the roof. Edging onto the tiles just above the gutter, he leaned past the upturned boat hull into open space.

"Got it?" Amelia asked.

"Do you have it?" Robbie boomed when Theo took longer than a nanosecond to respond.

"Shut the hell up!" Theo responded.

Wyatt leaned into me with a conspiratorial look in his eye. "They all need to stop shouting, bro," he said. "They're scaring the signal away."

When I ignored him, his mind made an almost insurmountable leap. "You know what's good for a bad leg? A good walk. Stretch it right out!" He scanned the small patio and stroked his chin. "Hmm, not much room here, though. How about a climb!" His face brightened. "Oh my God, I think I've just thought of a way out of here! It's so simple! We need to get up that mountain." He pointed at the roof.

Blocking out his drivel, I focused on the others.

"Everyone get back," Theo warned the others. "You're making me nervous. I'm gonna have to reach a bit further."

"Isn't that dangerous?" said Amelia. "I mean, you could–"

"Just… a little… further… Nearly… there…. Now – whooooaaaa! Jesus H. Christ in winter – that wind almost got me!" Flapping his arms, he reined himself back in and climbed shakily down to the waist-high railing. "It's too far."

"Argh! If only you'd let me send it when I had the chance."

"Oh, please. With one bar? Give me a break! What we really need is a high-frequency radio. The army use 'em all the time."

I stopped listening at that point. The cold had spread above the bandage tied around my thigh and a dull ache had started pulsing in my abdomen. If it weren't for the fact I was already wet from the rain, I knew I would have a cold sweat over my top lip.

I'm dying, I thought to myself. The world blurred, a trail of ghostly shapes following every object as my eyes passed over them. *This must be what it feels like to turn.* Even though it was probably only minutes away, I still didn't feel the urge to munch on a human face. *Maybe you have to wait until you die. I guess I'll find out soon enough.*

It seemed I'd find out sooner than I realised. Without warning, the door to the rooftop patio split down the middle and compacted bodies blundered onto the flagstones. While they lay in a heap, ghouls crawled through the body-sized cavity they had created, squirming over them.

"Woah! Quick, we've got company!" Theo hollered.

Forgetting the camera, the gang burst into action. Fire exploded from the end of Theo's shotgun and a handful of corpses fell as shrapnel obliterated them. Monty jumped up from where he was perched near the overhang.

"Good Lord!" he yelled. Unarmed, he hesitated. "Anyone see where I left my barbell?"

"Downstairs!" Amelia confirmed.

"Damn! Cover me while I plug the gap, will you?"

I wasn't sure how he expected that to happen. Among us, only Theo was suitably armed, and bodies were pumping through the gaping hole at a panic-inducing speed.

Rushing to rescue him, Robbie reached for his belt, and unveiled a huge meat cleaver. Slicing it through the air, he caught one of the leading monsters between the eyes. After it fell limp, he pushed the bottom of his boot into its chest to dislodge the blade.

"Take this!" He tossed a large carving knife to Monty.

"Where've you been hiding those?"

"Amelia gave them to me, bro. She found them in the kitchen."

As they entered the clearing, I eyed the monsters with a woozy mind. They seemed to bubble, their skin writhing with life. I blinked, wondering how hard I'd hit my head.

"Woohoo!" a shrill voice howled nearby.

I snapped my sweating face around and spotted Wyatt. He had climbed onto the sloping roof and was now straddling one of the hulls. The rain drove harder again, the tributaries it created on the roof washing past the upside-down boat. My mind couldn't comprehend the vividness of the colours glistening in the water. It looked like the roof itself was melting, forming a glistening waterfall of liquid rock.

"What are you doing?" I screamed as Wyatt stepped off the hull into the gulf. "You'll die. You'll fall off the roof!"

"What roof, Kitten? We're lost at sea. Does the kitty not like water? Come on! Get those paws wet with me." Wyatt's voice sounded tinny as though he were shouting at me from the back of a deep cave.

Strange whorls appeared in the light and the world contorted around me. I looked to Amelia for grounding. What greeted me instead was a pair of bloodshot, yellowed eyes and veiny skin. Tar-coloured slime dripped from a taut face. There was a zombie on me!

Squealing, I thrashed and kicked to get away. Molten heat burned in my thigh. All my struggling did was throw the creature into a frenzy.

"Just go with the floooooow, bro!" Wyatt urged off to one side. "Let the motion of the ocean carry you home."

The monster's jaw gnashed, a cocktail of dark bile and saliva dripping from its cracked teeth.

"No!" I tried to reason, feeling out of my mind. "Don't eat me! I'll be with you soon anyway." Concussion or some other nonsensical force compelled me to show the creature my bite mark as proof. Wedging a knee between my body and the zombie's, I propelled it back several feet. While it recovered, I fumbled with the t-shirt. The knot was so tight.

All I have to do is show him the mark and he'll stop attacking, my brain reasoned. *He'll know I've already been compromised.*

Snapping my eyes up, I screamed. The monster had recovered faster than I expected. Dropping onto all fours, he grabbed my throat. I yelped, but the sound set like concrete in my windpipe. The creature's head zeroed in on its target, and I closed my eyes. Warm fluid cascaded down my chest.

I'm dead.

I opened my eyes again to a dazzling light. Warmth rushed back into my body, and the sounds of the struggle faded from my mind.

There was a figure behind the light. I couldn't make out any facial features, but the outline was definitely humanoid. It was beautiful. Strands of flowing hairs whipped in the wind around a porcelain head. It topped an athletic and yet delicate body, like that of a Greek goddess. The figure loomed over me.

And then the light went out.

I gasped. "Are you an angel?"

"Close, but no cigar."

Amelia slipped the torch back into her pocket, having inspected my pupils. Behind her, the others were still fighting. Their grunts, as they thrust and swiped at the horde, sounded more laboured than ever. Clutching my cheeks between her hands, she glanced back into my eyes one more time, then turned to Wyatt.

"Wyatt! Get down from there before you hurt yourself. And what in God's name did you put in Milo's water?"

"Chill, babe," Wyatt sung back to her. "It was an emergency. I gave him some of my best stuff to numb the pain." His attention focused on me. "Hey, Milo? Can you smell colours yet? I'm pretty sure I can smell yellow, but I'll have to practice to work my way up to blue."

I said nothing, just firing him a look that screamed 'deer in the headlights.' It appeared my face had become incapable of any other expression. He was still on the upside-down hull, his feet dangling in the waterfall of rain so colourful it had to be packed with E-numbers. Oddly, I got a waft of grapefruit, which I assumed was the yellow he mentioned.

Glancing down, I jabbered in a moment of panic.

"Shh," Amelia hissed, trying to calm me.

The zombie lay on my chest, his neck contorted at an angle guaranteeing he was dead. The iron spike of Amelia's four-pronged grappling hook protruded from his face. As she dragged the rotting mass off me, my skin tingled. I shivered, almost missing the extra warmth.

"We need to get out of here," I mumbled. It was true, but not the most helpful suggestion.

"I know, Milo." Amelia's glanced over her shoulder at the carnage.

The others had formed a protective wall, but I could see they were melting. Or the rain was eating them. Either way, the attacking zombies would make light work of them the minute the weather and fighting ground them down.

"No," I insisted, scrambling to climb to my feet.

I caught a glimpse of the lake of souls below us and completely lost my mind. Through my eyes, they had become one amorphous mass, a bubbling pit of limbs and heads and filth. Screaming, I grabbed onto Amelia.

"Milo!" I could hear the panic in her voice, too. "I have to go help the others. I really need you to be calm right now."

I thrashed and stamped the foot of my bad leg. A shotgun blast of pain radiated through it and I shrieked in agony, crumpling back into foetal position. I was hyperventilating badly, shivering. Wyatt watched me with a dumb expression.

He's done this to me.

I scowled, but he didn't seem to notice. His face was clown-like now, contorted into a horrific grin stretching to either ear. His familiar cocaine laugh pumped up the vein throbbing in his forehead. As the wind hooked its invisible fingers under the boat, he cackled, riding it like a rodeo bull.

"Milo! I need you to focus, Milo! If you don't focus right now, we're all going to die. Milo!"

I refused to listen. She didn't understand the chaos going on around her – the curtains of light, the odorous colours, the screaming whale song drifting on the wind.

She placed her hands on me, and I jolted, throwing her off, and screaming. The rain felt like ants on my skin. I couldn't take my eyes off Wyatt. He seemed to be having the time of his life in the rapids.

Amelia blocked my view with her own face. I knew at that moment I'd completely lost all sense of reality, when the fighting behind her hit slow motion and all shouts became moans, indistinguishable from the zombies.

Unable to breathe, I stared into Amelia's dark eyes. A white shine swam in her pupils. Following the silvery shape, I watched it morph into some kind of white animal. A rabbit. Then I fell in, tumbling down the rabbit hole.

PART THIRTY-SIX
STRANDED

Tearing my eyes away from the burrows into Amelia's soul, I focused back on Wyatt. He had become a full captain now, the capsized boat under him a raft on the open ocean.

"Are you calm?" I heard Amelia yell at me. "Milo, are you gonna stay here, or are you gonna do something stupid?"

"Stay here," I mumbled, mimicking her, my gaze fixed on Wyatt. "Stay here."

"Good." And with that, she disappeared.

The narcotics had surrounded me with wild fantasies. Where Amelia walked, she left glowing footprints. Robbie had become a Norse god, his beard flashing orange as he cleaved open the heads of the undead. A bedraggled pack of zombies staggered through a gap that opened between the others, breaking their wall. Monty and Theo were a two-headed monster, fighting back to back, shotgun blasts firing like solar flares into the dawn sky.

With hampered movements, I pulled myself upright, testing my leg on the flagstones. The monsters heading my way looked unnaturally gangly, salivating and snarling like pit bulls. Leaning back over the railing, I eyed the sea of corpses. Their features glistened now, the rainwater and blood flicking off their grasping fingers like white horses at the crests of waves.

This was it. Whether or not my mind was showing an exaggerated version of reality, there was no doubt our situation had become hopeless. The abstract world my drug-addled brain had created showed the pandemonium for what it was: an apocalypse.

Despite their valiant efforts to protect me and staunch the flow of corpses, my friends were fighting a losing battle. The stream was endless. Every time they ducked in near the doorway, a fresh surge of attackers drove them back. Stuck between an endless army and a sea of death, I toyed with the idea of just ending it all.

After all, they didn't look unhappy. Just hungry. Falling into the sea of monsters would be a lot quicker than fighting for my life.

"Feel the rush! Just go with the flow!" Wyatt howled with glee.

Go with the flow.

I tilted my head to get a better view of the fantasy.

Go with the flow.

The boat Wyatt sat on bounced, caught in a wave that might have been the wind.

Go with the flow.

Two things hit me at once. One was a living corpse, the other was an idea.

"Wyatt, you genius!"

Wyatt looked offended. "What'd you call me?"

"You're a genius!" I repeated.

Laughing, I wrapped my arms around the zombie's waist, and lifted it high into the air. At first, it looked thrilled, its arms flapping in the G-force like a child at a fairground. The next moment, its eyes widened, as I tipped it over the patio railing, and it vanished into the murk.

Dragging my bad leg behind me, I shuffled towards Wyatt, waving my hands in the air. "Bring the boat closer!" I shouted. "We need to go with the flow."

A dead-eyed ghoul appeared next to my head. Black, viscous fluid, speckled with grit, dripped down its chin. With surprising dexterity, it pounced, then stopped dead. A barb-like prong exploded from its mouth.

I frowned for an instant, wondering what bizarre tangent my hallucinations had taken. Then the monster's head cracked, and one half of its skull came away. A final yank severed the skin and the zombie dropped to the floor. I realised it wasn't another hallucination.

"Now what did I tell you?" Amelia demanded, swivelling on her heels, and lodging the grappling hook like an ice pick into a second head. "You said you'd stay put – argh!"

She batted away a monster, ducking under its clutches and drawing it away from me.

"You don't understand!" I wailed. "Wyatt's a genius!"

Even with the drugs pumping through my system, I realised I looked like an escaped mental patient. Something warm trickled down my leg. I realised it was probably blood. My movement had loosened the t-shirt knotted around my wound.

"Just sit down."

"No," I insisted through slurred thoughts. Trying to find the right words was like searching for an eel in a mire. "He can save us all! The boat!"

"Just sit down, Milo!"

Another ragged mass of flesh and torn clothes piled into her. As she stumbled backwards, Monty charged the creature, swiping his large knife in a diagonal arc. It found its target, and the monster collapsed to one knee, the ligaments in the back of its leg severed in two.

"What the devil's going on?" he growled. "If you don't stop messing around, we're all going to die. I can't babysit all of you!"

"Yeah! What the *devil*?" repeated Theo, his copy-cat tone sounding odd as he tried to mock the British accent through the filter of a bad American one.

It seemed the word 'devil' triggered something in my mind, morphing his aggressive features into a rippled snarl. I saw a darkness in his eyes just as terrifying as the zombies.

"Can I get some help over here?" Amelia said. "That buffoon on the boat's slipped Milo something and I can't keep him still."

"The boat!" I screamed, ignoring her panic as more zombies pushed their way onto the rooftop patio. "Go with the flow!"

"Yeah!" Wyatt nodded wildly. "Cowabunga! Go with the flow."

"We'll sail the seven seas," I said, pointing at the vortex of bodies below us, in the hope it offered some sort of an explanation.

Suddenly, it looked like the nerves had broken in Monty's face. Glancing at the unmanageable build-up of corpses heading our way, he watched them crush each other against the railing and flail as they spilled into the army below. Sooner or later, the living dead would completely flood the confined balcony.

"Go with the flow?" I heard Monty whisper. His eyes shot open. "Go with the flow! Right, guys. Cover me. I'm getting on the roof."

Finally, I thought. With my job done, my leg gave out, and I collapsed.

"What!" blurted Amelia. "You, too? You're all mad!"

"Just hold the fort, chaps. I've got a plan."

A bolt of fire exploded from the muzzle of Theo's shotgun, taking three corpses off their feet. He hurried to reload as more took their place.

Monty ignored the blast, mounting the railing over the pit of gore-thirsty monsters below him. Next, he stepped onto the sloping roof. Spreading his arms for balance, he traversed the slippery terrain until he reached the upturned boat.

"Wyatt, get off the damn boat!" he shouted.

"Fine, bro. Whatever you say. It's all yours."

From my limited vantage point on the patio, my mind swam. As Wyatt stepped off the boat, I gasped, astounded that he could stay upright in the rapids created by the rain. It didn't matter to my mind that the torrent trickling down the tiles was actually no higher than the soles of his shoes.

"Grab the other end, old sport!" Monty yelled over the howl of the wind. "And, whatever you do, don't fall off the roof."

Wyatt did as instructed. Untethering the ropes securing the boat in place, and detaching it from the hook, Monty ensured they flipped the hull quickly. That way, it wasn't carried away by the wind. Together, they eased it closer to the patio. There was a moment where they blocked out the sky, lumbering its reinforced plastic structure directly over my head. Finally, they settled it on the railing with the front half overhanging the crowd.

Monty disappeared for an instant, and then returned with a long oar.

"Come on! Get in!" he yelled, turning to the others.

"Are you crazy!" said Amelia. "What are you even trying to do?"

She swiped her hook at face height as more zombies than she could handle lunged in close to get her. They had painted the floor with their black filth now. We were locked into one small corner, using the roof next to us to protect our flank.

"I know what I'm doing. I rowed competitively for years, and I was trained to kayak by one of the best instructors in Monte Carlo. Wyatt and Milo have the right idea. It's dangerous, but I think the bodies are packed closely enough for it to work. It's our only chance at survival. Now, get in!"

Hesitation flashed in Amelia's face. I didn't need as much convincing. I was going to die anyway from the zombie bite, so throwing myself into a potentially lethal situation meant little to me.

Fighting through my fever and the excruciating pain in my leg, I hoisted myself up next to the railing. The heat from the wall of decomposing bodies was surprisingly potent – like standing at the edge of a volcano. Far beneath us, they bubbled with the same burning ferocity and hunger as flowing lava.

Clambering into the hull, I rolled onto my back. The interior was both wider and longer than I expected. Although mostly open, one end was covered with a tarpaulin, which I assumed was meant to cover a lunchbox of emergency supplies. Sprawled on my back, I stared at the sky.

Why does it have to be cloudy?

I'd always hoped I'd die looking at the stars. Unfortunately life didn't work that way. Having said that, as a zombie-to-be, this wasn't necessarily my only chance at death. The thought made my lips crack a dumb smile. It only got bigger when I noticed the gigantic lion's head my warped mind convinced me was developing in the clouds. Just when I expected it to open its mouth, and spout some wise advice in a booming voice, the boat jolted and Wyatt clambered in next to me.

"Hey, Kitten."

The lion roared and withdrew into its nimbus body. Sitting up, I assumed the meerkat position to watch the action playing out behind me. The others piled into the boat, knocking me back onto my back. The last to arrive was Monty, who had delegated himself the role of holding the boat steady so it didn't fall off its knife edge.

As the zombies filled the boathouse's second-floor patio, Monty gave the boat one monumental heave and dived in with us.

I experienced the lurch of weightlessness as we slid off the lip of the roof and plummeted into the lake of ghouls. Contrary to their presumed inability to be shocked by anything, I was certain I heard a zombie scream. Either that, or its head squealed as its innards were forced through the top of its skull like toothpaste.

Thrown wildly, my delusions took over. What might have been hands on the vessel's nose became splashes of sea water. There was a terrifying moment in which we all screamed, tilted almost vertically, facing down at a crowd of monstrous heads.

Fortunately for us, Monty had rooted his feet firmly in the boat. Thrusting his oar into the crowd, he crushed an attacker's ribcage with the paddle and pushed the boat free of greedy hands. His quick thinking righted the hull and propelled us along the top of the crowd.

"Everyone still on?" he shouted.

"I think so, bro. That was close, though. Who's that?" someone said.

A familiar streak of white raced past my face.

Ghost Girl! I thought.

Judging by her dead features, she must have been bitten, found her way onto the roof, and reanimated while hiding in the boat's tarped section.

Crashing into Robbie at full force, their bodies entwined, and they tumbled together. Two devastating things happened at once: blood squirted from Robbie's face as she bit into it, and his ankle snagged on the edge of the boat. Contaminated and screaming, he overbalanced and disappeared under the surface of the horde.

"Robbie!" I yelled, unable to grab him in time thanks to the fog in my mind.

Wyatt actually attempted a lunge but was far too late. He yelped as a long arm shot out of the crowd and grabbed his shirt, threatening to wrench him under alongside Robbie. That was when Amelia interjected. She brought down her heavy grappling hook without hesitation, and severed the zombie's arm at the wrist.

"He's gone!" Wyatt cried. "Such a nice guy, and he's gone!"

Amelia withdrew on autopilot – possibly in shock.

"For Christ's sake, stay away from the sides!" Monty ordered through gritted teeth. "The zombies lash out at whoever's closest. We need them to punch up at the boat evenly from all sides to keep us afloat." An arm hooked over the edge of the vessel and threatened to capsize us. Moving with tiger-like aggression, Monty elbowed a waif-like head in the face, and the arm sunk back into the murky depths. "As long as I keep rowing, and we don't get overturned, we can crowd surf our way out of here."

"Just like Sophia at Glastonbury!" I said.

He winced, but agreed. "Yeah, something like that."

For the next few seconds, we advanced over the crashing waves of knuckles. My vision blurred – which I guessed was something to do with the gash on my leg – and I almost passed out. Between the biting wind and the lung-sapping heat of the crowd, it was impossible to get comfy. Despite that, we were safe – relatively speaking. It was more than we could have hoped for, given the circumstances.

Then everything came crashing down around us when Amelia said, "This is unbelievable. I've gotta get it on camera." Patting herself in search of the device, she frowned. "Argh, I must have dropped it!"

She fired a forlorn glance at the rooftop, then screamed.

Startled, I sat bolt upright and followed her gaze. *Can't I rest for a second?* I thought, feeling woozy.

I caught sight of what she was looking at and realised she wasn't being dramatic. It was worse than I thought. We'd left a man behind. Too far away to jump aboard, Theo was still on the boathouse roof.

PART THIRTY-SEVEN
BLAZE OF GLORY

"Turn back!" Amelia insisted with a frantic look in her eyes.

"We can't," said Monty. "Milo's bleeding to death, and I'm not sure I can turn this thing around."

She dived on his arm and tried to force him to change course.

"Get off, or you'll kill us all!"

"I'll go," I found myself saying. "Just drop me off anywhere near here."

They ignored my deluded babbling, instead choosing to argue amongst themselves.

"We're coming back for you!" Amelia hollered at the top of her voice.

"Don't!" Theo replied, his voice carrying over the wind and moans. He was perched on the ledge where he'd tried to pick up internet signal on Amelia's camera. The camera was in his hand. Slipping a cigar out of the inside pocket of his jacket, he saluted us from his perch, just out of the corpses' reach. "I always intended to go out in a blaze of glory," he called. "This is how I make things right!"

He placed the cigar between his lips and pulled out a lighter – the stainless-steel kind with the flip-up lid.

Holding it to the end of the cigar, he ignited the flame and waited until the tobacco glowed furnace-orange.

Ghouls scrambled at the end of the rooftop patio, stepping on each other to climb onto the roof itself. Theo didn't seem to notice. Completely lost in his insular world, he lion-kinged the camera at the end of the roof, as though taking a selfie.

The world blurred around me. I wasn't sure how much longer my vision would last. Still, I focused on Theo, waiting to see what he would do next, rooting for him to come up with a way to get free. Unexpectedly, his plan involved talking into the camera.

"People of the world! If y'all are watching this, I'm already dead," he started with a self-assured grin. "I know I'm not your regular cam girl, but this is the apocalypse, so you better get used to it." He spun the camera, facing the lens at the sea of bodies. Then he turned it back to himself.

"You see them?" he continued. "They're zombies. Thousands of zombies. Not a disease. Not a gas explosion. Not a terrorist attack. Zombies. The government have known about 'em for years. At least seven years, actually, since the Necroville incident. That was zombies, too, by the way, so don't none of you let some smarmy suit behind a lectern tell you otherwise."

Coming to a natural break, he lingered, sucking a long drag from his cigar as he squinted into the camera. When he was good and finished, he said, "I've been Theo Grayson, reporting live from the front line of the zombie apocalypse. They're hungry and coming your way. If you wanna survive, you better get ready. Now, peace out, suckers!"

Saluting the camera, he pressed a button and ended the recording. Then he turned to us and saluted a second time.

"Mission complete!" he growled, barely loud enough for us to hear. "Now, let's blow this hell hole to kingdom come."

With that, he raised both arms and swan dived into the open void. The screen of Amelia's camera flashed green as it hit the reception sweet spot and sent the video.

"Theo!" Amelia shrieked.

He didn't hear her. Showing no fear as he plummeted out of the sky, he disappeared into the pit of ghouls. What happened next was unexpected. As he lay dead on the ground his cigar must have struck oil, because a fireball erupted from where he had disappeared. Flames quickly engulfed the creatures near the blast radius. With so many monsters soaked in oil from the moat, the blaze spread like a pathogen.

"Row faster!" Amelia barked.

"I'm going as fast as I can, woman!" Monty snapped back.

"Get out of the boat, dude!" Wyatt shouted at me.

"What?"

"Get out!"

At first, I scrunched up my face in confusion. Then I opened my eyes and realised I must have blacked out for a few minutes. Disorientated, I lolled, facing the moat. We were on the opposite bank, beached on damp grass. Flames stretched in both directions.

Before I had time to make a full survey of my surroundings, Monty's hand closed around my lower back and my thighs, and he hoisted me out of the hull. Dawn was breaking but it was still dark, and it felt like I was floating through shadow. All I saw was the underside of Monty's chin for some time, and not much else.

"Take the key out of my pocket," he ordered someone. "We have to get moving or that tanker's going to blow."

A satisfying click signified the opening of a car door. I was pushed onto the back seat of a four-by-four. Cool leather eased the pain in my legs. No doubt they were far too expensive for me to be resting on them, covered as I was in blood and grime.

As my vision swam, my eyes focused on a net pouch attached to the back of the driver's seat. Tucked inside it was a university prospectus, an empty water bottle, and a small, grey item that looked oddly familiar.

Typical.

An asthma pump – probably left there by a friend or family member of Monty's. If I wasn't heavily sedated by injuries, I might have laughed. As it was, all I could do was offer a morbid smile and slouch further into the chair. My chest was clear. It seemed the universe had one twisted joke left to tell.

"It's okay, Kitten. We're gonna live."

Wyatt sounded worried. It took a lot for him to be concerned. Barely breathing, I stared at a light in the ceiling. It glowed white, then green. Then a pair of iridescent insect wings unfurled from it, and it giggled at me.

I felt life slipping away through the drain in my leg.

"Wyatt," I croaked.

"What?"

"You were right about the fairies."

He sniffed. "I know, bro. I know. Just keep watching them dance. Don't die."

Monty got into the driver's seat, and I heard the roar of the engine as the four-by-four pulled out of the campus carpark. There were several blunt *thuds* which I assumed were bodies bouncing off the bonnet. We had only travelled for a few minutes when more fairies joined the one looking down at me. These ones were bigger, flashing red and blue.

I could only see the world through two slits. Feeling the vehicle skid to a screeching halt, I watched Monty let down the window. A pockmarked man in a glossy black hat and a white shirt poked his head into the jeep.

"Alright, sir. Are you aware of the speed you were driving back there?" he asked Monty.

"Old chap, you see—"

"Not to mention you were swerving on the wrong side of the road."

"Yes, Officer. I can explain. I'm drunk."

"Sorry?" the officer said.

Amelia interjected. "We've had a hell of a night. The campus back there is on fire. We're all drunk, but our friend in the back is bleeding to death. He needs a doctor. He's been stabbed in the leg and will bleed out if he doesn't get medical attention soon."

Stabbed? I thought I'd been bitten.

Searching my memories, I remembered the dead body in the boathouse pantry. The fight had been over quickly – too fast to take in any details. *Did I get bitten?* I remembered a boy and a whirlwind of limbs, but no teeth. There was just a searing pain as we'd crashed into the wall together. Then an explosion.

Realisation struck me.

He wasn't a zombie.

I'd stabbed myself, and Monty must have let off the gun.

It was at that exact moment more fairies whizzed past the windows. Giant blue ones. They were wailing, heading in the direction of the university. One stopped.

I didn't register much of what happened next. All I remembered was being engulfed in cold air again as the door nearest me was yanked open and a troop of fluorescent paramedics heaved me onto a stretcher. Tilting my head, I saw a giant hand of smoke reaching from the university campus into the sky. Obviously, that must have attracted the attention of the police and ambulances. Fire engines raced past us at near-bullet speed.

While being hauled into the back of an ambulance, I heard the wingbeats of a giant insect. Staring at the early-morning sky, I winced as a helicopter torpedoed overhead, flying towards the smoke. It was red, with a news channel's logo pasted on the bottom. I stared at it, confused for a moment. Then I remembered Theo's broadcast. After that, the ambulance's ceiling blocked my view.

Paramedics piled around me, cutting away the t-shirt around my leg with surgical scissors. I winced but was too weak to call out. Looking down at the road beyond my feet, I saw Monty, Amelia, and Wyatt standing outside the car with two police officers. The first officer we had encountered had a notepad open in his hand.

"You lot have some explaining to do," he said. "Start at the beginning, and be as thorough as you can. What's happened tonight?"

"That's a hell of a question," Amelia said. "Something tells me you won't believe us, even when we tell you the truth. But you will soon enough. The whole world will know the truth."

EPILOGUE

A sphere of strong wind blasted outwards from the centre of the zombie horde. Surging in every direction, it snuffed out the lake of fire as though it were nothing more than a candle. Lying dead in the midst of the devastation, Theo's body lurched.

He awoke.

His skin was paper thin, having bubbled into hard blisters under the heat. Unable to move for fear of snapping the flesh at the seams of his joins, he lay dormant, pretending he had never come back to life. It wasn't hard. After all, he was an exceptional actor.

As he lay in the darkness, slimy bodies picked over what little patches of uncooked meat he had left. He waited, allowing them to do what their natures compelled them to do, unsure of what was to come.

Just when he thought nothing would happen, the zombies parted like cockroaches under a boot, and a shady figure entered the crowd, striding with purpose towards him. When the figure was within a few feet of his corpse, it ordered the last handful of zombies to get out of its way. They obliged, jabbering snarls at each other in some private language.

"Theodor," said the figure. It had a woman's voice. Silky smooth, and yet unmistakably deadly. "Get up."

Testing his ability to move, he splayed his fingers. The burns around his knuckles were particularly painful, but his hands worked. That was more than could be said for the last time he'd encountered the woman. Falling off that boulder had dislocated four fingers, and he'd been forced to snap them back into place himself.

"As you wish."

Fighting excruciating pain, he staggered to his feet. His skin crinkled like tin foil. Around him a sea of dead faces, each equally burnt and mutilated, stared back at him.

Poor souls, he thought.

They had no idea they were mindless land-clearing machines. Essentially, biological bulldozers bred to exterminate pests.

"Did you complete your mission?" the woman asked.

Her face was obscured by a long shadow, a look for which she was infamous. Even in the early hours of dawn, when the stars still twinkled but the sky was turning deep blue, she wore the dark like a veil. It somehow wrapped around her, tailoring itself to her form.

"Ma'am, yes, Ma'am."

He felt her eyes flair behind her veil of shadows. Although she didn't raise her voice or show any outward signs of fury, the quiet only made her warning all the more unsettling.

"Drop the commando act. You're a puppet. Start acting like one. Now, answer my question properly."

His throat tightened. "Sorry… Yes."

"Better."

Theo had learned not to argue or say more than was asked of him. He offered only prompt answers, and then returned to a subdued position, head bowed low. The consequences of stepping out of line were dire.

He was lucky. After sparing him from a brutal death, his mistress had favoured him over the others. He intended to keep it that way, knowing the fate of his predecessors.

Her slender hand, so white it shone like ivory, reached out and tilted his face upwards. Their eyes met, but she said nothing, and he dared not start a conversation. Cold ran through him, radiating from the tip of her finger over the burnt skin of his face, and down his neck.

A massage of tingles pushed its way over his flesh as the wounds began to scab up and heal at an unnatural rate. He stifled a cough, feeling the cooling sensation stop halfway down his crispy throat. A sharp ridge of burnt flesh caught in his windpipe.

She withdrew. He moaned slightly, unable to hold back his disappointment. Wiggling her index finger playfully, she tutted.

"Theo?"

"Yes, my lady?"

"Do you love me?"

Desperate to be freed of his agony and feel her healing touch again, he nodded. Ruby-coloured lips smirked behind her veil of shadows.

"Good."

With that, she headed back in the opposite direction. Zombies scrambled over one another to get out of the way as she parted the sea. All were silent, their minds no longer impartial killing machines.

Theo gulped, left behind with the image of his reward dangling in front of his mind's eye. A carrot he couldn't eat. His scorched skin was starting to itch but he knew scratching it would trigger crippling pain.

"My lady?" he croaked.

She stopped but didn't turn around. "Yes, Theo?"

"Aren't you going to heal me?"

Another pause. Then she asked, "Now, why would I do a thing like that?"

"Well... I did what you wanted."

He didn't see the second smirk – the smirk only a fellow sadist could appreciate.

"Yes, you did," she replied. "So, why would I waste the energy? You're no longer needed."

"What?"

Theo's stomach flipped. The word had come out involuntarily, like vomit. Some of the zombies nearest him actually looked startled. Nobody ever showed such insolence in the presence of the woman; nobody who wanted to survive, anyway.

He gulped. It hurt a lot. Thankfully, she didn't change direction. Commencing her walk, she vanished into the darkness of the dawn. Left alone, Theo breathed a sigh of relief.

Then a reedy whistle sounded from somewhere at the back of the crowd. At first, he paused, trying to work out what it meant. He noticed a glazed look in the zombies' eyes. Well, more glazed than usual.

Inching away, he backed into the boathouse's garage door. Within seconds, the monsters had reverted back to their previous shark-like selves. Their lips curled. It was like they were seeing him for the first time.

"Easy now," he said, raising his hands defensively.

It was no use. As one, the wall of bodies rushed forward, and he screamed. His flaky skin popped and cracked as they broke the burnt exterior to get at his gooey insides.

Striding away with a stoic expression on her face, the woman thought nothing of the tortured screams. Her mind was already focused on the next stage of her plan.

GET YOUR FREE STARTER LIBRARY!

If you like *Last Crawl*, follow the link below to get the prequel, *The Dead Woods*, for free! Joining Daniel's no-spam newsletter will also get you exclusive freebies and promotions you won't find anywhere else.

To get your free starter library, visit:

www.danielparsonsbooks.com

Also, why not review *Last Crawl* on Amazon? Authors depend on reviews to reach new readers and gain promotional opportunities. Support Daniel Parsons by writing a review today.

ALSO BY DANIEL PARSONS

Have you read them all?

THE DEAD WOODS

Graduating university is an emotional time for everyone. When a group of ex-students decide to spend one last night together at a zombie experience facility to create lasting memories, however, none of them anticipate just how memorable it will turn out to be. It quickly becomes apparent that the undead actors are very good at what they do. Too good.

Armed with only an arsenal of Nerf guns, the group quickly figure out that they'll need more than foam bullets and sandwiches to get them through the night.

BLOTT

Thirteen-year-old Blott Meritum has hidden his freakish ability since he was a toddler. However, as his people hurtle toward starvation, he has no option but to risk exposure and take action.

He commits a forbidden crime to save his people, and soon discovers that the world outside the village harbours unexpected perils, and that his ability means he can change his people's whole existence. However, a sinister voice inside his head has other ideas.

Will he keep his humanity and save his people? Or will he be consumed by the monster inside him?

THE WINTER FREAK SHOW

After twelve-year-old Toby Carter escapes a brutal workhouse at Christmas, he can't believe his good fortune. Adopted by a band of travelling performers called The Winter Freak Show, who put on spellbinding shows each night, he finally believes he's found the family he always wanted. Then everything falls apart.

Children are disappearing throughout the city. All evidence points to those Toby trusted the most and he finds himself caught up in a conspiracy far more sinister than he ever imagined. Defenceless and on the run, he's confronted with two options; uncover the kidnapper before another child falls victim, or stand by and watch as the shadowy criminal becomes unstoppable.

The fate of Christmas rests in the balance.

THE #ARTOFTWITTER

In *The #ArtOfTwitter*, fantasy writer and Twitter coach Daniel Parsons explains how he grew a 90,000+ strong army of loyal followers and gained real-world influence as an indie author. Breaking his tactics into short chapters and simple, actionable steps, he demonstrates exactly how any creative professional can achieve similar results.

Whether you're a writer, artist, musician, or any other creative professional, *The #ArtOfTwitter* will show you how to:

- Understand the changing world of social media
- Avoid common mistakes
- Grow your popularity without being suspended
- Gain a bigger audience by using hashtags
- Build strong relationships with your followers
- Nurture follower engagement
- Save time with Twitter apps
- Implement a strategy for sustained growth
- Make money with Twitter ads
- Ensure every tweet is a hit
- Get real-world influence

Printed in Great Britain
by Amazon